Unleashed

Books by Eileen Brady

The Kate Turner D.V.M. Mysteries

Muzzled

Unleashed

Unleashed

A Kate Turner, D.V.M. Mystery

Eileen Brady

Poisoned Pen Press

First Edition 2015

10 9 8 7 6 5 4 3 2 1

Library of Congress Catalog Card Number: 2014958051

ISBN: 9781464203947 Hardcover
9781464203961 Trade Paperback

Poisoned Pen Press
6962 E. First Ave., Ste. 103
Scottsdale, AZ 85251
www.poisonedpenpress.com
info@poisonedpenpress.com

Printed in the United States of America

To my parents, Marie and Michael Brady,
whose example shaped my life

Acknowledgments

Writing a book is like running a marathon that lasts for six months. My family deserves praise for their patience during endless rewrites, especially my long-suffering husband, Jon. Much love to both sisters, Rosemary and Margaret, and my daughters, Britt and Amanda, for their understanding. The efforts of Barbara Peters and Annette Rogers, my editors at the Poisoned Pen Press, made *Unleashed* a much better book and I'd like to acknowledge Tiffany, Beth, Diane, Pete and the rest of the staff for all their support. Special thanks to Maryglenn McCombs for her public relations and publicity work. This book wouldn't have been possible without insight and suggestions from my fellow writers and Tuesday night critique group members—Sharon Magee, Art Kerns, Scott Andrews, Bill Butler, Louise Signorelli, and that wonderful writing wizard Betty Webb. Being a veterinarian for over twenty years has only deepened my love and curiosity about animals. Thanks to my readers for their kind words and funny animal stories. Not a day passes that my own pets don't make me laugh, especially a certain Cornish Rex cat, Lily, who thinks every glass of water I pour is hers.

"The love of all living creatures is the most noble attribute of man."

—Charles Darwin

"I had been told that the training procedure with cats was difficult. It's not. Mine had me trained in two days."

—Bill Dana

Prologue

The killer took a final look around the townhouse. Empty vodka bottles in the garbage and lying on the carpet by the bed. Percocet, Oxycontin, and Ecstasy pills added near the prescription bottle of Vicodin on the bedside table. A broken vase still in the garbage. Keep it obvious and simple.

In the living room the extra wineglass had been removed, washed, dried, and put away behind the rest of the glassware. It would look like Claire Birnham had been drinking by herself before her suicide. The glazed stoneware lamps cast pools of light over the purple sofa and acid-yellow accent pillows. Decorated in modern clean lines, the living room shone with personality. On the walls hung her minimalist artwork. A pity, the killer thought. So talented. Did she understand what she had gotten herself into?

The suicide note would appear as soon as the computer screen on the desk refreshed but, taking no chances, the killer printed it. A scrawled signature completed the lie.

In the breakfast alcove Claire slumped in a chair, forehead on the kitchen tabletop, her dark curly hair cascading over the edge. She snored gently, full of booze and pills. By pretending to need advice, the killer had lulled her into letting down her guard. Once she swallowed the doctored cocktail the rest was easy. Now to get her into the car for her final curtain call.

As if sensing what was coming, the girl stirred for a moment, then sank back into oblivion.

The killer helped Claire stand and, supporting her around the waist, walked her through the back door into the garage. A silver Honda Civic was parked on one side of the two-car structure; the second bay set up as a work space, packed with art supplies and tools. As planned, the driver's side door was open, making it easy to slide the victim into the front seat. Once there her body slumped back against the headrest. Perfect.

Reaching across the seat with a gloved hand, one turn of the key started the motor. A quick press of Claire's fingers on the car key fob dangling from the dashboard finished the job. The other hand, the one with the bandage, draped over the steering wheel.

Satisfied, the killer walked to the garage side door, brushing against a pegboard bristling with more tools and canvas stretchers. A thin leather leash hung next to a row of screwdrivers. A twist of the knob locked the door from the inside. Behind the townhouse a sidewalk led to a parking lot devoid of cameras. At three-thirty in the afternoon on Friday, it was deserted so no one saw anything. A fast left out of the parking lot, then a right put the truck onto a main road. With the townhome complex rapidly fading from view, a smile crossed the killer's face.

A perfect murder.

Wait.

Something was missing. That leash.

Where the hell was Claire's nasty little dog?

Where was Toto?

Chapter One

After kicking my cheating boyfriend to the curb I needed to find a job far far away from him.

Quickly. With $150,000 worth of student loans left to pay for my veterinary education, I couldn't afford to be without an income. That's how I ended up in the tiny town of Oak Falls, about two hours from New York City if you put the pedal to the metal, but light years away from the crowds. Hired as a relief vet while the practice owner, Doc Anderson, took an around-the-world cruise, I lived in an apartment attached to the office. At least it was a short commute.

Now, seven months of house calls later, I thought I had seen just about everything.

I was wrong.

Friday morning, my veterinary technician, Mari, and I piled into the office F-150 truck and drove to our first appointment of the day. Seventy-two Chestnut Lane turned out to be an older farmhouse-style home on an acre of land that bordered the state park. Mature elms created a canopy over the front walkway, lined by low-lying junipers and daylilies. A pretty setting, but we were there to take care of a sick pug whose owner had called for an early morning appointment.

An attractive young woman in her twenties with light brown hair and a gentle face opened the door. "Are you the vet?"

Nodding, I introduced myself. "Yes, I'm Dr. Kate Turner and this is my assistant, Mari."

"Nancy Wagner. Come in." She stepped aside. "Don't let anyone out."

Both Mari and I are masters at not letting dogs, cats, or any other type of pet escape through exits of any kind. Watching carefully, we snuck through the door, using our legs like goalies at a soccer game to block anyone trying to flee.

Nancy watched us close the door. Satisfied none of her pets had gotten out, she led us down a fairly narrow hallway.

Unfortunately our progress abruptly stopped when a large gray and white pot-bellied pig with a pink nose turned the corner, effectively throwing a block.

Oops.

Could the sick pug we were supposed to be seeing actually be a sick pig? Had our receptionist Cindy made an interesting typing mistake?

"Is this the patient?" I asked.

"Yes. This is my Angel. He's almost a year old and he's got a terrible rash on his belly."

Just because veterinarians treat all kinds of animals doesn't mean we have every species' medical problems right at our fingertips. Luckily, I knew quite a bit about pot-bellied pigs. During vet school several had come into the university's small animal clinic with various problems. I'd also gone on farm calls to a pot-bellied pig breeder, and babysat one named Daisy for a friend for a month. Most of the pigs I'd handled were gentle and surprisingly smart.

"All right. Where can I examine him?"

"I guess we could use the living room." Nancy made a kissing sound and the pig turned and trotted off behind her. My guess was he had the run of this part of the house.

Without much trouble Angel rolled over on his back and presented us his belly to scratch. A diffuse red rash spread across the pale, almost hairless skin on his abdomen and halfway up both sides. The lack of any raised diamond shaped lesions or pustules quickly ruled out some of the bad pig diseases—which left anything from fungal to contact dermatitis to a million other things. To be certain I took several skin scrapings which Angel seemed to enjoy.

"Is he healthy otherwise? How is his appetite?"

"Perfectly normal."

Maybe this was a husbandry problem, having to do with diet or his environment.

Mari, Nancy, and I sat on the wooden floor. Angel loved having his belly rubbed and grunted with pleasure. I listened to his heart and lungs and continued my exam. "What are you feeding him?"

Nancy pointed over to the kitchen counter. "He gets his pig chow plus vegetables and fruits, and some of what I eat every day. Then I let him root around in the yard outside."

Since pigs are omnivores, which means they eat everything, it sounded like a fairly balanced diet. Except for the rash he looked like a healthy piggy. Digging a little deeper I questioned her further. "Did you spread any chemicals or fertilizers outside recently, or add any new plants or trees?"

"Absolutely not. I'm very careful because of all my pets." Nancy sounded indignant.

"What about his sleeping pen?" Since our animal patients can't talk to us, I found taking a detailed history is of huge importance. "Do you change the hay frequently? Is there any evidence of mouse or rat infiltration in his stall?" Skin lesions could be a result of moldy hay or damp unsanitary conditions.

His concerned owner continued to stroke Angel's belly. "I'm sure everything is fine. I don't have any skin problems."

Not sure if she understood I tried to reassured her. "From a preliminary look, I don't think this is contagious to people, but I'm curious if it has something to do with where he sleeps.

Again she looked up at me, eyes wide. "He sleeps with me."

For a moment I thought she sometimes camped in the backyard.

Mari subtly nudged me with her elbow.

I persisted. "Where exactly does Angel sleep at night?"

"In bed. With me," Nancy said in a matter-of-fact voice, as though everyone sleeps with their pig.

That's when a rooster walked into the room. Brightly feathered, brown and black with a red comb, he strutted past us, barely glancing at the pig on the floor. "Hi, Tommy," Nancy said to the chicken.

Mari poked me again and whispered, "That's odd."

I was there to figure out what was wrong with Angel, not the owner, so continued. "Does he sleep on top of the bed?"

"No. Under the sheets. He gets cold at night." she explained, "Besides, he likes to cuddle."

Picturing her spooning with her pig seemed all wrong. I kept going.

"Have you changed your detergent or fabric softener?" Since pigs have sensitive skin I went with one of the most common causes of rashes—contact dermatitis.

Nancy frowned and pursed her lips. "Oh my gosh. I changed my fabric softener to Lavender Fields right around the time I noticed the rash. Do you think that might be it?"

"It certainly could be a cause. Would you be able to wash him with a hypoallergenic shampoo?"

"Sure, Angel likes taking showers with me."

Of course he did. Another place I didn't want to go.

"Great. Mari will get the pet shampoo for you. Follow the directions and wash all the linen and whatever else he comes in contact with in hot water. Use your regular detergent but skip the fabric softener. If that's the cause of his skin condition you should see a difference in about ten days. Meanwhile, we'll call you with the results of our tests. There may be some other type of diagnostics to run, depending on how he responds."

Angel rolled over, then pulled himself up onto his relatively slender feet. I noticed a large doggy door leading out into the backyard. As we watched, the pig aimed his snout into the door flap, pushed it open, then squeezed through.

"Thanks so much, doctor," Nancy said, relief in her voice. "I was worried it might be something serious." She hesitated for a moment. "Do I have to wash Tommy, too?"

For a moment I was confused. "Who is Tommy?"

"My rooster." She smiled a sweet smile. "He sleeps with me too."

◇◇◇

After saying goodbye and getting into the truck, Mari couldn't hold it in. She laughed her butt off. What exactly was going on in that house? I wasn't sure. Nancy appeared to be a normal person, but lonely. Maybe her surrogate animal family filled the gaps in her life. The animals were healthy and well looked after, so who was I to judge her? After all, I talked to my dog Buddy, and he often slept at the bottom of the bed. During thunderstorms I let him crawl under the blankets. Whatever gets you through the day. Still, I couldn't imagine sleeping with sharp piggy hooves in the bed with me.

"Is there a Mr. Nancy in the picture?" I wondered, turning the corner onto Scenic Drive.

"No such luck." Mari entered something into the laptop. "She confided in me that she doesn't get that many second dates."

I tried not to crack a smile. "Gee, I wonder why?"

An hour later we arrived back at the animal hospital and I immediately looked at the skin samples. Everything checked out fine, no nasty scabies or demodex mites, no yeast or any of the other common skin problems that might cause a rash. Knowing Nancy would be worried I called her back while writing up my records.

"Thanks, Dr. Kate. I'll give you an update in two weeks. She took a moment, then continued, "Why don't you check out my Facebook page and follow the link to our website and my blog?"

Six o'clock rolled around before I had an opportunity to go into Doc's office to check my email. For curiosity's sake I looked up Nancy on Facebook.

To my surprise there were lots of postings on her page and a professional looking link to her website. When I clicked on it I got another surprise. Nancy wrote a blog about her pets and her life, a pretty popular blog, and now I was part of it.

Obviously taken from an overhead cam, the posted picture caught me rubbing Angel's tummy. It was a toss-up who sported the bigger grin, me or the pig.

Chapter Two

Seven-thirty on Saturday morning my alarm rang. Still half asleep, I stumbled into the animal hospital through the connecting door to my apartment, dying for that first cup of coffee from the office Mr. Coffee machine. Try as I might I've never been a morning person. The shrill barking of one of my patients, a wire-haired Cairn terrier named Toto, woke me faster than usual.

"Good morning, Dr. Kate." Our cheery office manager and chief receptionist, Cindy, handed me a stack of messages. "You're going to be busy today."

"Thanks." I stuffed the notes in my pocket. After taking a blissful first sip of java I made my way over to Toto's cage. The barking turned into fierce growls. Obviously the little guy felt better today. He'd been admitted early Friday morning for observation after his owner found him doing something totally in character with his breeding, running around with a recently dead rat in his mouth. Multiple bite wounds on his lip and face needed to be cleaned and medicated under anesthesia. After taking blood, plus giving him a shot of Vitamin K, I'd kept him in the hospital overnight in case he'd been exposed to rat poison. Happily for all, Claire Birnham, his anxious owner, had arranged for an early pickup of her furry baby this morning. A one-person dog, he loved his mommy and hated the rest of us.

As the staff started to drift in I retreated to the doctor's office to check lab results, review the appointment schedule, and answer my messages. With the practice owner, Doc Anderson, enjoying his round-the-world-cruise, I was the sole veterinarian at the hospital. While I was in the middle of sending an email to a client whose cat was diabetic, Mari poked her head into the room.

"Have you heard?"

"Nuhh," I managed to answer, concentrating on the last sentence I'd typed. I felt sleep-deprived, having spent the night locked in a vivid dream about mega-sharks inexplicably chasing me on their fins through Grand Central Station. Too much Sci-Fi channel.

Used to my morning pattern, Mari didn't need much encouragement to continue. "I heard it from my cousin, the EMT. Claire Birnham committed suicide last night."

"What?" A face flashed before me. Intensely blue eyes full of energy, glossy dark hair curling past her shoulders and an easy brilliant smile. Slender artistic fingers splattered with acrylic paint holding Toto close to her heart.

"She did it in the car. Hooked up a hose to the exhaust and died of carbon monoxide poisoning. A neighbor smelled the exhaust and called the police."

"I can't believe this. We just saw her yesterday."

Both of us stood in silence for a moment, not knowing what to say. A familiar high-pitched bark brought me back to the present.

"What about Toto?"

Mari looked at me and shrugged her shoulders. "I guess she wanted him here with us."

The news seemed strange, almost unreal. My email half-finished, I stared at the screen. I'd last spoken to Claire yesterday afternoon. We'd joked about Toto, named after the famous terrier in the Wizard of Oz. Not only did he look identical to the dog in the movie, with his short brindle coat, but he behaved in a fiercely protective manner, putting himself between her and the rest of the world. I had mentioned that the Cowardly Lion could have gotten his courage from her little dog.

My coffee suddenly tasted bitter. I didn't need it anymore to wake me up. "Did she leave a note?"

"I think so," Mari replied, then paused for a moment, a pensive look on her face. "Claire always seemed so full of life. I guess you never know."

I guess you never know. That phrase kept repeating in my head. Upset at the news, I excused myself and went back into the apartment to think. Buddy, my King Charles spaniel, nuzzled up to me.

"Let's go out," I told him and smiled for a moment at the excitement that statement always brings. A former show dog who'd fallen on hard times, he now resembled a mutt, which was fine with me. Only the shape of his head hinted at his refined breeding. As Buddy went and did his business I sat in one of the patio chairs and remembered Claire.

Mari was right. Every once in a while you meet someone so full of life they sweep you up in their enthusiasm. Claire was like that. An artist with her master's degree in art history, she worked two jobs, one at the Quahog Art Gallery in town and the other setting up exhibits in the Edington Museum in Rhinebeck. I'd known her as a friendly and devoted owner to her fireball pet.

Unfortunately, suicide was something I had first-hand knowledge of. One of my classmates at Cornell University killed himself by jumping into a gorge on campus. He seemed the least likely person to do such a thing. A married father with two kids? Who does that? No one saw it coming, not even his wife.

I tossed the ball for Buddy. He took off after it, ears flapping up and down, eye on the prize.

The news about Claire struck me as bewildering and inexpressibly sad. The living may ask why, but the dead don't answer.

Her death put the hospital in an odd position. Who did her dog belong to now? A family member needed to come forward and claim responsibility for Toto. I reminded myself to talk to Cindy about this sad situation.

A chime from my cell phone alerted me to an emergency that just arrived. Putting the suicide out of my mind, I called to Buddy and ran back into the hospital.

The hit-by-car or HBC ended up taking up most of my day. A typical story. Someone didn't close the front door all the way and the family pet ended up running into the street. Queenie, a Siamese-mix cat, had been hit after crossing a busy road. The driver, a cat owner herself, felt terrible and gave us her phone number for reference. Meanwhile, we called the person listed on the kitty's collar and she was astonished that her pet had gotten outside.

Although we found only minor injuries, the cat did have blood inside her chest, probably from contact with the car or the road, so it was touch and go for a while. By three in the afternoon Queenie was out of danger and bravely telling us all about her near miss, and how many lives she had left, in cat language. I was beat.

That's when I noticed Eugene about to walk Toto.

Doc Anderson had hired eighteen-year-old Eugene after a terrible horseback riding accident left him with permanent brain damage. I'd gotten used to him cleaning the cages and kennels, a silent cipher who didn't interact much with people. Some of the staff avoided him, but I liked him and found his silence relaxing to be around. No one doubted his compassion and excellent care of our animal patients. Whenever I felt an animal needed additional attention I could rely on Eugene. As I followed him into the treatment area I noticed how muscular his back and arms looked.

With his dirty blond hair and hazel eyes he must have been a good-looking kid before the accident. Now his facial muscles were slack on the left side and he wore thick glasses to correct his vision.

Before I could warn him, Eugene opened the cage and pulled a thin leash out of the back pocket of his scrubs.

"Eugene, be careful," I cautioned. "He can be very grumpy." Grumpy was my euphemism for biting the living daylights out of you.

"Toto." Immediately the dog stopped fussing and looked up expectantly. Then the brindle terrier placed two front paws on

Eugene's chest, let him attach the lead to his collar, and wriggled into the boy's arms.

"He likes you." The little dog snuggled up to him, took one look at me, and growled.

"Toto, no." Eugene said, then headed toward the fenced-in yard we use to exercise the dogs.

When Eugene stopped to open the door, Toto turned his head and glanced back into the clinic, as though looking for someone.

I knew who he was looking for.

His mommy, Claire.

He didn't know he'd never see her again.

And he'd never know why.

◇◇◇

By six o'clock when Queenie's owners left, I was too exhausted to do much more than microwave some leftover Chinese takeout and sit in front of the television. Buddy jumped up on the sofa next to me, doggy eyes fixated on my food. I slipped him a little piece of chicken, and made him promise not to tell any of my clients that I gave him some people food. We sat together and watched another cheesy science fiction movie about a swarm of giant alien bee-creatures trying to take over the planet. By nine I could hardly keep my eyes open. After taking Buddy out for his final bathroom break, I climbed into bed, determined to relax and kick back tomorrow. After all, Sunday is supposed to be a day of rest. Annoyed that I moved around too much, Buddy jumped off the foot of the bed and took a drink of water. Since my dog didn't have much on his doggy mind he immediately fell asleep on his fluffy bed. Between my twelve-hour workday and little sleep the night before, I barely finished two pages of my well worn Clive Cussler thriller before conking out.

◇◇◇

"Help me," a voice screamed in my dream. "Not in the car. I can't breathe. Please don't do this to me." I felt awake and asleep at the same time, my heart pounding, frozen in place. "Let me out of here. Somebody help me. Please help me," screamed the girl. Curly dark hair pressed against a car window. A splayed hand pushed on the glass.

I bolted upright in bed fighting to catch my breath. Claire's face. White as a ghost. Pleading. In my dream Claire had cried out for help, her dark eyes wide with terror.

In my nightmare she was being murdered.

◇◇◇

I'd only been awake for twenty minutes, but it felt like an eternity. After pacing back and forth in the apartment I called my buddy on the police force, Luke Gianetti. From the sound of his voice, I guessed I'd interrupted him. Rumor had it he was dating up a storm now that his fiancée had broken off their engagement. With the horrifying dream fresh in my mind I didn't care about his suddenly active social life.

As soon as he answered I started talking. "You're going to think I'm crazy but I had a dream about Claire Birnham. Someone put her in her car and started it. Then I began thinking about it and I really feel Claire's death couldn't be a suicide. She wouldn't have abandoned her dog. Toto was like a baby to her."

"Hold up a minute." Music sounded in the background. "What's going on?"

"Well, Toto is here at the hospital. Claire was supposed to pick him up today. Why would she kill herself? This whole thing feels wrong, Luke."

"Calm down, Kate. You wouldn't have any hard evidence to back this up, would you?"

"No." I stammered in frustration. "But my staff thinks it's strange, too."

"Okay." His voice, annoyed. "Does anyone on your staff have any evidence?"

"No," I admitted.

"Kate, the investigation is still active so I can't discuss it with you. I know you mean well," Luke sounded like he was deliberately picking his words, "but with suicides, you never know."

"But..."

He interrupted me. "Having someone close die like this is very traumatic. Your mind is probably trying to work through it by using that dream."

His words made sense but didn't help much.

It always came back to that phrase, I thought, after we hung up. You never know. I'd taken enough psych courses to recognize the validity of his point, but the dream felt so real. My nerves on end, I poured myself a glass of cold white wine.

Luke asked me if all I had was a feeling. I guess that was true. I didn't know much about Claire's personal life or family situation that could have brought her to such a fatal decision. Her mother lived in town somewhere, but I'd never met her. What was I going to do, call her out of the blue and have a chat? Ask why her daughter killed herself? Wasn't everything bad enough without me adding to her burden?

As I turned out the lights to go to bed an unsettling thought hit me.

Maybe Claire couldn't rest in peace yet.

Maybe she wanted to tell me something.

Chapter Three

My fears that Claire might haunt me over the weekend proved groundless. After a dreamless night's sleep I woke up to my pager going off, alerting me to another Monday morning emergency call. I pulled on my scrubs and ran for the door without even taking a shower. Mari peeled out of the parking lot before I realized I'd forgotten something very important. Coffee.

Mari filled me in as she drove. Our receptionist, Cindy, had received a frantic call that blood was pouring out of a cocker spaniel's ear and the owner couldn't get it to stop. A gruesome story, but it turned out to be a slight, no, make that a gigantic exaggeration.

Bitsy, a blond six-year-old cocker spaniel, greeted me enthusiastically at the front door. Her wiggling body matched the synchronized shaking of her head. A "stinky feet" smell rose from her ears and wafted up to me while I stood in the entrance. Her owner, a thin fortyish woman in paint-splattered clothes, looked panic stricken. Clutched in her hand was a Kleenex with one drop of blood on it.

"Hi, I'm Dr. Kate Turner from the Oak Falls Veterinary Hospital. You called about Bitsy?"

"Yes. Do you see it? She's bleeding." With that she brought us into the foyer and dropped to her knees on the marble floor. Bitsy slobbered all over her, oblivious to the drama.

I couldn't see much of anything in the dark foyer, plus Bitsy kept sliding on the slick surface.

"Don't worry. We can take care of that." I tried to reassure the owner. People who take their own injuries in stride sometimes fall apart when their pet is hurt. "Could we go into the kitchen?" I asked. "The light is usually better plus I can examine her on a table or countertop, if that's okay. It makes clean up much easier."

"Sure. That's a good idea. I'm Althea Kent, by the way." After slipping a leash on Bitsy I offered Althea a hand up.

We walked into a large, bright kitchen. One of the walls sported several paintings of fruits and vegetables. As I looked around I noticed decorative touches of glazed pottery and a Merlot wine-colored accent wall.

Althea cleared off the kitchen island and put newspapers down to protect the granite from Bitsy's thick nails. "This is where I groom her," she explained. "She's used to standing here for me." Before I could help she scooped the dog up in her arms and deposited her on the table. Bitsy thanked her with a brisk shake of her head. A clump of gunk flew out and dropped on the *New York Post.*

"Oh my God. Is that part of her ear?" Althea's voice went up three notches.

"No, not to worry." With exam gloves on I picked it up and slid it around between my finger tips. "This is debris from her ear canal." I lifted up one of Bitsy's ears and snuck a quick peek. My nose already told me what was wrong. The long-standing ear infection had thickened the inside of her ear, effectively narrowing the ear canal. A glance at the other ear confirmed that it was bilateral, affecting both sides. Most likely not a primary tumor or polyp. "Bitsy has a bad ear infection. The blood probably came from her scratching and shaking her ear. Take a look."

Althea came around the side of the table and hazarded a brief glance at the exposed ear. She made a squeak and retreated back to the other side. "I'm sorry. I'm usually much better than this, but it's been a terrible couple of days for me."

"Let me finish and I'll explain what we have to do to help her." An examination of the rest of the happy cocker showed no other problems but a slightly dry skin coat and a pudgy body. I took a separate culture and sensitivity swab from each ear, labeled them and put them in two separate lab pouches. When I inserted the long cotton tip into the ear the cocker spaniel groaned.

We put Bitsy down on the floor. Althea gave her a dog biscuit. I gathered up the newspapers, threw in my exam gloves, and put the whole thing in a garbage bag. After taking a moment to wash and disinfect my hands, I came back and sat down at the table.

"Ear infections can be pretty painful," I began. "Bitsy needs to be admitted to the hospital for the day for an ear exam and cleaning under light anesthesia. I'm also going to culture the stuff in her ears and do some blood tests, especially a thyroid test, to make sure everything is okay. Has she been tested for low thyroid before?"

"No."

"We also will teach you some massage techniques that will make her more comfortable."

Althea seemed like a nice person so I didn't want to insult her with my next question. I searched for a diplomatic way to tell her Bitsy smelled. Really bad.

"Have you noticed an odor coming from her ears?" I kept my tone very professional.

Her forehead wrinkled up. "No. But my friends tell me she stinks."

"You don't smell anything?" My voice was incredulous.

"I had a high fever when I was a kid," she explained, "and it left me with almost no sense of smell. That's probably why."

Lucky for Althea in this case, but unlucky for Bitsy. Another owner would have noticed the ear infection immediately. "I'm going to recommend a high quality hypoallergenic diet for a while, in case she has any food allergies that are contributing to her problem. Now, this isn't going to go away overnight." I paused to let that unfortunate truth sink in. "You'll need to medicate her and come back to the office for some rechecks."

Althea nodded. "Anything for my Bitsy."

"Great. I'll have the office call and set up an appointment for you." I got up from the table and noticed the paintings again.

Looking closely I read the signature at the bottom. A. Kent. "Are you the artist?"

She joined me and straightened the frame. "Yes. It's my hobby. These are acrylics."

The four paintings hanging together depicted a ripe tomato, a shiny purple eggplant, a green striped zucchini, and a lemon with leaves still attached. Painted in an impressionistic style, they looked good enough to eat.

"I like these," I told her truthfully.

"Thanks. I did them in an art class two years ago." She reached out and straightened another one of the canvases a touch.

"That sounds like fun." Maybe I should paint something—like a wall. Every room in my apartment was a dingy shade of beige.

Mari sat down at the kitchen table and started typing my treatment notes into our laptop.

"I was just about to make coffee. Would you like some?" Althea asked.

"Absolutely." My two vices left in life were coffee and homemade pie. Oak Falls had plenty of both.

"Me, too," my assistant chimed in.

Soon the smell of hazelnut crème coffee perfumed the kitchen, temporarily masking the odor of cocker spaniel.

With a wave of pure joy I finished a second delicious cup then stood up. Finished for now, Mari packed up everything and started to say her goodbyes. "Thanks for everything, Althea. Don't forget to confirm an appointment for Bitsy. And no food or water the morning of the procedure."

"Okay," she promised.

Mother Nature had played a dirty trick on some cocker spaniels by giving them heavy droopy ears that trap moisture and heat, creating a perfect environment to grow a host of nasty stuff. Most likely Althea would need to monitor Bitsy's ears for the rest of her life.

"By the way…"

I turned back for a moment expecting a question about her pet.

Althea looked slightly embarrassed. "It's just that…has anyone told you, that you look like a young Meryl Streep?"

"Yes, but not today." I tried to make a joke out of it. Personally I didn't see it. Maybe it was my longish nose and straight blond hair.

She squinted her eyes at me. "Only less dramatic."

"Great." I guess.

Mari honked the horn, which meant we were late for our next appointment and I should hurry up. With a wave goodbye I made my way down the walkway and got in the driver's seat. Busy entering the next address in the GPS, Mari stopped to remind me to make the first left out of the development.

When we turned onto Silver Hollow highway I mentioned the Meryl Streep thing.

"Hey, it's better than what that client told me yesterday."

My assistant was super athletic, ran marathons, and lifted weights in her spare time. She had impressive, actual muscles in her arms. Did they tell her she looked like Wonder Woman?

"So, what did they say?"

"She said my face reminded her of her basset hound, Dr. Watson."

"What?" It came out as almost a shout.

"My eyes were the same as his." Mari gave me a soulful glance. "I think she considered it a compliment."

Chapter Four

"Leave well enough alone!" Gramps yelled into the phone. A coughing spell quickly followed.

I'd heard those words before. It was Tuesday night. Luke Gianetti had dropped in with Chinese food, Buddy was barking at a storm rolling in, and I was trying to hear what my grandfather was saying between coughing spells.

"Listen to your grandfather," Luke commented. He neatly lifted a snow pea with his chopsticks and popped it into his mouth.

"Save some for me." I covered the receiver with my hand and tried for a stage whisper but it came out like a hiss.

"What did you say?" This time when Gramps spoke there was more wheezing than coughing.

"Nothing." Leaning back on the living room sofa, I waited for everything to calm down, wondering why I blurted out my concerns about Claire's suicide during our phone conversation. Gramps had limited mobility due to his COPD. Any excitement set him off and lately that was every time I talked to him.

"So, Gramps. How do you like the new place?" I blatantly changed the subject. Fried rice and orange chicken appeared in front of me as Luke slid a plate onto the coffee table, then went back into the kitchen. Buddy trotted after him, tail wagging in anticipation of a handout.

"It's okay. Not too bad."

An independent living facility was his new home and my grandfather wasn't sure about it. At the relatively young age of sixty-eight he'd ended up tethered to his oxygen tank after working first as fireman, then an arson investigator, for the City of New York the last thirty-five years. I'd set up a camera on his computer so we could video chat but he grumbled that he was too old to learn those new tricks.

It took a few minutes for him to catch his breath.

I used the opportunity to sample my food. My previous six months as a relief vet in outwardly bucolic Oak Falls had been quite an adventure, which is why Gramps wanted me to mind my own business. Quite by chance I'd stumbled onto two elderly clients who had been murdered.

"Katie. Are you there?" Gramps bellowed.

"I'm here. Did you take a puff from your inhaler?" Lately, that was all that would stop these coughing spells.

"Yeah. Works great."

"Sorry to get you all riled up."

Despite the puffer it took a moment for him to reply. "I'm just worried about you. This amateur detective stuff is dangerous. I don't know where you get it from."

Laughing I reminded him. "Gramps, I get it from you. Don't you remember those poker games—bringing home your buddies and talking about all the cases you were working on? That NYPD sergeant named Ray and your high school friend, Phil, the detective. Most nights you'd scatter your notes all over the coffee table then fall asleep in the La-Z-Boy. Once you were snoring, I'd go over and read everything. Some of those crime scene pictures were kind of gruesome for a teenage girl."

I realized Luke was sort of listening to our conversation. He didn't have much of a choice. Gramps used one of those amplifier things on his phone.

"You didn't." There was shock in his voice.

"Oh, yes I did. That's why I never objected when you made me take all those self-defense and karate lessons."

The wheezing began again then calmed down. "I suppose you're hard-headed and stubborn enough to want to find out the truth. That's what pushed me. Following the truth, no matter where it led. You scared me when you got mixed up in that other murder. It almost got you killed."

He couldn't see me smile. "What's the odds of that happening again? A million to one? Like being struck by lightning."

"You're probably right. But I worry anyway. Why don't you take up some nice hobby, like knitting?"

Clouds rolled past the kitchen window as the sun set behind the hills. A sudden gust shook the tree branches and skittered leaves across the parking lot. A windstorm was kicking up.

"Don't worry," I pleaded. "Love you, Gramps."

"Love you back, kid."

Before I hung up I assured him once again that I intended to be careful and not get into any trouble. I'm not sure he believed me.

"I'm off the phone," I yelled in Luke's general direction. Impatient with the chopsticks, I switched to a fork. The blanket that was supposed to save the sofa from dog hair had ended up in a bundle at my feet.

"Sorry, I couldn't help but hear your conversation." He opened the cabinet next to the sink and took out a glass.

"That's okay. It's only what you tell me all the time." My Gramps and local policeman Luke Gianetti were on the same page as far as my ever playing detective again was concerned.

"He's a great guy, Kate. You should listen to him." He poured himself some water, then sat next to me on the sofa. Buddy jumped up between us, hoping someone would drop something.

"Did you get egg rolls?"

"Of course I brought you egg rolls. I'd be afraid to show up without them."

Luke had a pre-law class at the community college on Tuesday night and he'd gotten in the habit of stopping by with Chinese food, so he wouldn't have to eat alone. Weekends were another story. Those he spent hanging out in a major way with different ladies in the neighboring towns. Since most weekday nights I worked late, then pulled on my sweats and sat in front of the television eating something from the freezer, it worked out well. Tuesday had became my Saturday night.

"I bought you some of that cream soda you like. It's in the fridge." Even though I ate takeout from Lucky Garden Restaurant at least once a week, it always tasted fantastic.

Luke stood up again and opened the refrigerator. "Got it. By the way, how's Jeremy?" The last part of the question got kind of muffled from his head being behind the door, but I figured it out.

"Fine. I've got a Skype date with him later this week."

"Romantic." He barely masked his sarcasm.

"How are Krissy and Missy and…I'm forgetting one…is it Sissy?"

"Lacey. Very funny."

"Right. I don't know how you keep them all straight. I'd find dating so many people confusing and rather exhausting." After my pronouncement I made a point of checking the takeout container for any goodies stuck on the sides.

"Very funny. They're friends. No drama, just fun. A whole bunch of us hang out together." He poured himself the cream soda. "You should join us sometime."

I could picture that. Me standing around watching him flirt with girls dressed in pretty clothes and lots of makeup. Making chit-chat. "Maybe. Our schedules don't really mesh."

"Speaking of meshing, I've got to get going. Want me to toss everything in the dumpster?"

"Sure. That way the whole place doesn't smell like Chinese food all night."

"Happy to oblige." He picked up his coat from the kitchen chair.

"See you next Tuesday. " I handed him my trash in a paper bag.

"Tuesday it is."

He pulled open the door. A wind gust rattled the screen, blowing a few leaves with it.

"Drive carefully," I cautioned him.

"Always."

I looked at my watch. His visit came out at a record forty-five minutes from start to finish, including the time I spent on the phone.

The dumpster lid creaked and then made a sharp slamming noise when it closed. After a few moments I heard Luke's SUV start up, his bright headlights shining for a moment through the curtains. Next, a crunch from gravel under his tires, and he was gone.

◇◇◇

A crack of thunder woke me up. I'd fallen asleep on the sofa in front of the television. No rain coming down yet. I needed to take Buddy out before the storm hit.

"Let's go, boy." We walked to the side door that led to the patio and parking lot. I reached for a flashlight hanging from the coat rack.

My mind wandered back to the conversation with Gramps. Maybe Claire had been secretly depressed. What if she used antidepressant drugs that altered her state of mind, and made her forget about Toto? How well did I know her, anyway?

The wind kicked up. Buddy disappeared, heading for his favorite tree.

Lightning raced sideways across the sky. It reminded me how fragile our time here on Earth was. Anything could happen at any time.

The first raindrops fell, followed by more sharp cracks of thunder.

"Buddy, come on." A pungent odor filled the air. Ozone. A flash of lightning lit the sky directly above us. Buddy raced across the grass to me, whining. He hated storms.

◇◇◇

A deafening crash, followed by another bolt of lightning startled us both. Alone in the distance, a towering pine tree burst into flames. Even with all the doors and windows closed I could hear the fire engines coming up the road and smell the sharp tang of smoke. It probably crept under the door or slid through cracks in the window frames. Worried, I'd called the fire department only to be told that the blaze was contained, and that residents should stay inside and not get in anyone's way. With the flames smoldering, the smoke smell got worse before it started to dissipate.

Buddy decided to sleep in my bed, smack up against my leg. He needed the companionship of someone pressed close to him to reassure him everything was all right.

He wasn't the only one.

Chapter Five

Out of respect for our client and friend, Cindy canceled morning appointments so we could attend Claire Birnham's funeral service. I'd stuffed half the staff in Doc's old Ford 150 truck with the others squished into Cindy's new VW bug. The only one who didn't show up was Eugene. Once there, we hurried up the steps of Blessed Heart Catholic Church as the hearse rounded the corner.

The chilly air inside smelled of smoke and incense. Morning sunlight streamed through the stained glass windows depicting the Stations of the Cross, its warmth only a promise. Above the main altar brilliant reds and blues from a large glass panel of Christ's Ascension Into Heaven created rainbow prisms. Claire would have liked the effect.

The casket rolled down the aisle blanketed with white roses. A woman with dyed red hair walked heavily behind it. She clutched the arm of a muscular man with a buzz cut and almost stumbled. Despite the scarlet hair, the resemblance left no doubt in my mind that this was the bereaved mother. As they passed by I recognized Althea sitting across from us, a Kleenex clenched in her fist. The organ played a hymn I didn't recognize, then ended with a flourish when the priest stepped up to the podium to address the crowd.

Funerals are all different and all the same.

I found myself thinking about my mom's and brother's funeral, surprised I remembered anything about that day. Gramps had sat on my right, eyes red, smelling of cigarettes and

Sea Breeze aftershave, his big hand awkwardly holding mine. On the other side, bolt upright, sat my father, dry-eyed and aloof. People kept coming up to me and talking, trying to hug me or whisper condolences, not sure how to comfort a fifteen-year-old who'd lost most of her family. They didn't know I was mad, mad at my father for buying a small car that could be so easily smashed, T-boned by a drunk driver's truck. Mad that my doctor father stayed late at the hospital that night doing surgery. Mad because mom had indulged my baby brother, Jimmy, with a trip to the ice cream place, because he liked to watch them mix all the additions into his cookies and cream. Mad that I had been snotty to them all and decided to stay in my room and sulk.

Gramps told me later in an anguished voice that the police found a takeout bag next to her purse. Always loving, my mom had brought home butter pecan ice cream, my favorite.

At the end of Claire's service we all filed down the aisle. Ahead of me I saw Luke, his arm around his grandmother, and recognized some clients scattered among the somber crowd. By the time we reached the huge church doors Luke had vanished. At the bottom of the steps a cluster of mourners surrounded the woman with red hair. As our group walked toward them the crowd thinned out and for a moment she stood there alone.

An usher who had greeted Cindy by name hurried over and touched Claire's mother on the shoulder. I saw him look our way, then bend down to whisper something in her ear. She nodded, seemed to sway on her high heels, then made a beeline for us.

Her gentleman friend reached us first. "Mrs. Birnham wants to thank all of you for taking such good care of Claire's dog."

"That's right." A slight slur gave her away.

She was drunk. Not the kind of one-time reaction to tragedy drunk, but the broken capillaries under the makeup kind of alcoholic. The smell of vodka oozed from every pore. People think vodka has no odor but they're wrong. When she spoke I could smell it mixed with the sharp tang of breath mints.

"Thank you," Cindy replied, on behalf of the hospital. "And thanks, Buzz." Obviously the bereaved mother had no idea who I was.

"I'm Dr. Kate Turner, Claire's veterinarian. I'm so sorry for your loss." The male friend who had stood next to her turned away for a moment to speak to the limousine driver waiting at the curb.

Claire's mother stared vacantly at me. "Where is the little monster?"

"Beg your pardon. What did you say?"

Mari caught my eye, a puzzled look on her face.

"That nasty rat dog, Toto." She spat the words out. "Where the hell is he?"

I was at a loss for words.

Cindy came to the rescue. "He's boarding at the animal hospital, Mrs. Birnham."

Strangely, Claire's mother didn't say anything in reply.

Feeling as though I needed to respond I said, "I'm so sorry. Please don't be concerned. We can talk about this some other time."

"How much is the bill?" She shook her head as though trying to chase the cobwebs out.

Again, I was taken aback. "Uh, I think it's about two hundred dollars," I stammered, not really sure, trying to catch Cindy's eye.

"Too much." She stepped away, her black dress swishing as she moved. Over by the limo we saw the man with the buzz cut signal they were about to leave.

Mortified, I didn't know what to do.

Abruptly she turned back. A mean expression pulled one side of her mouth down.

"Keep the little fur ball or get rid of him. I could care less."

Now in a hurry Mister Buzz Cut put his arm around her waist and guided her down the walkway toward the funeral lead car, directly behind the waiting hearse. She twisted away from him for a moment. Inexplicably she waved goodbye with the tips of her fingers.

Chapter Six

We rode in stunned silence all the way to the hospital.

"That was awkward." Cindy said when I got back to the office. She handed me my afternoon schedule. Because of the funeral all my appointments were squeezed together, one after another, leaving me without a lunch break.

"Sorry, Dr. Kate. I did the best I could. " Her normally sunny disposition dimmed. "Do you want some of my potato chips or a banana?"

"Don't worry about it." My stomach growled as I peeled the offered banana and tried to talk at the same time.

"That was awkward." Cindy said for about the fifth time. "At the funeral."

"Extremely. I'm glad you're handling the paperwork instead of me." Picking up the chips, I stuffed an apple in my pocket, and Mari and I made our way out to the truck. During the short walk I thought about that bizarre exchange with Claire's mother. I wondered why she hated her daughter's dog so much.

"Turn right in point-five miles" chimed our GPS in its charming British accent.

We turned onto Neeton Drive, then made a quick left to Reddick. The homes in this area all had at least an acre of land surrounding them, resulting in a spacious and appealing neighborhood. Most of the original ranches had been renovated and turned into large sprawling buildings with three-car garages.

All had artfully landscaped front yards surrounded by stacked bluestone walls.

"Leaves are starting to turn." My assistant rolled down her window. Patches of bright red or yellow leaves signaled fall would be here soon, followed by the long cold winter.

"Mari, what did this client call about?" I retrieved my stethoscope hanging from the rearview mirror.

"Some kind of skin thing." She looked at the computer screen and pulled up the appointment notes. "A lump on the dog's back."

"Okay, let's go." As always, out of habit, I ran through the many diagnostic possibilities before I saw the patient. This time I didn't even come close.

The furry mixed-breed dog in front of me with pale hazel eyes looked like a combination of Old English Sheepdog and a certain British rock 'n' and roll star. His abundant hair flew in all directions, as did he.

"Jagger," said his owner, Tracy. "Sit." She tried pressing on his hindquarters. "Down, Jagger, down." Her commands ignored, the dog continued to leap up, twisting and turning in undisciplined joy. Slobber dribbled from his thick doggie lips. "He's a little excited to have you here."

"Why don't you let Mari hold him?" I asked the increasingly frantic owner.

Mari looked at me and nodded. I stood back, ready to witness something truly extraordinary.

"Jagger, sit." His eyes rolled and locked with Mari's. Nothing happened for a moment. Then he sat.

She held up her hand, palm open, then pointed. "Down."

The dog lay down and stayed still.

I almost burst into applause. Mari was one of those technicians you run into once in a while if you are lucky. She had the whammy on dogs. No physical force needed with her, or any kind of extra restraint. When she spoke they listened. It was a thing of beauty.

"Where is that lump?" I asked the astonished owner. A three-foot sea of tangled fur on his back loomed before me.

Tracy immediately bent down and walked her fingers to a spot to the left of the spinal column. My fingers confirmed the position, then I trimmed some hair with my bandage scissors so we could easily find it again.

With Jagger cooperating, I palpated his lymph nodes with my gloved hands, checked his mouth and teeth, and then listened to his heart to get an idea of his general physical health. Satisfied, I zeroed in on the lump. Parting the hair further, I uncovered a firm mass about two and a half inches across and spongy to the touch right on top. There was no sign of infection. I shined my penlight on the skin. As I suspected, there was a small hole in the center. A breathing hole.

"Are there any horses around this area? Or has Jagger been around a barn or farm in the last two weeks?"

Puzzled, Tracy's high forehead wrinkled in thought. "My daughter rides. We head to the stable once a week for her lesson and I usually take Jagger with me. They have a fenced-in dog run out back and I let him play with the stable dogs. Why?"

Mari let our Old English patient up. Ecstatic with joy, he immediately ran around the room, long pink tongue hanging out of his mouth.

Putting my penlight back in my pocket I gave Tracy the good and bad news. "First, he doesn't have a tumor."

"Oh, thank God," she interjected.

"That's the good news. What he does have is a fly bot, a larva called cuterebra that is living under his skin and growing. It needs to be removed."

Again the frown, then a look of pure disgust. "Is it dangerous? Can we catch it?"

"No to both questions. It's more of an annoyance, although rarely some animals can have severe allergic reactions to them. He'll have to come in to the hospital and be given a light anesthesia or tranquilizer so we can remove it."

"Will it leave a scar?"

"It might, but once it heals, with all that fur you probably won't notice it. Can I use your phone? I'm going to call our receptionist, Cindy, and see when we can fit you in on the surgery schedule. I don't want this thing causing any more damage."

While Jagger's mom arranged things with Cindy, Mari and I played with the energetic dog who only needed consistent training and routine exercise to be a better pet. Very often the owner needs as much training as the dog. As we made him sit for the tenth time, the front door opened and a blond teenage girl, long hair pulled into a tight ponytail, came in. She was dressed in riding clothes. This must be the daughter Tracy mentioned.

"Oh," she said, looking up from her phone. "Who are you?"

"I'm Dr. Kate Turner, from the Oak Falls Veterinary Hospital. Your mom wanted me to check the lump on Jagger's back." By now the dog looked like he would wiggle out of his skin, greeting his teenage master.

"Oh, yeah. What is it?" She absentmindedly petted the dog's head while texting on her phone.

"A fly bot."

Surprisingly she knew exactly what it was. "Ick. One of the horses had that about a month ago. It was gross."

Mari nodded her head in agreement. "Totally gross."

"Hi, honey." Tracy came back into the room to greet her daughter. "How was your ride?"

She glared at her mother. "Mom, it was a ride. How do you think it was?"

To her mom's credit she didn't even flinch.

"Well, I think we'd better be going. They booked us pretty tight today." One really awkward encounter a day was my limit. I'd leave them to fight it out.

The teenager tore herself away from her phone for a moment. She got a sly look on her face. "Someone who rode at my stable just died."

"Oh my gosh, did they get thrown?" Tracy asked, concern in her voice.

"No. This chick named Claire killed herself." Her matter-of-fact tone might have been meant to shock her mother. If she expected a horrified reaction from us, she didn't get it.

To change the subject Tracy asked Mari a question about billing. As they spoke I focused on the girl and decided to snoop a little.

"Did you know Claire well?" It was odd carrying on a conversation when the other person was staring at a screen.

"Not well."

"Suicide is very sad."

No reaction from the girl whatsoever.

"I'm sorry, I didn't get your name." At least she could tell me that.

With an annoyed look on her face, she reluctantly gave me her name. "Lark. Like the bird." Her voice dripped with sarcasm. Then her attention drifted back to her cell phone.

The reticence of some teenagers to talk about anything with an adult killed me. But at her age I was just as bad.

"Did she ride alone or with a group?" I had the feeling this was a losing battle.

"Some guy."

"Can you describe him?"

An exaggerated sigh followed as though I was taking up precious time that could be better spent texting.

"Ah. Tallish, dark curly hair, jeans, cowboy boots with crescent moons. Cute for an old dude."

I was okay until I heard about the boots. I knew those boots. In fact, I'd seen them on a semi-regular basis over the last few months.

Those boots belonged to Luke Gianetti, my Tuesday night Chinese takeout buddy and contact at the local police department. Why would Luke go riding with Claire Birnham?

And why would he hide it from me?

Chapter Seven

The thought of Luke and Claire riding together filled my imagination with unanswered questions. Had they been a couple? With my appointments finished for the day I loaded Buddy into the truck and took a ride downtown.

Luke and I had settled into an easy friendship. I was in a sort-of long distance relationship with an anthropologist I knew from college, Jeremy Schaeffer, and Luke was in multiple rebound flirtations with women whose names ended with the letter "y". It wasn't hard to understand how he felt, being free to date for the first time since high school. He definitely wanted to sow some wild oats, needed to sow those oats and get them out of his system. We were both on the rebound from failed relationships and not eager to move into anything serious. For now, being friends felt like the perfect solution.

What baffled me was why he didn't confide in me, tell me the extent of his relationship with Claire. Maybe there was a reason he accepted her death as a suicide.

It only took fifteen minutes to reach the village of Oak Falls. The town spread out over several miles, but the small historic center only filled a couple of blocks along Main Street. On most weekend nights the stores stayed open late, luring the many visitors who drove up from the metropolitan New York City area. I eased into an empty parking space near the gelato store. With Buddy on his leash next to me we started a slow stroll around town.

Besides walking off my nervous energy I had an ulterior motive. The art gallery Claire had worked at was somewhere here on Main Street. Maybe I could casually drop in for a visit and speak to the owner. I joined the many people browsing the shops and stopped to get Buddy an organic homemade doggy bone from the Love My Dog store. The owner had crammed all kinds of dog-related items into the small store, a new addition to Main Street, plus she had set up a cute patio with pet friendly tables outside. She'd recently begun selling coffee and desserts for her human customers, too.

Buddy and I were both enjoying our treats, his a peanut butter-flavored dog bone, mine a double espresso, when someone paused next to us.

"Dr. Kate?"

I looked up to see Althea standing next to us.

"I wanted to thank you. My Bitsy is doing great."

"That's wonderful. No problems? "

"None. I spoke to the office yesterday and gave them an update."

A couple with a stroller ambled past us.

"Is this your dog?" She bent down to say hi.

"Yes, this is Buddy." I noticed she carried a plate with a brownie, and balanced a coffee in her other hand.

"Would you like to join me?"

Her face broke into a smile. "Sure. Thanks."

We sipped our coffee in silence for a moment.

"I don't know about you but I had a chocolate attack. These are so so good."

I nodded in agreement. "Believe me, it's taking all my will-power not to get one."

She gazed out to the street. "My friend Claire and I always stopped here when we went shopping. These brownies were her favorite."

The funeral. I remembered then that Althea had been at Claire's funeral.

It turned out not only did Althea know Claire, but they had been close friends for the last few years, going out to lunch once a week and frequently taking art classes together. Their tastes were eclectic, she told me, from slump glass work to figure drawing. Both celebrated their creativity.

"So, were you surprised to learn about her suicide?" Eager to hear what she'd say, I forgot about my coffee.

"Completely." Her clear blue eyes welled up with tears.

"We don't have to talk about it if you don't want to."

"No, I want to." Althea looked away and spoke in a soft voice. "We had made plans to go into the city together, after she picked up Toto. Just for the day. She needed to get away."

"Why is that?" I finished my last sip of coffee, very dark and bitter.

Althea used a corner of her paper napkin to blot her eyes. "Her boss at Qualog is a perfectionist. Claire organized the exhibits, did the publicity, and manned the phones. This new exhibit took up a huge amount of her time. Between the artist's demands and Gilda she barely got everything done on time."

"Who is Gilda?" Although I'd been in Oak Falls a little over six months I wasn't familiar with the name.

"Gilda Treemont. The owner of the Qualog art gallery. We called it the Q spot behind her back." Again, her eyes filled with tears as she remembered her friend.

I wanted to keep Althea talking if possible. "Was there anything else troubling her? Boyfriends? Family?"

She reached down and gave Buddy a little attention before answering. "I've been going over and over all of this in my head since I heard about…since, you know. Claire broke up with her boyfriend, A.J. about ten months ago, but she's the one who called it off. She told me she was ready to expand her horizons, whatever that meant." Althea smiled at the thought. "Her mom got back together with Buzz, who Claire hated, but that's no surprise. They've been on and off for years. Her mom, Bev, is an alcoholic. Most of the time she's on the wagon but when she slips—she slips in a big way."

I nodded. "She introduced herself at the funeral."

"Yeah, that was bad." Her voice trailed away. Picking up her trash she took one more wistful look around. "Claire kept a lot of things to herself. I keep thinking if she'd only told me I could have helped."

What do you answer to that?

She hoisted her purse over her shoulder. "Well, thanks for listening, Dr. Kate."

"No problem. Any time."

"I meant to ask you. Who is going to take Toto? I would but he's nipped Bitsy a couple of times. They really don't seem to get along with each other."

"We're working on it."

"Thank you. I know she trusted you, and she loved that dog so much. He was her baby." Again, she shook her head in frustration. "I guess you never know." Holding all the plasticware, she walked over to the recycle pail and pushed it through the slot.

After saying goodbye and letting Buddy sniff some new dog friends, we continued on our way. The Qualog Art Gallery ended up being a few doors down, the exterior painted a sleek black and white. A massive antique door, the birch wood elaborately carved and gnarled with age, contrasted with the modern storefront. The juxtaposition between new and old made a strong and pleasing statement. A small sign by the door said "We welcome well-behaved dogs." According to the sign the gallery would close in less than an hour. Keeping Buddy by my side, I went in, and a tiny bell chimed to announce a visitor.

The open space in the front displayed only one painter. This must be the show Althea told me about, the one Claire worked on before her death. The paintings hanging on the stark white walls had a gorgeous vibrancy, landscapes with imaginary plants and vines forcing your attention with unexpected color and texture. No simple flowers in a vase for this artist. The effect was bold and compelling.

Before I could take in the entire effect a woman's voice called out from the other room. "Please look around. I'll be with you in a moment."

Uncertain, I waited in the middle of the room. Above the paintings small metal lights illuminated from several angles. Drawn to one canvas in particular I decided to take a closer look. As I approached I noticed how thickly the paint was applied.

"Amazing, aren't they?" A tall slender woman with slanting dark eyes and long silken hair appeared behind me. "His technique is impeccable. We're going to host his first major show."

"What is the artist's name?"

She seemed perturbed for a moment, as though I should know the answer to that question.

"Andrei Roshenkov." Her eyes darted around the room, then stopped. With a furious frown on her lovely face she strode to the far wall and picked up an easel leaning against the corner. I watched as she began texting someone. When she noticed me staring she briefly turned her back to me. After a moment the annoyed look vanished, replaced by a certain level of concentration. A salesperson hoping to make a deal.

"Are you interested in purchasing something for yourself?"

"Not at this time." The price tag on the painting in front of me was $13,000, definitely out of my range. A print from Marshalls for $19.95 was more my speed at the moment, but if I had the money I'd certainly be tempted.

"Perhaps you'd like to view some of our other works?" She led me into another large room subdivided by moveable screens. "I'm Gilda Treemont, by the way." Her offered hand felt smooth and cool.

"Kate Turner."

Please, take your time, Kate. I'll be right back."

I could see no evidence that anyone was mourning Claire here. Not even a picture of her in the window.

Gilda walked briskly into what looked like an office at the back of the gallery and shut the door. Even through the walls I could hear her yelling at someone. After a few moments a young woman bolted out of the room and ran past me, head down, a streak of blue prominent in a mass of mahogany dyed hair.

Buddy noticed her movement, then whimpered.

I started to double back to the exit but Gilda caught up with me.

"Do you have any questions?" Her calm face showed no evidence of the angry confrontation that had just taken place. In a simple beige silk dress with a tooled leather belt slung around her narrow hips, she radiated exquisite, slightly bohemian taste.

I took a deep breath and went for it. "Actually, I came in to see what my friend Claire had been working on before she died."

Her pupils dilated for a moment, then she brought her hand to her neck. The scrolled silver bracelets around her wrists made a dull ring. "Forgive me. It was so unexpected. She did a wonderful job presenting Andrei's work. The lighting and placement of the canvases were all her idea."

I nodded my head and kept my eyes on her. Gilda shifted and absently played with a delicate turquoise ring on her finger.

"Claire was very gifted and a fine artist herself. I'm thinking of doing a retrospective of her work. Maybe next month." The gallery owner became slightly more uncomfortable and slowly started drifting back toward the entrance.

"She never hinted she was unhappy?" I walked alongside her.

"Well, you know young women, one minute up and the other minute down. She worked very hard, though. We'll all miss her." Gilda's face composed itself into a polite version of sorrow.

On my way out I passed the antique easel again, but now it held a three-foot by four-foot publicity photo of a handsome man in his thirties. The black and white portrait caught him grinning at someone off-camera. With longish blond hair and a slight stubble on his cheeks he reminded me of a young Brad Pitt with a hint of Russia in his cheekbones.

Gilda's eyes rested on the portrait, her face gentle for the first time. "This is Andrei. Did you want to meet him? I expect him very soon. He is as beautiful as his work."

I wondered if she knew she had said that last sentence out loud. Was their relationship more than a professional one? With a quick thank you I took one last look around, and noticed the young girl who had fought with Gilda now busy with a feather duster. Our eyes met briefly. Her body language signaled a beaten dog. Althea had said Claire's boss was a perfectionist.

Did a violent argument with her boss push a depressed Claire over the edge? I needed a mood elevator, which in my case isn't pills—it's either chocolate or a piece of pie. I decided to stop fighting with my sweet tooth and give in.

Oak Falls is pie heaven thanks to Mama G., the owner of the Oak Falls Diner and grandmother to the Gianetti family. For the last ten years or more her pies have won awards and acclaim from the *New York Times* to Yelp. Most of the restaurants in the area carried her pies, proudly advertising them on their menus.

Judy's served freshly cooked breakfasts and lunches plus Mama G.'s pies. They closed each evening at six-thirty and reopened at seven the following morning, so if I wanted to get anything, I'd have to move fast. Luckily a table outside opened up as I approached. I headed toward it, then realized I was in competition with a tall man in dark sunglasses walking a French Bulldog. Short of racing to the table like a round of musical chairs, we were both on an intercept path and arrived at the same time.

"Would you like to share the table?" he asked. "Wilson is a little tuckered out." Sure enough the black and white Frenchie was panting up a storm.

"That would be wonderful. My guy Buddy is ready for his water break." I sat down under the umbrella, then took out a dog bowl and thermos from my backpack. "Maybe Wilson would like some water too," I suggested. The dogs sniffed noses and other body parts, then, slurped up most of the water, before lying down at our feet in the shade.

"Nice day," he said politely after we gave the server our orders.

"Yes."

His phone chime rang, possibly indicating a text message or email. Turning his chair, he slipped off his sunglasses and proceeded to speedily work the keyboard in answer. Without the glasses on he looked familiar. I must have stared, because he stopped in mid keystroke, then continued texting. In one of those odd coincidences, I was sharing the table with the artist Andrei Roshenkov.

Our plates arrived at that moment, and he put his phone down on the table. He had ordered an espresso, while I had pigged out with a slice of peach pie and cup of tea. I waited for a moment, then took a chance, "Are you Andrei Roshenkov, the artist?"

He leaned his head to one side. "Yes. Do I know you?"

"No, but I just saw some of your work. I'm Kate Turner."

That elicited a broad smile. The publicity picture didn't do him justice. He was one fine looking guy. "Were you in the Qualog Gallery?" he asked. "I'm on my way there now to meet Gilda. They seem to be doing a great job with the presentation, and advertising. I've had several major reviews."

"Yes. I knew the woman who helped stage it. Claire? Claire Birnham?"

A puzzled look came over his face for a moment, as if he had to place the name. Then recognition seemed to click in. "Oh yes, Gilda told me what happened. Terrible. I didn't know her well. We met a few times to discuss the show. Such a sweet young thing."

"Were there any problems at the gallery?"

Again, he seemed puzzled. "I don't think so. Everyone got along fine."

I continued, since he didn't seem to object to my questions. "Are you familiar with her work?"

"Yes. She lit the canvases in a very creative way using different light spectrums. I may experiment with that from now on. It gave what they call 'a punch' to the colors." He smiled at me.

Obviously he'd misunderstood. "I meant her artwork. She painted abstracts I believe."

"That's very popular now," he laughed. "In my opinion, with abstract art you don't have to worry about composition or drawing skill, you can call anything art. In Russia teachers require great discipline from their students, unlike here in the United

States." After tasting his coffee he continued. "So you liked the arrangement of my work? Which one did you like best?"

"I liked them all."

"Interesting. I find it hard to choose between them myself. I would be embarrassed by my fantastic reviews if they weren't true."

Self-centered and oblivious to everything going on around him, Andrei obviously didn't have an artist's tortured soul, but creativity blossoms in unexpected places. It took persistence and drive to paint those canvases plus a great deal of hard work to corral a gallery show. So what if he seemed more like an actor or model than a stereotypical artist dressed in worn clothes dotted with paint?

The French Bulldog whined under the table. Immediately, his master bent down to slip him a small dog biscuit from his manicured fingers.

At least his dog had a reason to like him.

Chapter Eight

The next two days at work were crazy, busy, hectic where-did-the-day-go kind of days. Each night I fell into bed, not needing anything to lull me to sleep. In the morning I would wake up, have my coffee, slip into a new set of scrubs and set off running. One day blended into the next. The intense workload pushed Claire into the back of my mind.

We were X-raying a Dalmatian with a bladder full of stones on Friday afternoon when Mari mentioned something that brought everything home again.

"Are you going to the yard sale tomorrow? You know, Claire's stuff?" Despite the clumsy lead-lined X-ray gloves and apron, neck thyroid guard, and goggles she wore, Mari effortlessly positioned the dog on his side for the first view.

With a click of the remote button the lateral view was done. Now to roll the dog over for a ventral dorsal view with the patient on his back. As I helped turn him I said, "I didn't know anything about it. What time does it start?"

"I think the paper said eight, but I can't get there till around noon. I'm looking for a coffee table." Satisfied with Spots the Dalmatian's position, kept in place by weights on both sides, we retreated behind the lead-lined door and took the second view.

Together we slid the dog onto a stainless steel rolling table and after drawing bloods, taking a sterile urine sample, and clipping his toenails, we moved him onto the blankets set up in his cage. Normally Eugene would be watching Spots come up from anesthesia, once the endotrachael tube was removed, but without him to help I hung out with one eye on the dog and the other on my data entry notes.

Mari began to clean the cage next to me when a bolt of brown fur flashed past her head, accompanied by a terrible yowl.

"No," she yelled out. "Bad boy." The furry obstacle turned to look at her, eyes glowing, from the safety of the rolling IV stand.

"You've been pranked by Mr. Katt." At the sound of his name our hospital kitty gazed innocently at the ceiling.

"Do you think he knows he's scaring people?" She bent down and continued using the spray bottle of cleaner.

"I think he knows exactly what he is doing. And he likes it." Mr. Katt had a cat smirk on his face. If you believed cats can smirk at you.

Soon the young Dalmation was up and banging his tail like Calypso steel drums on the sides of the cage. Mari moved him into a large run and we started getting ready to close. Until we got the lab tests and culture samples back, Spots would stay with us and have his urine output measured and recorded. He needed to be on a special diet to control the increased uric acid found in his bloodstream, similar to gout in people. Unfortunately, the modern Dalmatian breed possesses a genetic mutation that contributes to the formation of bladder stones in some dogs. Breeders and veterinary geneticists are hard at work trying to eliminate this problem from their bloodlines.

"You would never know he just had anesthesia." Mari came back into the treatment room, drying her hands with a paper towel.

"He's a happy camper, that's for sure," I commented. "Are we ready to lock up?"

Mari glanced at the treatment board. "Looks like it."

"Have a great weekend. Don't party too hard at the wedding."

Since a former employee was getting married on Saturday night during the Labor Day weekend and several staff members were participating, Cindy decided to close the office early, and limit appointments to half a day on Saturday for current client emergencies only. The answering service would pick up our calls and refer them to the emergency hospital, which meant that after noon tomorrow, no work for me until Tuesday. Maybe I would run over and join Mari at the sale. Most likely, morbid curiosity on the part of people in the community would pack the place.

My premonition turned out to be correct. When I pulled into the address advertised for the yard sale, cars lined the street on both sides. I'd gotten there a few hours after it started but obviously there must have been lots of early buyers. Red SOLD tags sprouted on many of the large items while the tabletops looked picked-over. Like every yard sale when you get there late, most of the cool things were gone. Card tables held miscellaneous items and impromptu shelving popped up all over the front yard. A hand-lettered sign said "More Indoors" so that's where I headed first, thinking I might find Mari inside.

Claire's townhome turned out to be an end unit with a soaring two-story living room and elegant stairs leading to the second floor. At one point it must have been lovely, bright white walls, a spacious room beckoning with its purple sofa and loveseat. Now those pieces and most of the furniture had been pushed next to the wall. A dining room table and chairs were being carried out as I entered. Dodging them, I moved off to the left near the gas fireplace.

"Hey, Kate," someone yelled above me. I looked up to see Mari leaning over the second-floor landing railing. "Come on up." She gestured toward the stairs, then disappeared.

As I walked up the steps I noticed the carpet looked a little dingy, unlike the rest of the house. The walls up here were also white, but with nail holes and vague outlines of paintings clearly visible on the paint. Probably Claire had hung some of her artwork there. When I got upstairs I noticed a vague smell of paint or turpentine. Not overwhelming; only a faint hint in the air.

I glanced into a small but cozy bedroom, where Mari was busy speaking to someone about the two nightstands for sale. The next room had been converted into an art studio with hardwood floors, wooden shutters on the windows, and a skylight. The tall ceiling matched the peak of the roof. Most people would have used it for the master bedroom, I thought. Stacked along one side of the wall were paintings arranged according to size. A cork bulletin board bristled with notes and doodles, plus articles cut from various newspapers. An adjustable easel stood in front of the window overlooking the backyard. On it rested a large painting, less abstract than some of the others. I recognized the stepping stones and curve of the water. This was the path to the small island in the river, near the Tube Depot in town. The water mesmerized me, swirling around the rocks and outcropping of reeds before dashing toward the Hudson River and eventually the sea.

A price tag of one hundred twenty-five dollars dangled from the wooden stretcher on the back of the picture. The artist's painted canvas wrapped around the corners of the frame making it look like the water flowed off the surface. Sprawled at the bottom in black paint I could make out Claire's initials.

"Like it?" A woman with a fanny pack strapped under her stomach came up behind me. As I stood there she judiciously slipped several bills into it. "My bank," she said, pointing to the leather pouch almost hidden by a large roll of belly fat.

I'd never seen her before. Was she a friend of the family helping out? My gaze went back to the canvas. "Yes. Actually I do like it, very much."

After zippering the pouch shut she moved toward the easel. "We can probably do a little better on the price. There are lots of paintings to get rid of."

"Doesn't Claire's mother want to keep some of them?" I looked around the room. At least thirty other works leaned against the walls.

The woman made a grunting noise. "That kid scribbled and drew from the time she was little. Bev told me she had enough of her stuff." A crafty look stole over her face. "It's a tragedy, but hey, you got to pay the bills. We can do one hundred on this."

I hesitated.

"Okay, for you, I'll go ninety, but that's my last offer. So, you want it?"

"Yes," I said, on an impulse. "Do you have bubble paper to wrap it up?"

"Maybe." She stood and waited expectantly. I realized she wanted the money first.

Before coming over I'd made a stop at the ATM in case I found something I liked. Once the transaction had been tucked away in her bank she began wrapping the picture.

"Are you a member of the family?" I asked as she taped down the hanging wire.

"No, I'm Evie, Bev's friend. We used to work at the factory together. Go out, have a couple of drinks, some laughs."

She put the painting down on a big piece of bubble paper, then proceeded to wrap it like a present. The two ends didn't quite meet so she pulled some newspaper off the bulletin board and made a patch.

"It just has to hold till you get it home." Evie certainly was optimistic.

"So you didn't know Claire that well?"

"No," she admitted, "but I heard a lot about her from Bev. I guess she put her mom through the wringer with drugs and guys when she hit her teens. Thank goodness I don't have kids." She stuck a red SOLD sticker on the wrapping and stood back.

Mari stuck her head in. "What did you get, Kate?"

"A painting. How about yourself?"

She grinned. "I made out like a bandit. A coffee table, two nightstands and a big soup pot."

It struck me that we were pawing through Claire's things, like going through a dead person's pockets. Even though the yard sale was practical, that didn't make it any more palatable.

"If you want I'll help you down the stairs with that," Mari said. "Be back in a few."

Already Evie, the lady with the money pouch, had latched on to some other buyers. The top floor became quiet as people meandered out with their prizes. Through the big windows

I could see that the line of cars parked along the road had dwindled. Curious about Claire's home I decided to look into the bedroom. The first adjective that came to mind was serene. A large faux stone Buddha head on the floor contributed to the feeling. I wondered if she did yoga in front of the calming statue. Wall-mounted swing lamps with SOLD signs made use of every tight inch of space. Both nightstands were gone, probably into Mari's truck.

The room was painted a matte gray-blue color. I noticed tiny silver stars adhered to the white ceiling surface. Claire had placed them to form the constellations. From her bed she'd have the heavens twinkling above her.

I'd done the same thing when I was twelve.

Most of her personal items had been removed. On the top of the dresser dusty imprints hinted at treasured items that once rested there, now probably displayed on the long tables set up on the front lawn. For a moment I wondered what my stuff would look like scattered on a table for people to pick through. Pretty sad.

"Kate," Mari called, "are you still up there?"

"Yeah. Can you help me with the picture?" Wrapped up, the picture slid easily along the wooden floor until I got it out onto the landing. It wasn't heavy at all, just awkward, since it must have measured four feet by five feet. Mari met me at the stairs and together we lifted it over the stair treads, being careful not to go flying ourselves. With Mari walking backward we carried it out to the truck where I wrapped it in blankets for the short ride home. Buddy watched from the front seat, jumping back and forth and wagging his tail. I'd rolled all the windows down to keep him comfortable in the sixty-degree weather.

"I'm taking off." Mari wore a big smile on her face. "This was the best, and see, you ended up with something too."

"Thanks to you. See you on Tuesday." Striped bungee cords tied tightly around her purchases, Mari backed up, then took off in the direction of her house. I decided to look at the last of the items set out on the front lawn. It was obvious Claire enjoyed traveling. There were two pieces of Italian pottery with vivid floral designs, a pyramid souvenir from the Louvre, a miniature replica of Stonehenge made out of textured plastic, and several framed pictures of Claire in front of various well-known sites, like the Eiffel Tower and Buckingham Palace. In all the photos she stood by herself, posing for the person behind the camera. Who had she traveled with? The rock musician ex-boyfriend ? Or a mystery man?

The prices on items ranged from twenty-five cents on up to two hundred dollars. I picked out a green bud vase with an elegant long neck marked two bucks and a leather-bound book of Emily Dickinson poems for five dollars, then called it a day. So far no emergencies waited on the horizon, so it looked like I had the weekend off. A cool breeze reminded me the sun would be setting soon, earlier and earlier the closer we inched toward winter. Buddy woofed at me from the passenger seat of the truck, his head and front paws hanging out the window. A former champion King Charles Spaniel, he now was just a happy-go-lucky, can-I-come-for-a-ride-please-please-please, kind of dog.

Fall was in the air but for the life of me I couldn't figure out a pattern to the leaves starting to change. Sometimes only one tree turned bright yellow in a field of green. More often a cluster of leaves hinted at a color to come. According to the locals the road along the Hudson River past Bear Mountain Park would be breathtaking in a few weeks. But along with the leaves came more visitors clogging up the roads. Everyone complained about the tourists but no one complained about the cash they spent.

I'd saved quite a bit living in Doc Anderson's converted garage apartment, I thought, as I pulled into the parking lot. I'd even sent in extra payments on my student loan. No commute, since it was attached to the animal hospital, meant no gasoline bill. The interior, however, still looked forlorn. Doc obviously didn't spend much time watching HGTV, the Home and Garden TV network. Slowly I'd changed some things to my own taste. The old squishy sofa now had a soft, colorful spread draped over it. The mismatched linens had been banished to the storage closet and a luxurious Ralph Lauren bedding package bought on sale made sleeping a pleasure. After taking Buddy for a walk I gave him a treat for being such a good traveler, then hung the picture on the wall near my bed. I checked the back to make sure the wire was secure and noticed an inscription. Across the back Claire had written "Life's Little Mysteries" and a date in a black pen. An odd title, I thought. I put the book of poetry on the nightstand and then placed the bud vase on a shelf in the pantry. By now it was five o'clock. Maybe I'd get into my sweats, make some soup, and watch a movie.

I wondered what Luke was doing tonight, then felt guilty about not thinking of Jeremy instead. Dutifully I fired off a quick hello to his email from my phone, figuring with the seven-hour difference he'd see it tomorrow.

Buddy suddenly jumped up from his bed and walked over to the side patio door that served as my front door. His tail slowly wagging, he barked a few welcome barks. The doorbell chimed. I took a look through the peephole, then opened the door.

"Hey. Watch out. Hot stuff." Luke Gianetti strode into the apartment, immediately making it feel smaller. Maybe Buddy was happy to see him but I wasn't. Recently all we did when we got together was argue.

"Don't put it there," I told him as he headed for the kitchen table. I could see a red greasy stain spreading across the bottom of the takeout bag. "It's leaking. Put it on the counter."

A grin spread across his face. "No wonder my hand is hot."

"Hey, what's going on? It's not Tuesday."

"Are you complaining?"

He started to unpack everything and spread it all over the kitchen I'd just cleaned up. Sure enough a small plastic container of Chinese hot sauce had opened and covered the bottoms of most of the cartons. "Here's some paper towels." I quickly ripped a few squares off the roll. The pungent smell of vinegar and chili spilled into the room.

"Thought you might be hungry." Not waiting for an answer he began dishing out shrimp in lobster sauce and something I didn't recognize. Like a magician he dug into a separate container and pulled out an egg roll. "Want one?" he offered.

Hunger overrode my annoyance. "Got any hot mustard?"

"Oops. Forgot that."

I was about to protest when I saw the smile on his face. "Why do you do that to me?" I asked as I found the little plastic container and opened the lid. The image of plum sauce spread on the crispy egg roll made me ravenous. "Come on. Let's sit down at least."

"Okay." He opened another container and spooned some of it onto the rice. His plate piled high, with the egg roll riding the top like a surf board, he sat down. "Chopsticks?"

"Got them." One hand juggled the plate while I handed a pair to him. For a couple of minutes only the sounds of our appreciative eating and the faint click of chopsticks filled the room. Buddy had stationed himself next to Luke. Even though I told him a million times not to feed the dog at the table, it fell on deaf ears.

He looked up from his plate and gestured with his head. "What's that?"

I followed his stare. "A painting. I bought it today."

Those dark eyes gazed thoughtfully at me for a moment. "One of Claire's?"

"Ummm," I replied, mouth full of food.

He rightly interpreted that as yes. "Yard sale?"

"Um hum."

He shifted his eyes back to the painting. "It's nice."

Finally finished chewing I answered his question. "Mari went this morning so I met her there. This was only ninety dollars, down from one hundred and twenty-five."

"I was going to go but I figured it would be pretty…pretty sad. " He turned away from me and looked back at the picture.

"It's a way of remembering her." I explained.

"True. I see your point."

"Good."

He shifted slightly in his seat, one hand at his side. I knew he'd given Buddy some chicken under the table. In a halfhearted attempt to distract me he said, "Remember what you promised your grandfather. Stay out of this Claire thing. I don't want to get any calls complaining about you stirring things up."

"Relax, will you. It was only a yard sale."

Any hope of a carefree dinner with Luke vanished with that comment. Should I question him about his horseback dates with Claire? Maybe now wasn't the best time.

My guest seemed intent on finishing his food at a new record speed.

The silence between us was deafening. I decided to wait and get my information from Rosie, who worked at the diner. To be thorough, I'd ask her about all his lady friends. I made one last attempt to be conciliatory. After all, he'd brought me dinner. "Don't worry, Officer. I don't intend to make things difficult for you. I'm much too busy."

Chopsticks suspended in the air, his suspicious brown eyes met my innocent blue eyes.

Obviously he didn't believe me for a minute.

Chapter Nine

The following Friday afternoon we had our monthly staff meeting which consisted, as always, of people stuffing enormous quantities of free pizza into their mouths. Amy, a part-time staff member and vet tech student, made a big deal out of eating her healthy lunch, a leafy green salad with tomatoes and cucumbers. Halfway through the meeting, however, she snuck a big greasy slice of pepperoni and sausage pizza when she thought no one was looking.

As office manager, Cindy worked from an agenda hastily made up the day before. My contribution was a request to please write names on all samples submitted for lab work, whether in-house or being sent to an outside lab. That would include the plastic supermarket bag of poop, the coffee cup with no lid full of urine, plus all our blood tubes and miscellaneous samples brought in by clients.

Mari spoke up immediately. A staff member for three years, she was known for being meticulous about paperwork. "On that same subject, I would like to remind everyone to make sure the samples are in a correct container."

"Can you give us an example?" The most even-tempered person around, Cindy always saw both sides of the picture and strove for tranquility amongst the staff. Like that was ever going to happen.

"Last Saturday morning Nick put a fecal sample in a Kleenex on the lab countertop and left it there. I had to run around to find out whose it was and what tests to run." Mari sounded both indignant and accusatory. "Plus it smelled up the place."

All eyes turned to our weekend tech, Nick Pappadreus. I was looking forward to his reply, since he excelled at wiggling out of any difficult situation. On the defensive, Nick quickly explained. "I was releasing the ear surgery cat and when I walked back through the waiting room this lady was sitting there holding the sample, hot off the presses. So I offered to put it in the lab, in case Dr. Turner wanted to check it out."

Everyone nodded along. There was nothing like a good poop story.

"It felt a little sandy through the Kleenex, but I wasn't sure. That's why I waited until the doctor saw it to do anything." Once again our crafty tech and kennel help had turned a negative into a positive.

Mari looked unconvinced. "You could at least have wrapped the whole thing in plastic."

"Good idea," Cindy bubbled, sounding like a kindergarten teacher. "When in doubt slip the whole thing in a large zip lock bag and write the client's name on it."

I smiled. Cindy thought everything in life was better in a zip lock bag.

"Well, I didn't know the client's name so I believe I asked someone to take care of that for me."

All heads swiveled back to Mari.

"Don't look at me." If there was anything my head technician hated to do, it was to admit she was wrong.

Cindy raised her hand. "You know, I believe you asked me, Nick."

Nick smiled a triumphant smile. "I believe you are right, Cindy."

"Oops. My bad. Well, no harm done. I'll be more careful next time." As always nothing ruffled her optimistic personality. Meanwhile Mari glowered at Nick. I wasn't sure what the deal was between the two, but I was certain someone would tell me the latest gossip. Obviously I wasn't up to speed with all the latest interpersonal workplace drama.

"Can we talk about our uniforms?" Amy shifted in her seat. "Cindy, did you get Doc's permission to buy us new scrubs?"

This was an ongoing issue. Like most hospitals, over the years the staff had worn several different colors. The old olive green had been replaced with a navy blue, then a light green which everyone hated because you could see their underwear lines. Next the staff retaliated by mixing hospital colors with their own scrubs, usually covered with bunnies or jumping dolphins or whatever was on sale the day they went shopping. It resulted in an eclectic look, rather than the desired team look pushed by the veterinary management magazines. In fact, as I glanced around at the staff they sported a crazy patchwork of old and new uniforms, with the prize going to Cindy, who for some reason was wearing an orange top with pumpkins on it—in honor of Halloween, still over a month away.

"Well, in my last email I asked Doc and gave him an estimate. We should hear back soon."

Everyone had heard that before.

Mari swung into action. "Did we decide on a color? I liked the purple."

Amy countered immediately. "That purple is the color of grape jelly. All we need is to wear brown shoes—then we'd look like walking peanut butter and jelly sandwiches."

Nick jumped into the normally exclusively female conversation, showing symptoms of temporary insanity. "What about khaki-colored?"

"Yuck. It'll make our butts look huge. Tan is the worst. Except for white."

I laughed. Someone always worried about the size of their butts, when truthfully scrubs were the most unflattering thing you could wear, period. It didn't matter how you dressed them up. Plus, in veterinary medicine your clothes needed to be extra loose because of all the bending and lifting we did throughout the day.

"Whoever orders, please make sure I have cargo pants," I reminded everyone. My longtime habit of writing notes to myself and shoving them in my pockets made that a necessity. The office was trying to go paperless, but I was losing the battle. At the end of the day I usually had a scrunched-up little pile of hastily scrawled reminders.

"What color do you like, Doc?" That loaded question came from Nick. As the doctor I wore a long white coat over my scrubs so I didn't care what color they decided on, especially since my butt was covered up. Of course I had been known to wear my own pants or jeans with a scrub top, just to liven things up or when I forgot to do the laundry, thereby contributing to the mess.

"I'm butting out of this conversation, no pun intended." I waited for a laugh but no one even cracked a smile. This was an extremely touchy subject. No pun intended.

"Maybe that steel gray color?" Nick said hopefully. Truth be said, it didn't much matter what color scrubs I wore. At the end of each day, despite using the pet hair roller, I ended up covered with fur.

"Anyone else?" Cindy eyeballed us. "Okay, I'll put a uniform catalogue in the break room. Pick out your two favorite colors and give me your selections. The most popular one wins."

"I don't think part-timers' votes should count the same as full-time, because they won't be wearing the scrubs the same amount of time," Mari chimed in.

I had to give it to her, she was always precise. On some level this made bizarre sense.

Cindy wisely decided to wrap up the discussion. "Interesting. I'll think about that. Now, I've got a pleasant surprise for all of you."

All eyes shifted to our office manager in anticipation.

"We got a new…microscope!" She popped out of her chair and gestured to the lab countertop. There nestled among all the other machines was something with a black plastic cover sporting a red bow on top.

Mari and I immediately went to look at the new piece of equipment. I couldn't have been more excited if someone had handed me the keys to a BMW.

"It's state-of-the-art so don't go spilling Diet Coke on it," our receptionist cautioned us.

Mari sat down on the stool and took the cover off. The various stainless steel parts gleamed with newness.

"It's heavy," I slid the base toward her.

"Remember to cover it when you're done to keep the dust and hair off it." Cindy paused for a moment and surveyed the room. "Also, don't forget to turn the light control switch off."

Most of the staff bit their lips. I was betting the cover would be lost in one, maybe two weeks, tops. The light, well, that's why they make replacement bulbs.

"Okay, if there's nothing more, let's get back to work." Cindy smiled at us like a grade school teacher.

Eugene raised his hand.

Everyone stared. Eugene had never said anything at any meeting. His eyes locked onto mine, pupils large behind those thick glasses. He pointed up.

All eyes followed his finger to see a huge tarantula crawling across the ceiling.

"Okay," Mari said. "Who let Spiderguy out?"

◇◇◇

After finally capturing our de facto hospital pet, the elusive and hairy Spiderguy, and depositing him in his terrarium, we finished up treatments and closed for the day. I had the entire afternoon off, with no particular plans. As I contemplated what to do next the text chime rang on my phone.

Luke.

R U busy?

No.

Meet me at diner in 1 hr

I stared down at my phone screen. Then a final word popped up.

Plse

What could he want?

Sharing Chinese takeout occasionally was one thing, going out to dinner something else.

After a messy breakup with my former boss I'd given up on men for a while. Moving away and getting this job at Oak Falls Animal Hospital had helped me get over the jerk. Recently I'd reconnected with a college friend, Jeremy, a nice guy I hung out with in school. He qualifies as a long distance relationship, since he currently lives near an anthropological dig his university is excavating in East Africa. So now whenever anyone tries to set me up with a neighbor, relative, or ex, I trot out Jeremy. He had proved very useful.

Luke obviously had his own issues, being on the rebound from his high school sweetheart. Deep down, part of me expected him to get back together with her.

Annoyed at his abrupt text I had a dilemma. Should I even bother to change my wrinkled clothes or put on any makeup? That way he'd know I'm not interested in dating him. Or should I look great so he'd regret we aren't dating, even though I didn't want to date him on the rebound anyway? Or should I stop over-thinking it and just get dressed?

My decision ended up somewhere in the middle. After a quick shower and a liberal coating of lemon mango body lotion, I pulled on old jeans and a clean white T-shirt, tied my hair back in a ponytail, and did a careful but natural makeup. Of course, I could have texted back no, but hey, it's not like I had anything else to do. Besides, now would be a good time to ask about those riding dates with Claire.

On the way to the diner Mother Nature reminded me relentlessly that the seasons were changing and changing fast. A pale yellow leaf fell onto the windshield and hitched a ride with me.

The parking lot looked packed but I got lucky when someone began to slowly back out. As always the Oak Falls Diner was busy. Between the great foodie reviews in the local and national news, enthusiastic blogs from diners and its local historical status, the old silver railroad car and subsequent addition was a popular place. While updating their menu they still made space for the old diner favorites, like gravy and fries.

Inside I saw my friend Rosie managing the cash register. She gestured over her shoulder.

"He's by the window." Luke must have told his cousin to keep a lookout for me. I nodded thanks and pushed past a pack of tourists waiting to be seated.

Luke stood up as I approached the booth. His mother and grandmother had raised him with excellent manners. However, after I sat down it was another story.

He started right in on me. "What are you doing, Kate? Althea told me you've been asking her all kinds of questions. Claire committed suicide, plain and simple. Don't start making it into something else."

How small a town was this? Did everyone but me know everything that happened in Oak Falls? That got my back up. "Listen, I accidently bumped into Althea and she's the one who wanted to talk about Claire. She brought up their plan to go into the city together on Saturday. You don't have all the facts, Officer."

"Neither do you." We sat across from each other like matador and bull, almost huffing at each other in anger.

Rosie strolled over with her coffeepot but stopped when she saw our faces. "I don't think you two need any more caffeine. Dinner menu?"

"No. I already ate. I'll have a decaf and a piece of today's pie, please," I told her, trying to smile but not succeeding.

"Same here," Luke said.

"It's too early in the day to fight, cousin. Why don't you both start again?" With those wise words she went back into the kitchen to place our orders.

I didn't know what to say so I took Rosie's advice. With a forced smile on my face I said, "Hi, Luke. How are you today?"

He tilted his head and glanced up sideways at me. "Doing well. How are you?"

"Truthfully, I'm confused," I told him, letting him see how I felt. "I have a friend who won't confide in me, a friend who went horseback riding on a regular basis with Claire. Do you know who that could be?"

There was a stunned silence. He gazed past me at nothing, sadness in his dark brown eyes. You could see the wheels turning when Luke looked like this.

Then he confessed, "I don't think you're aware of my history with Claire. She tried to kill herself once before."

My face must have registered shock.

"I know, because I helped pick up the pieces."

Chapter Ten

The diner was too public a place to discuss anything personal, so we went over to my apartment and sat on the small bluestone patio outside, looking over the parking lot at the distant trees. Buddy chased after tennis balls while I supplied some hastily made iced tea.

It wasn't what I thought.

"Claire was five years younger than me, and like another little sister," Luke began. "My baby sister, Teresa, and she were best friends all through middle school and high school. With Teresa married and out in California now, I've tried to stay in touch. I swear, when she was a kid, Claire hung out at our house more than at her own home. Since you've met her mother I'm sure you understand."

"Bev was drunk the day of the funeral. Mean drunk."

"Then nothing's changed."

He continued after a moment. "Even back then Claire liked to paint and draw. She always took the lead if they had any kind of homework that involved artwork. Usually she ate dinner with us—at least, my mom always set a place for her. She blossomed during that time. Teresa and Claire were the same size so they even wore each other's clothes, except Claire didn't have many things to contribute."

Buddy brought the ball over to me, wagging his tail in anticipation. Too bad life wasn't as simple for people as it was for their dogs.

"Didn't her mom mind?"

Luke laughed. "Not a bit. After Claire's dad died, Bev went to pieces. The drinking got worse. She worked the ten a.m. to seven p.m. shift at the factory, so she didn't care. Every morning she slept in so Claire got herself off to school. Basically Bev saw her kid for only about an hour or two each day. After work she'd change clothes and head out to the bars, to unwind, she claimed. By the time she crawled home with her latest boyfriend, Claire was asleep."

"What a life."

He poured another glass of tea and took a long drink. "She asked me one time to put a lock on her door."

I bolted upright. "The boyfriends?"

"Maybe. There was one in particular she hated named Buzz. I installed a deadbolt and put a latch lock on her window. She told my sister that sometimes she pushed her dresser against the door at night."

I felt sick to my stomach. "Was she that frightened?"

He looked at me with anguish in his eyes. "Yes. I tried to talk to her, my sister tried to talk to her, even my grandmother, but she gave us all the silent treatment. One night while Bev was at a bar she slashed her wrists. We barely found her in time."

There was nothing for me to say.

"She got help from the school psychologist and guidance counselors. Bev's insurance from the factory didn't cover any mental health stuff, plus Claire wouldn't consent to any kind of therapy. But in the last few years everything changed for her. I think when she turned eighteen she received a settlement from her father's estate. Then she got her degree, started working at the gallery, and now she seemed fierce. Like you."

The compliment stunned me. No one had ever called me fierce.

Buddy came up to us and sat on my feet. "So, what can I do?"

"You don't do anything." His voice was emphatic. "Almost everything at the scene points to suicide. Leave it go. For her sake."

"Did you say almost everything?"

Luke looked like he wanted to kick himself. "It's just the toxicology report. She had so much alcohol and pills in her, the coroner doesn't see how she could have walked to the car."

I thought for a moment. "Maybe she swallowed everything, then went into the garage before it took effect?"

"Maybe." He picked up the tennis ball and threw it. It bounced off Buddy's favorite tree and rolled into the bushes. "It was something technical, having to do with how much was left in her stomach, how much was metabolized...that kind of thing."

I watched my dog's head disappear into the shrubbery. "Do you think...?"

Luke interrupted. "Can we stop talking about this now? Please."

"One more thing. Where were the bottles of alcohol found? In the fridge? At the kitchen table?"

Luke's dark eyes turned toward me. "No. That's the other odd thing. There was one bottle of vodka and one bottle of whiskey next to her bed. Empty. The pills were in the bathroom and on the nightstand. Her favorite wine was in the refrigerator. Unopened."

"Why is that strange?"

He waited for a moment, almost as if he were trying to decide whether to tell me. Then he rolled his neck for a moment, to ease the tension. "Alright, I'll tell you. Claire hated the smell of beer and vodka and Jack Daniels, because that's what her mother always drank. I've never seen Claire drink anything but ice cold white wine and an occasional designer-style cocktail."

"We had something in common."

"Then there's the blood."

"No one said anything about blood."

He gave me a look like I shouldn't have been surprised. "A vase was broken. The techs picked up two sets of DNA on the shards and some partial prints on paper napkins in the trash. We have no idea how long they'd been there."

"You ran them, I suppose."

"Of course. No matches in the local or national databases."

Maybe someone had been with Claire that night. Someone who liked hard liquor, like her nasty ex-boyfriend. Then I remembered the smell of vodka on her own mother.

A small whirlwind blew dried leaves across the bluestone and into the yard.

Buddy ran out from under a branch, triumphantly carrying the tennis ball. Luke leaned over and retrieved it, putting it on the table to let the panting dog rest for a while.

"Even if we wanted to pursue it, Claire's body has been cremated. All we've got are a couple of bags of trace evidence from the scene. But the guys were thorough. They even kept the bloody bandage on her hand."

How much more confusing could it get? "Luke. What bandage?"

Chapter Eleven

Eugene didn't show up to work the next day. This was very unusual. Because of his head injury he lived at home with his parents, who diligently kept him to a rigid schedule as recommended by his doctors. If he was sick they always let us know. Although his job consisted of mostly cleaning and exercising the animals, it played a vital role in keeping the hospital running smoothly.

"Where's Eugene?" I asked Cindy, between bites of a bagel. One of our clients had dropped off a dozen this morning as a thank you. The staff was now in bagel heaven, slathering the specialty cream cheeses on raisin cinnamon, sesame, and everything bagels. Crumbs and seeds littered the treatment room and reception countertops.

Cindy's spinach bagel sat on a napkin next to her desk, broken into bite-sized pieces. "I don't know. I was about to call." She interrupted herself to answer the phone.

"I'll call him." I pantomimed talking on the phone, then went over to the employee list on the wall. As his home number rang I suddenly wondered exactly what I would say to his parents.

"Hello."

"This is Oak Falls Veterinary Hospital," I answered. "Can I speak to Eugene?"

"This is Wendy, Eugene's mother," the woman said. "He's not going to make it in to work today."

"Oh, I'm sorry to hear that. Is he ill?" I walked in to the pharmacy area so I wouldn't bother Cindy on the other line.

There was an embarrassed silence on the phone. "Is this Dr. Kate?"

"Yes. We were all concerned about him."

Again Wendy hesitated then asked me a question. "Eugene has been very sad these last couple of days. He won't talk to us about it. Did something happen at work?"

I searched my memory of the last few weeks. The only thing I could come up with involved Claire and Toto. "Did Eugene know Claire Birnham, by any chance?"

"Of course. She rides at the stable Eugene works at."

Wendy had used the present tense when referring to Claire. "Perhaps he's upset about her death."

There was a gasp, as if someone had punched her in the stomach. "Oh, no! What happened? She didn't fall off a horse, did she?"

Strange that she jumped to that conclusion, then I remembered her son's story and understood. I chose my words carefully. "They say she committed suicide."

"Suicide? The poor girl. She was so kind to Eugene. He used to follow her around and always helped her groom the horses she rode."

I heard a sniffle on the phone and knew she was crying.

"Who is taking care of Toto? Eugene loves that little dog so much."

"We have him here at the hospital. He might be up for adoption."

"Our family would take him in a heartbeat. Can you let us know?"

Maybe we'd struck pay dirt on our search for a home for the little cairn terrier. "Eugene is one of the few people Toto really likes. If it's up to me you'll be the first in line." This time Wendy couldn't control the sobs. She mumbled a goodbye and hung up the phone.

I drifted back to reception where things had quieted down.

"What's up with Eugene? Is he coming in today?" Cindy resumed munching her bagel and finishing her cup of coffee. By the time she left she would drink at least three more mugs but it never interfered with her mellow nature.

"No, he won't make it today. That was Wendy, his mother. He's under the weather for a few days."

She made a note in the computer, most likely keeping track of any sick days to put in the employee record. "That's okay. The regular staff can take up the slack. It's almost the end of the week, thank goodness. Did she say what was wrong?"

"Not really." I felt a little white lie was in order. Eugene's mother would eventually find out how to help him through this situation, and then she could tell Cindy if she chose to.

Everyone deserved a little privacy.

Chapter Twelve

The next few days I settled back into my animal hospital routine, work, work, and then work some more. Eugene didn't return, which meant techs doubled up on kennel duty. It was only at night, if I poured myself a chilled glass of white wine that I thought of Claire. Questions remained, but who was left to supply the answers?

Finally it was Friday, almost the end of a terribly long week. Because morning appointments were running late as usual, Mari and I ended up dining al fresco in the truck. Being the driver, I could only listen while Mari chomped away at her Italian sub, filling the truck interior with the smell of ham, salami, and Italian dressing. My turkey sub with mayo beckoned to me from the backseat.

I veered over to pass a gaggle of serious bicyclists encased in brightly colored Spandex. Sponsor names on their clothing tempted you to read them like a newspaper. Clusters of these racing bikes could be found on the back roads and state park bike trails more and more, especially on the weekends.

"That reminds me," Mari said between bites. "I've got to start serious training for my twenty-five K ride." Finally recovered from a knee injury, her goal was an Iron Man marathon next year in Hawaii. Each morning she biked five kilometers before coming to work, which is why she could eat all day long without gaining any weight.

Another group of cyclists passed us going the opposite way.

Every time I saw them I felt guilty and vowed to exercise more. However, nothing on earth could get me into a head to toe Spandex jumpsuit. "Is there something going on this weekend?" I asked. "We're seeing lots of bike people on the road."

"There's a river run and bike race tomorrow from Rhinebeck to Peekskill, all along the Hudson."

"That should cause a traffic jam," I commented, slowing down for a small group of three in front of us. Our trusty British-accented GPS was silent for once. We didn't need his help today since we were headed for one of our favorite clients.

"I wonder what they'll be wearing?" Mari finished her sandwich and stuffed everything back in the plastic bag after carefully picking pieces of lettuce and onion off her scrub shirt.

We turned onto a quiet street and parked in front of a cozy English cottage-style house with a white picket fence and beautifully manicured shrubs and flowers.

"No idea. But I know they will match."

When the front door opened we had our answer. Daffy and her Chihuahua, Little Man, wore identical Hawaiian shirts, flower leis, and floppy straw hats decorated with more flowers. Used to our sweet but eccentric client by now, Mari and I marveled at the professional quality and attention to detail Daffy brought to her creations. As always Little Man growled, trying to be as macho as possible while wearing a tiny straw hat with two holes that skillfully allowed his bat-like ears to stick out. For some reason the Chihuahua wasn't as grumpy as usual. I think the dog was glad not to be forced into a hula skirt.

We were here to trim his nails, check his rear end, and generally chat with the owner. The little dog was her world, albeit a color-coordinated one, so after a few health issues cropped up she decided to book an appointment every six weeks for a checkup and nail trim. Little Man rarely wore down his own nails since he was carried around most of the time.

"That is so cute," Mari exclaimed as she studied the tiny lei around the dog's neck, carefully staying out of lunging distance. As if he could read minds, Little Man showed us his teeth.

"Right," I said. "Can you distract him, Mari?" Like a pair of ice dancers we took off in opposite directions to later meet in the middle, where the toy dog waited. Mari waltzed over to the front end and dangled my stethoscope. As it drew near him, he immediately reacted, deepening his growls to Rottweiler intensity. Meanwhile I had stealthily slipped out of eye range, turned and slid a gauze noose over his nose before he could react. After tying the ends in a bow behind his ears Mari picked him up and pressed him into her body, making sure to keep his front legs away from the homemade muzzle. Another smoothly executed Chihuahua restraint completed. To make things easier for us I took his hat off, but left the shirt on. It looked kind of cute on the little guy.

"Be good, baby," Daffy interjected. "Mommy loves you."

With his bulgy eyes bulging even more, his thin skin stretched across his head and his giant transparent bat ears showing a highway of veins, he got the ugly baby award. Ugly-cute, of course. To retaliate he released a poisonous dog fart.

"Let's get this done," I told Mari, who was trying not to breathe. Unfortunately she stood at the epicenter of the polluted zone.

I plugged in my grinder and got to work on his nails. After experimenting with all kinds of clippers and files we'd found he tolerated the electric grinder very well. After a quick exam of his anal glands I cleaned up his tushy with some hypoallergenic baby wipes. Maneuvering around him we repeated our dance, but backwards, and soon Little Man perched happily in his mother's arms, growling at the world.

We washed off our hands and Mari started typing in her notes. Daffy offered us some fresh coffee and blueberry pie. She and everyone who knew me were aware of my addiction to homemade pie. Pretty soon if I kept eating this way I'd have to join those Spandex guys on their bikes. I used my fork to full advantage while we were given all the local news and gossip. The conversation eventually focused on Claire's suicide.

"She'd broken up with that awful man," Daffy said, cutting another pie of pie and inching it over to me. "I think she planned to move into New York City, to be closer to the action."

Hearing that phrase come out of this very proper lady put a smile on my face. But she'd also told me something I was interested in. "What man are you talking about?"

Daffy lowered her head and looked around the room as if spies were everywhere. "A man in Rhinebeck. A rock 'n' roll musician." She may as well have said "the devil" from her tone. "He's been arrested for assault and domestic abuse before."

"How do you know all this?" What I didn't say out loud was how did she know so much when she spent most of her time in her cottage with her dog having dress-up parties.

Her bright eyes twinkled at me as if she knew a secret. "Bridge club."

Mari turned to me with a knowing look. "Bridge club. That explains it."

"Explains what?" I asked my tech, bewildered.

"Tell her about bridge clubs in small towns." Mari settled back in her chair with her arms crossed.

"Well, there's nothing much to tell, really. We meet twice a week for bridge and we rotate houses to be fair. Our group has three tables of four each, which is twelve ladies."

So far I had no idea what Mari knew that I didn't. A quick glance only confirmed the knowing smile on her face. Turning to our hostess she said, "Tell Dr. Kate what you talk about."

Daffy straightened up in her chair. "This is a serious card game. We mostly talk about bridge." Then she paused, "But we do gossip a little between sets."

"Like what?" Mari prodded.

"Oh, the usual. How the kids and grandkids are doing. The weather. Who's had plastic surgery and which husbands are sleeping around." She giggled as if caught at something naughty. "Let's see. Whose relatives are having financial difficulties or been arrested or is being investigated by the police. Which families are remodeling and how bad the place looked before the contractor stepped in. What the nannies say about their rich employers in the city. Couples everyone thinks will get divorced." Again she giggled. "We should make that one a board game."

Mari gave her approval of that with a thumbs-up.

Daffy continued without a pause. "Who is a secret hoarder. Little things like that."

"In other words," Mari said, "They know everything happening in town."

Daffy looked coy. "Well, not everything."

I had to ask. "What don't they know?"

"That you're dating Luke Gianetti."

"What? You never told me that?" Mari said, accusingly.

No wonder Luke came over to my place. He must have know about the local gossips. And here I was sitting in the living room of Gossip Central.

"We're not dating." I rose and started to get ready to leave.

"That's all right, dear. I explained to the bridge club they were wrong."

Finally, someone standing up against idle chatter. "Thank you, Daffy."

She smiled sweetly at me. "You're welcome. I told them you were one of those nice lesbian ladies."

◇◇◇

Mari could barely breathe from laughing so much. I opened the driver's side door. The truck reeked of submarine sandwiches. Half of my turkey sub plus a soda were heating up in the backseat.

"Pull yourself together, Mari. You drive for a while." I reached behind me and picked up my lunch. "I'm going to finish eating."

We switched seats, and after moving an empty super-sized chip bag from the passenger seat I settled in with my sandwich. Daffy had provided us with entertainment but more importantly, information. I wondered if the police had even investigated Claire's ex-boyfriend.

Mari held her comments until we turned the corner.

"Come on, you have to admit that last comment was pretty funny. She said it so seriously."

I took a big bite out of my sandwich then mulled it around in my head.

"Maybe it's the cargo pants."

Chapter Thirteen

I knew Oak Falls was a small town but didn't think I'd hear details about Claire's love life from a salesgirl at the local feed store. The small building with the tin roof smelled of animal food and polished leather plus an overlay of fly spray. With the back door to the attached shed propped open, the sweet smell of alfalfa and timothy hay added their perfume to the mix. I'd dropped in to pick up some apple wafer treats for my horse patients. The store sold all kinds of gear including used saddles, mounting them on blocks near the front window. It was late afternoon, and I was the only customer in the store. A beautiful tooled leather saddle caught my eye. After I stopped to admire it the salesperson said, "That's the owner's personal saddle. If you're interested I'll give you her number."

Before I could say anything she wrote down a number on a piece of lined paper and handed it to me.

"We're also getting in two used saddles, one English and one Western, tomorrow on consignment, if you're interested. They might be good if you're starting out. I think there's some tack, too, but I'm not sure. The owner picked it up at an estate sale."

"What estate sale?" I moved to a different aisle and found a small bag of apple wafers on the middle shelf.

"Claire Birnham."

"Did you know her?" Maybe Claire bought her riding supplies here.

"Yes, I did. Very sad thing." The salesgirl came out from behind the counter and walked over to me. Petite and wiry, she was dressed in jeans and cowboy boots. I took a chance and asked, "Do you ride?"

"Like the wind." She bent down to straighten some items on a shelf. "I met Claire a few times at the stables and here at the store, but we didn't ride together, so I didn't know her that well. I wasn't surprised at what happened, though." Her voice took on a knowing tone.

"Why is that?" I leaned up against a display of fly masks, hoping no other customer came through the door. The salesgirl, whose name was Kaila according to her nametag, showed no discretion at all.

"That boyfriend of hers, A.J. Janssen. Very good looking, but what a piece of work. Thinks he's going to be a famous rock star."

"Oh?" For once I didn't have to ask any questions.

"They had a big fight, I heard. They were always fighting," she confided. "Last year just before Christmas he punched her in the face. Gave her a black eye."

That sounded familiar. Another woman in an abusive relationship. On the outside Claire had seemed smart and focused, like she had her life figured out. But at least she had enough courage to put an end to it. I wondered who else knew her secret.

Finding a sympathetic ear, Kaila kept talking.

"Anyway, she said she broke up with him and he said he broke up with her. But this time A.J. started seeing someone else, a rich groupie from Rhinebeck. I guess he proposed 'cause she's wearing a big ring on her finger. I figure that when Claire found out she lost him for good she got depressed and one thing led to another." Kaila's face had a smug expression. "She also had these weird guys hanging around her. That Eugene gave me the creeps."

"Where did you get your information from?" I asked, wondering who she'd talked to or if most of it was simply made up.

Her smug expression never wavered. "I've got my sources," she said, then clammed up as two guys in jeans came through the door.

Even being dead doesn't guarantee you any privacy. Having to get the dirt on Claire was leaving a bad taste in my mouth.

◇◇◇

That night in a dream it happened again. Claire frantically calling out for someone to help her. The car motor running, the garage filled with exhaust. My heart pounded as I sat bolt upright in bed. Was it my subconscious that kept sending me these dreams?

As a scientist I didn't believe in ghosts.

But in case I was wrong—I whispered, "I'm trying Claire, believe me, I'm trying to help."

Chapter Fourteen

On Saturday night I decided to check out Claire's former boyfriend and put a face to the name. Kaila at the feed store had reminded me his band would be playing at The Rocket, a popular club across the river, just outside of Rhinebeck. Two shows, one at seven and one at nine, then a jam session until closing. During the quick trip over the bridge I tried to plan out how to approach him. Damp air smelling of boat exhaust and fish rose up from the water below. A lone speedboat with its running lights on was making toward the dock in Saugerties.

My goal for the night was twofold, to see if the ex-boyfriend had an alibi for the night Claire died, and to find out what kind of relationship they'd had. From the look of the ad I'd seen, Tuesday Night Road Kill played heavy metal music. I love all kinds of music but it had been years since my last loud concert. Vet school didn't leave you a lot of time for partying. As the far side of the bridge loomed toward me I tried out different scenarios to get close enough to ask him questions about Claire. Then I wondered if he'd answer them.

Not really prepared for either, I drove past the fairgrounds until I spied a neon sign depicting a hot pink rocket endlessly lifting off into space. I'd found The Rocket Club. Pickups and old cars packed the parking lot, with some sports cars and expensive SUVs mixed in. Clumps of kids drinking beer sat on the hoods of their vehicles or leaned against the bumpers. I pulled in and found a space in the fourth row. When I opened the truck door, super loud music accosted my ears. The bass thumped like a monster heartbeat. It made the thin metal over the engine vibrate. The windshield glowed with a pinkish-purple light from the sign, blinking out of sync with the music.

Immediately the sweetish unmistakable aroma from a joint being smoked close by floated past.

With my keys and wallet safely zipped in my purse I dodged the cars and walked through an acrid cloud of cigarette smoke left from patrons smoking just outside the entrance. The bar door was old and made of thick wood darkened from a thousand sweaty hands. When I pushed it open a blast of hot air smelling of beer and sweat pushed back.

Wooden tables filled the sizable space while a mirrored bar ran along the far wall, stopping about six feet from the stage. I settled on a single vacant seat at the bar just as a screech of feedback echoed from the onstage mike.

"Testing, testing. Feedback," said a pale skinny guy with dreadlocks hanging past his shoulders, probably the sound engineer. With their backs to us, five musicians were tuning up, until the drummer hit an impromptu solo. When they all moved toward him I immediately spotted A.J.

Various people had described him as gorgeous. From where I sat that was an accurate statement. The guy had sculptured features with broad cheekbones and ice blue eyes. Streaky blond hair in a loose ponytail fell halfway down his back. A thin white T-shirt exposed muscular arms, tattooed from shoulder to each wrist. Sitting at the bar I couldn't make out much detail, but the tattoos certainly weren't run of the mill artwork. In the front row a girl popped up and ran over to him, a water bottle in her hand. With barely a glance he took it from her then leaned in to speak to the musician on bass guitar. When she returned to her seat I got a look at her face. Creamy coffee-colored skin, thick curly black hair, and a dramatic oval face. Model slender, her conservative but expensive clothes set her apart from most of the other groupies crowding the stage, who obviously thought clothes could never be too short, too tight or too revealing. I wondered how Claire had fit into this picture.

I quickly figured out you can't have a conversation during a live performance. My plan to first get info from the bartender didn't work. Luckily Tuesday Night Road Kill had a pleasing, if loud, melodic metal sound, pretty unique and interesting. A.J. growled and sang in a strong baritone. From the adoring faces looking up at him, this might be a stepping stone to better things. About an hour later, the first set finished. We had blessed silence for a short moment, until the pre-recorded music kicked in.

My non-alcoholic beer tasted flat in the mug by this time. As I waited to order another I noticed in the far corner by the stage, a table being set up to sell the band's latest CD. On an impulse I slid off my barstool and hurried into line. Four people sat at the table. The first took your money, then the second handed you your CDs along with the band's promotional bag of stuff. At the end sat the drummer and A.J., swigging beers and signing the discs. I forked over my twenty bucks and waited my turn.

"Who should I make it out to, darling?" asked the dark-eyed drummer, whose Southern accent sounded as thick as maple syrup.

"To Kate," I answered.

He signed with a black sharpie then slid the silver disc over to A.J. Without looking up A.J. signed the other side, glancing at the name before copying it into his inscription. When he went to hand me the CD his eyes registered surprise, then a glimmer of interest.

"You look familiar, honey," he said, trying to place me. "You kinda look like…"

I interrupted him. "She's my aunt," I lied, for once grateful I resembled a famous actress. "Please, I like to keep that private if you know what I mean."

Up close he was even better looking. "Our secret, Kate. Yeah, my agent is trying to set up some movie auditions in L.A. for me."

"Actor and singer," I told him, filling my voice with admiration. "Wow."

He gestured for me to move closer. The line of people waiting began to back up. "Maybe you could mention my name to her? Or bring her to one of our sets?"

"Uh, she doesn't go out much anymore." I scrambled to think of a reason.

"Hey, no worries. Hang around till we finish up tonight. We can get to know each other."

"Sounds good," I told him as I reached for my CD. Fame definitely opened doors for you, even such a marginal connection as I pretended to have.

"Hey, keep moving up there." The money guy stood up and angrily gestured toward me.

A.J. proceeded to give him the finger. "Later, honey." The next girl pushed me aside, then handed him the flyer to sign as well as the CD.

Silently asking Meryl Streep to forgive me, I shouldered past the crowd only to get bumped by someone pushing past me in the opposite direction. A thick cloud of hair floating above an Italian leather coat brushed past. I recognized the woman, slightly taller than me, as one of the groupies. Maybe this was my opportunity. Quickly I did a U-turn and followed the pair of black skinny jeans striding toward the door. Moving in her wake, I ended back outside on the porch, only to spy her closing the passenger door of a silver Land Rover.

A few seconds later a light flickered in the front seat, then all I saw was a pinpoint of flame. The woman I followed had been angry about something. In a few minutes I predicted she'd either be super mellow or ready for a fight.

Leaning up against the building I pretended to text on my phone. It kept me looking busy and let me keep an eye on the SUV. Inside, they announced that the second set would start in twenty minutes. The lead guitarist played a quick riff with a hint of the blues for emphasis.

After about ten minutes the Land Rover door swung open. I saw A.J.'s groupie slide off the seat, then keep sliding onto the asphalt, her hand still clutching the door handle. I hurried over and helped her up.

"You okay?" I asked.

"Fine," she whispered. "Oh, it's you." The Ms. Happy face turned into a Ms. Grumpy face.

"Sorry, do I know you?" I helped her to her feet, then released her elbow. She jerked away from me and immediately fell again. A funky mix of roses, vodka, and pot wafted from her.

"What were you and A.J. talking about?" She practically spit out the words at me as I helped her up again.

Jealousy had reared its head big time. Maybe if she calmed down I could ask her about Claire, although that didn't seem like much of a possibility.

"Nothing much. He knows my aunt," I lied once again.

"So?" She made it sound like an accusation.

"We were talking, that's all." Obviously she was jealous of every girl that got near her boyfriend. How could I get her to trust me? I bent down, pretending to tie my shoelace, pulling up my cargo pants leg. That's when I got the idea.

I slipped some anger and roughness in my voice. "I'm a little pissed off. The girl I came with ditched me."

"For another guy?" She seemed mildly interested in my made-up story.

"No, for another chick." I tried to sound tough, then waited. Let her jump to any conclusion she wanted.

She took the leap. Suddenly freed of suspicion I was after her boyfriend, the classy groupie smiled and introduced herself. "Sorry about that. Thanks again for helping me. I'm Bella."

"Kate. Are you feeling better now?

"A little like I'm on a tilt-a-whirl."

"There's a bench on the porch. Do you want me to sit with you for a minute?"

"Sure." This time when I held her elbow she didn't complain. After we got to the wooden bench she sort of crumpled onto it.

"I bet you thought I was coming on to him." I laughed, waiting for her reaction.

Her head went back and rested on the wall. "Yeah. I'm used to it but it doesn't make it easier. Of course, he eats up all the attention."

"Well, not to worry on my end." I patted her knee. She shifted her weight to move away from me.

Figuring our girl talk time was limited I got right to the point. "Yeah, the last time I saw A.J. he was still with Claire. I didn't know they broke up."

Bella appeared to listen to the canned music over the loudspeaker, probably figuring out how long before the set would start. "Yeah."

"He got tired of her, right?" I pulled at a loose string on my shirt. "She could be pretty bossy."

The girl leaned in to me, as if she had a secret. "That's what A.J. wanted everyone to think. But he got dumped!" That set off a cascade of giggles and hiccups. "He's so great looking he thinks nobody in the world could get tired of him. But Claire did. Little high school sweetheart miss goody-two-shoes Claire told him to take a hike. She had another dude waiting in the wings." She whipped out a lipstick from her jeans pocket and touched up her still red lips. "So, I moved in, quick as lightning. And I haven't lost interest, let me tell you, because the guy is fantastic in bed."

She winked at me.

"How did he react to being dumped?"

Again she caught my eye but this time there was a look of cunning in them. "He lost it. When she took off, someone said, he tried to kill her."

"That's terrible." What if A.J. carried out his threat?

Bella laughed at my reaction. "Hey, baby. A.J. is rock 'n' roll and sex and drugs. A little violence thrown into the mix only spices it up." She lit up a cigarette, cupping the lighter against a breeze. By the flickering light I saw purplish bruises that circled both wrists.

"Who was her new boyfriend?"

"Some guy she met at that gallery."

"Are you sure?" Whatever else she had taken in the truck started to kick in. Bella began to mutter. Her speech sped up and her eyes began to glitter. Before I could ask his name her arm went up and she tossed her curly long hair over one shoulder.

"No worries now," she crooned, repeating A.J.'s phrase. "Claire is dead and gone." She swayed back and forth to the music. "Who wouldn't kill to get a piece of his ass? Could you blame me?" As if she said something hysterically funny she began to laugh.

The loudspeaker kicked in announcing the start of the next set.

"Bella, Where was A.J. the night Claire died?" I stood up trying to get her attention. Over the loudspeaker the announcer began to introduce the band.

"Bella, where was he?"

She stared up at the night sky for a moment, a smile on her face. "They had a gig that night, I think. Check their blog. Always something about each performance on their blog."

Bella gathered herself up and made her way back inside. Despite her altered state of mind I suspected this new girlfriend told the truth. It would be easy enough to check on the computer. With no reason now to stay I went back to my truck and decided to leave before the crowd began pulling out. Once inside the cab I could still feel the music, then realized the beat pounded inside my brain. I gulped a couple of Advil and rolled down the windows to let the cool night air clear my head.

A little heavy metal night music went a long way.

As I left Rhinebeck behind me I wondered about Claire and these last six months. Two sources confirmed that she's broken up with her boyfriend, and that she wasn't depressed about it. Now someone hinted about a new boyfriend. Her friend Adele said Claire was excited about changes in her life and moving to New York City. Unless she had extra income I didn't know about, that took a lot of money. Where was she going to get that from? Not selling her artwork.

All along I'd assumed A.J. might be the killer, with his history of violence toward her, fueled by anger that she'd broken off their relationship. The only problem, if he killed her, I would have expected him to use his hands out of rage. But what if the killer had another agenda, one much more subtle. I wondered if Claire had been killed by a woman, a woman who wanted her out of the way. A woman who wanted A.J's complete attention. Would someone wealthy like Bella really kill for "a piece of ass" as she put it?

Or just hire someone to do it for her?

Chapter Fifteen

Safely back home by nine forty-five, I snuggled on the sofa with Buddy, watching reruns of *Say Yes To The Dress.* The phone rudely interrupted us. Tempted to let it go to voice mail, I looked at the caller ID, then happily picked up.

"Hi, Kate."

I recognized the voice of my veterinary school lab partner and old friend, but could barely hear him over the television. After taking one last peek at the tattooed bride determined to squeeze her ample chest into a sweetheart neckline I clicked it to mute.

"Hi, Tim. What's up?"

"Would you like to meet us in the village and have brunch tomorrow?"

"Sure." I didn't need to check my social calendar to know I was free. In the background I heard Tim's wife, Tina, say something that I didn't catch. The speaker phone projected their voices in a strange way. Both sounded like they were underwater.

"We want to go to that new art exhibit that's opening in town. The one getting so much buzz."

I sat up. "Do you mean Andrei Roshenkov?"

Tina's voice became louder. "I'm impressed. I didn't realize you kept up with the latest artist showings."

"I happened to meet him the other day, that's all," I confessed.

"Good for you, Kate. I'm glad you're getting out more. Does his picture do him justice? Very good looking guy."

"Tina." Her husband sounded indignant.

"For her, not for me. Why would I need anyone else when I've got the dogs and you." Tina's laughter bubbled through the receiver. "Just kidding. You come before the dogs most of the time." She laughed again but this time Tim joined in.

From the depths of the chenille sofa I half-listened as Tim told me where and when to meet them in town. Since he had a touch of OCD I felt pretty confident he would also send me a confirmatory email, maybe with a map.

"Okay, I'll see you both tomorrow. Love you guys," I told them before I hung up the phone. Tomorrow would be fun, since the two of them were a riot to be with. Of course, they'd bring their Papillon show dogs, a.k.a. surrogate children, since they rarely traveled without them. That meant eating brunch on an outdoor dog-friendly terrace, which was fine with me.

On the screen, a teary bride-to-be silently sobbed in the bridal store dressing room, frustrated at not finding a dress. With the television still on mute, the program took on a surrealistic tone. A burr on Buddy's coat stuck my finger and yanked my attention away from wedding drama. Since I had no immediate intention of getting married unless I didn't need a groom, I wondered what my fascination with the reality series was. Annoyed at myself I turned the television off and got up to throw the burr away in the garbage. Then it occurred to me that Tina and Tim lived just outside Rhinebeck. I wondered if they had any additional info on Claire's old boyfriend A.J. and his rock group.

With my mind hopping all over the place I brewed myself a cup of chamomile tea, in the hopes of calming down. Before I went to bed I checked to make sure I had something relatively clean, mostly unwrinkled and free of animal hair, to wear tomorrow. In the back of the closet, still on dry cleaner's hangers, was a stash of clothes I'd brought from the city when I first moved in. Problem solved. I took Buddy for his walk and stared at the night sky. The big dipper twinkled down at me, the crisp air smelling of night blooming jasmine. The last thing I remembered before I fell asleep was turning the page of my new mystery novel to see who the killer was. Thankfully that night Claire didn't haunt my sleep, although I did dream I danced the hula with the Wicked Witch of the West.

◇◇◇

Sunday turned out unseasonably warm and clear, blue skies hosting wisps of clouds. I checked on the animals in the hospital, walked and fed both Buddy and myself, then hopped in the shower. My new shampoo filled the damp stall with the smell of honeysuckle and lemon. For once I'd left plenty of time to meet my friends. Wrapped in a terrycloth robe I picked up my book and plunked down in the armchair. Just sitting and reading for a half an hour seemed like a luxury.

Fresh from the cleaners, the crisp cotton dress with an embroidered collar and hem felt light and airy. Slowly I brushed back my hair, did a careful makeup, then added an antique necklace made from carved wooden squares. When I looked in the mirror I paused for a moment. Most days I barely got out of my scrubs and certainly didn't put on any makeup. The confident woman who stared back at me from the mirror felt like some distant relative. She'd taken a leave of absence after my messy breakup. Time to bring her back.

Our meeting spot was in the center of the village, at the popular Barks for Bones specialty store. Through the crowd of pet owners and their dogs, I spied Tina and Tim checking out toys and beds and all the fun items the store stocked. Each had a Gucci shoulder strap bag with a perfectly groomed Papillon head poking out of it. They waved at me through the plate glass window.

"There you are, sweetie." Tina reached me first and gave me a hug. "You look scrumptious, doesn't she Tim? Like an ice cream cone on a summer day."

"What a nice thing to say. Thanks, Tina. You guys look great too." Both my friends could have stepped out of a Brooks Brothers catalog. White linen pants, pastel shirt, with an unconstructed jacket for him, and cream-colored linen dress and summer hat for her. Since I'd first known Tim in vet school he'd come into a sizable inheritance. Then a few years ago he met and married Tina, who came from a very wealthy old Rhinebeck family. Money became the two of them, with the bonus that they threw insanely good parties.

Tim stepped down the stairs and onto the street, his hands filled with packages. Both had taken advantage of the weekend sales. "Hey, Kate. Wonderful to see you," he said, rounding up Tina who'd dashed back inside the store for one last look. "The gallery is this way. I'm curious to see Roshenkov's work. Did you like any of them?"

"I don't know much about art but I found them very hypnotic." I gave his Papillon a pat on the head. Buddy whined and looked up at me.

"Hey, no need to be jealous, big guy." Tim bent down and introduced the dogs to each other, then broke out a few gourmet doggy treats that got everyone's tails wagging.

As we strolled along, Tina brought me up to date on all the exploits of her dogs and their latest ribbons. Then she told me who on the show dog circuit got loaded on margaritas and drove his car into a fountain and which handler was rumored to have had a rather intimate tryst with one of the judges. I didn't know most of the people she talked about but it didn't matter. The day was glorious, I was with my friends, and murder wasn't part of the conversation.

Up ahead a small crowd spilled out in front of the Qualog Gallery, many holding wineglasses. "Gallery shows are great for people watching." Tim guided us toward the entrance.

"I'll take your word on it."

People strolled back and forth out of the open door. A sign on the sidewalk announced the opening of Andrei Roshenkov's show and a free local wine tasting. With no need for invitations we scooted past several people chatting away and walked toward the reception area. If anything, the canvases looked more impressive than they had the other day, the natural daylight combining with the artificial light to give added depth to each brushstroke.

"Beautiful." Tim stared at a large landscape directly in front of him called *Afternoon Garden.* Somehow the artist had captured the riot of colors in an overgrown garden with the overlay of beginning shadows. Peaceful but full of strength. The price on the notice mounted next to the canvas read fifteen thousand five hundred dollars. "What do you think, honey?" He turned to Tina who stood transfixed, a sweet smile on her face.

"Love it. Let's get it before someone else does." Tina pointed to the red dots next to two nearby paintings indicating they were sold.

"You ladies mingle. I'll catch up to you." Tim set out, gradually making his way through the crowd toward the gallery office, while Tina and I wandered around. A waiter approached with a tray and offered us glasses of white wine.

"This is exciting," I confided to Tina as I tasted the chardonnay. "I think I see the artist over there." Leaning against a wall near one of his pictures, Andrei held court with four women.

"Great looking guy," Tina commented. She stroked her Papillon, lingering on the dog's silky ear fringes. "Let's go talk to him." Ahead and to the right we saw Tim in conversation with Gilda, the gallery owner who looked very pleased. Tim gave us a thumbs-up then reached for his wallet.

Andrei noticed us as we made our way toward him. I saw recognition dawn a moment later. "My coffee buddy," he said, taking my hand.

"Congratulations, Andrei," I said, "the show is lovely. This is my friend Tina. She just bought one of your paintings."

"*Afternoon Garden.*" Tina inched ahead of me to talk to him. "We adore it."

"That's the only reason to buy art." He took her hand in his, his pale blue eyes resting momentarily on her Rolex and Gucci carryall. "Paintings should be with people who love them." A movement in her bag prompted him to say, "What do you have here?"

An elegant slim nose and pointed ears dripping with fringe popped out of the carryall over her shoulder.

"Hello, princess," he said, delicately touching the dog on her head and ears.

"This is champion Marie Antoinette Texas T & T. We call her Teeny. She's almost as beautiful as your painting."

A genuine smile creased his face making him even more attractive, if that was possible.

"Andrei," called a voice over my shoulder. "Come meet one of your admirers." Gilda glided over in a sleek black dress with a cut out back and side. She didn't appear to be wearing a bra. Without pausing she edged herself between Tina and the artist like a quarter horse cutting the herd. Tim followed behind, a bemused look on his face. As Gilda attempted the artist extraction, Tim put her straight.

"Tina, honey. I see you two have met."

Quickly recovering, Gilda made nice, draping her arm proprietarily on the artist's shoulder. "Is this your lovely wife?" she asked Tim, applying the charm. It didn't help business to get off on the wrong foot with buyers.

Standing near Tina she became startled as Teeny popped out of the carryall again.

"What a cute little thing." With a tentative finger she touched the dog's long silky fur. "I love them so much, but I'm deathly allergic to them. Cats too." She excused herself and I watched her head straight to the ladies room, undoubtedly to sanitize her finger.

As the others drifted off to look again at *Afternoon Garden*, I went past the crowd to the back of the gallery, passing behind the temporary divider. The young employee I'd seen crying the other afternoon was texting madly and trying to open a box of wine simultaneously. Like her boss she too was dressed in black, but hers was a modest buttoned up affair. She obviously handled the nuts and bolts of the opening while Gilda worked the customers. I wondered who had taken over Claire's responsibilities. Behind the set of rolling partitions and out of sight of the customers, extra paper napkins, appetizer platters, and glasses littered the table set up for the event. Cardboard boxes filled with used glasses and plates had been shoved under the table to get them out of the way.

"Can I help you?" she asked anxiously, still in the middle of a text.

"I'm a friend of Claire Birnham."

Sorrow mixed with panic shown in her expression, an unusual combination of emotions. Her eyes darted around the room for a moment as if looking for someone to rescue her. Then she said, "What do you want?"

As I moved closer she shrank away like a dog waiting to be hit.

"Just a moment of your time, to talk about Claire. How she seemed on that last day." I carefully watched her reaction. She took a deep breath to calm down a little and gathered up her strength.

In a tight choky voice she answered my question. "She was normal. Fine. I didn't think anything was wrong. If I had, I would have helped her."

"I'm sure you would have. I'm Kate, by the way."

"Roxie. I've only worked here for a month," she explained, "so I didn't know her that well. I'm sorry."

I made my way to the edge of the table, then poured a glass of water. I noticed she'd changed the blue streak in her hair to a bright pink one. "What about Claire's boyfriend? Was she having guy problems?"

Before saying anything Roxie snuck another peek at her phone, then looked up at me. "I don't think she had a boyfriend, at least not a steady one. There was someone but she broke up with him recently. She didn't tell me who he was but she called him a jerk."

Sounds about right, I thought. That's the same thing her friend Althea said about him. "You're talking about the musician, correct?"

"No." Reluctantly the girl raised her eyes from her phone. "What musician?"

The sound of high heels clattered toward us. "Roxie," hissed Gilda as she came around the divider. Seeing me she stopped abruptly then asked, "Can we help you?"

"Just had to use the restroom. Thanks for the water." I handed Roxie my empty glass and went out to join Tim and Tina. Behind me I could hear Gilda giving more orders to her timid employee.

◇◇◇

"Now what were you asking us about?" echoed Tina. She lifted the last calamari from her appetizer and dunked it in marinara sauce before finishing it off. A big blue umbrella that said Casa Mia Ristorante sheltered us from the sun. The Papillons perched quietly on individual chairs, obviously at home with dining at a restaurant, while Buddy lay at my feet.

"Kate asked me if we knew of a band called Road Kill." Tim used a piece of bread to mop up the last bit of sauce from his baked clams.

"What a horrible name," she commented.

A slight breeze ruffled the tablecloth. "The full name is Tuesday Night Road Kill, I believe. They sometimes used an abbreviation, TN Road Kill." I pushed my empty plate to the side after finishing off the melon and prosciutto appetizer.

Tina scrunched up her face and turned to Tim. "Honey, isn't that the band that played for the opening of the Hudson Wellness Center?"

Tim mirrored her and frowned in concentration. "Truthfully, I have no idea. If you say so."

"I'm positive." She turned back to Kate. "Our friends were trying to pronounce the initials. We didn't know what it stood for, I'm afraid. If we did we would have gotten a good laugh."

"Do you remember anything about them? Especially the lead singer."

"He sang pretty well, and was nice looking in a rough sort of way." She turned her head away from Tim and mouthed "really hot" to me and giggled.

"Anything else?" Really hot wasn't what I was looking for.

"Wait." She tapped her manicured fingers on the table for a moment. "There was some gossip a few weeks after that show. Someone said Marilyn Fossman flew him down as her boy toy to the Caymans for some fun in the sun. When she came back she had a black eye and a bandage over her nose. Said she'd had some work done while down there."

"So?"

"So, when the swelling went down and the bandage came off she looked just the same. We think Marilyn lied about the surgery." Tina lowered her voice. "The girls think she got punched in the face by lover boy."

Chapter Sixteen

"But Gramps, it's not like that." Lounging in my apartment in my sweats I had combined sorting laundry with talking to my grandfather. "So far there's no real proof about anything." I'd made a big mistake telling him about Claire, and how suspicious I was of her suicide. Now he didn't want to talk about anything else. His raspy breathing rattled through the phone.

"It's probably useless to tell you to leave it to the professionals, but that's what I'm going to say. Leave it to the police. What about that officer who helped you out before? Luke? Go talk to him." By the end of the sentence he was seriously out of breath. I could almost see him, sitting in his favorite recliner, his gray hair standing up on end. Whenever he became agitated he'd run his left hand through his hair. Maybe I should have waited two weeks until our visit, but it sort of slipped out. In his day he'd solved plenty of cases, even had his picture in the papers a few times. I thought it might perk him up to have a mystery to solve, but, when it came to me and my safety, he had zero tolerance. If he could put me in a giant bubble he would.

I folded a couple of T-shirts and let him calm down. When his breathing sounded better I said, "Maybe I won't tell you about any of this. Is that what you want, Gramps? To be out of the loop?"

"Katie, you know better than that."

"Well, I'm a chip off the old block."

"I guess I'm the old block you're referring to," he answered with a chuckle. "Since you were a little kid you've been stubborn as a mule."

"And who do I get that from I wonder? Listen, if it makes you feel better I've already talked to Luke and he agrees with you."

"Good. You know, honey, the suicide thing. If that is a setup it might be difficult to prove. Especially with the forensic evidence gone."

"What can I say, Gramps?" I searched for a way to tell him how I felt. "She was my client and her dog Toto was my patient. My gut tells me she wouldn't leave her dog like that. I feel an obligation to them to at least be sure of what happened. Can you understand that?"

All I heard in answer was his wheezy breath and a clicking noise.

"I dreamed about her death." He'd probably think I'd gone off the deep end, but he surprised me with his answer.

"Some of the victims in the cases I investigated appeared to me in my dreams." His confession came in a somber voice. "They couldn't rest in peace."

A wave of emotion shook me. My grandpa raised me from fifteen on, after my mom and brother died and my dad remarried way too fast for comfort. As a lonely teenager I often quizzed Gramps on why he was working so hard on his cases. Why he stayed late and sometimes missed my basketball games or school debates. That's what I remembered him saying. They couldn't rest in peace until he solved the crime.

I nodded my head in perfect understanding. After our conversation ended and the laundry had been put away, I sat down at the computer and Googled "suicide." What I found troubled me. There were all kinds, from anguished family members swearing they didn't see it coming to suicides planned right down to the last detail with elaborate notes and clothing laid out for the funeral director. The reasons for killing yourself often varied by age. Teenagers wrestling with their sexual identity or sick of being bullied. Middle-aged men faced with a job loss or insurmountable financial problems who often took their unwitting families with them. The mentally ill, who didn't want to live one more day with depression. Cancer patients sick of chemotherapy or an elderly person with chronic pain seeking permanent relief.

But the ones that stuck in my mind were the suicides that seemed to come out of the blue. People who had their share of problems, but no more than anyone else, who decided to end their existence. One case in particular, a veterinarian like me, disturbed me the most. I read about it, tears welling in my eyes. She also did relief work and had talked to a clinic the day before, scheduling herself for the next few days and into the following week.

When she didn't show up for work the police were notified. Behind her locked bedroom door they found her hooked up to an intravenous drip. On the nightstand sat an empty martini glass and a note apologizing for any inconvenience. In the drip, a lethal dose of veterinary euthanasia medication. No one she had talked to had any inkling of her pain. Her clients and fellow employees noticed nothing unusual, just the same compassionate person they thought they knew.

Maybe I was wrong thinking I knew Claire.

Maybe none of us knows anyone else.

Maybe we don't even know ourselves.

Chapter Seventeen

"He ate how many pork chop bones?"

It was Monday morning and Mari and I stood in the ultra-modern kitchen of a young couple, staring at their black and tan German Shepherd who looked extremely uncomfortable. All eyes turned to the husband, a muscular guy gone to fat with a guilty look on his face.

"I'm on this high protein diet," he began explaining, "so I bought that big family pack of chops."

"Just tell them, Ed." His thin blond wife looked like she wanted to hit him over the head. Probably with a big pork chop.

"I cooked maybe, eight or nine?"

"You ate nine pork chops? Some diet," his wife huffed.

Acting as a mediator I jumped in. "So the pork chops were cooked?"

The guy gestured toward the backyard. "Grilled on the barbeque. I basted them with sauce. They were real good."

"Then what happened?"

"I, ah." The husband's head went down. He knew he was in for it. "I gave the leftovers to Brutus." The Shepherd's ears perked up after hearing his name, then he stretched back on the floor.

"You fed our dog bones? What kind of dumb ass are you?" the blonde yelled. "Do you know how much this is going to cost us?"

"Oh, come on now, Paula."

Hoping to head off a marital battle I jumped in again. "This is about Brutus and medically supporting him through this. We need to take him to the hospital and get an X-ray and see where these bones are. He might pass them or he might need surgery, but he's obviously in discomfort now."

As if holding up his end of the conversation, the big dog let out a groan.

Focused on their pet the two stopped fighting long enough to help us take the Shepherd out to the truck and put him in a transport cage. While Mari went through all the paperwork, I called ahead to the clinic to give them a heads-up on what we needed.

"Okay. We're good to go," Mari said as she swung up into the passenger seat of the truck.

"I feel sorry for the guy." We backed down the driveway, then, turned east toward the hospital. I drove slowly, conscious of the dog in the back.

Mari agreed. "I wouldn't want an intestinal tract full of bones, that's for sure."

"Me either, but I was talking about the husband."

"Yeah, he's definitely not getting any tonight," she said with a laugh, then began rooting around in a grocery bag behind her. "That's not what I was commenting about," I explained. "I guess I was thinking how one impulsive decision could screw things up so much." The delicious scent of potato chips escaped from the bag Mari opened. Being a runner she ate more than anyone I knew and still remained fit.

"Yeah. My advice to the guy…" she said between mouthfuls of chips, "become a vegetarian."

◇◇◇

Taking an X-ray of the German Shepherd turned out to be pretty easy. Brutus was more than willing to lie down quietly on the X-ray table for us. Our digital film showed good news. The big dog had taken his time and thoroughly chewed up the bones, so it looked like they would pass along with a little help. It was a great X-ray, with the bone remnants lighting up his whole intestinal tract. Quite an impressive sight.

"Maybe we should submit this to the X-ray contest sponsored by *Veterinary Practice News*." I told the staff. Their last contest included X-rays showing pets who ate light bulbs, rubber ducks, and the Internet favorite—forty-three and a half socks successfully removed surgically from a hosiery-loving Great Dane.

Thanks to small frequent feedings, some medication to lubricate and coat the intestines, followed by a brisk walk, we'd already begun seeing some poop action, and I swear the dog smiled up at us in relief. However, he wasn't out of the woods yet. I called his owners and told them he needed to stay with us at least until tomorrow. There was a particularly large piece we wanted to keep an eye on. Before we hung up they started to argue again.

With the day finally over and Brutus securely tucked in for the night in a large run, I slipped into my sweats and made some tea. The last few days had been sunny and bright, but tonight the air felt chilly. Early September was giving way to the beginning of fall in earnest. I looked forward to crisper weather with a bit of trepidation. Slogging through snow and ice was not my idea of fun. I preferred to watch the snow fall while snuggled in warm blankets on the sofa. I'd had enough snow for a lifetime in college and veterinary school.

Thinking of winter reminded me of all the mornings in vet school at Cornell when my roommates and I had to get up for large animal clinics. Braving the weather in scrubs and rubber boots, I'd stomp my feet to make sure I could still feel my toes. Once in the stalls, things heated up quickly, the musty smell of cow and horse clinging to my clothes and the soles of my boots. It seemed like yesterday, not six years ago.

Buddy jumped on the bed and circled, wrapping himself in the blanket I left for him at the foot of the bed. I ruffled his ears, then looked for something to read. Sitting on the nightstand was that book of Emily Dickinson poems I'd bought at the yard sale. I'd been reading her works on and off since high school, mostly off now with work and everything else taking up my time.

I opened the slim volume and read the list of contents. On the opposite page the only known authenticated portrait of the poet stared back at me with somber eyes. Strange to think of her voluntarily housebound in Amherst, producing poems even her family was unaware of. The paper of the book felt thin and fragile, so I carefully turned each page and glanced at the poems. Some of the titles were familiar even after all these years. When I turned the next page a folded note appeared. Maybe someone had marked this particular page. I looked at the poem. It was one of Dickinson's most famous: *Because I could not stop for Death, He kindly stopped for me.*

Sliding the note from book I opened it. A shock ran through me as I read the words written in a sloping hand. *Someone is so mad they want to kill me.*

I jumped out of bed and stared at the note in my hand. Buddy looked at me strangely, then settled back into bed. The writing had a familiar look. Could it be Claire's? Did I have a sample to compare it to? Then I remembered the inscription on the back of the painting. Sliding into my slippers I padded across the room, removed my new painting from the wall and looked at the back. I read the inscription again. *Life's Little Mysteries.* The note in my hand had the same sloping style, the m, s, and I appearing identical. I wasn't a handwriting expert but that looked close enough for me. Restless, I walked back and forth, not knowing exactly what to do. Finally I slipped the note back in place and slid the slim volume next to my well-worn Merck Veterinary Manual. Hiding it in plain sight.

Still not sure what to do I called the one person I could always rely on.

"Gramps, it's me, Kate," I almost yelled into the phone.

"Hey there, sweetheart," he answered with barely a cough. New medication had lessened the severity of his COPD symptoms. "What's up? Still coming to see me Sunday?"

"Of course, wouldn't miss it. Be there around ten or ten-thirty."

"I'll be here."

I didn't want to get him upset right away, so we talked a little about my cases in the hospital and I ended with Brutus gobbling bones in the living room while watching football with his owner. His laugh turned into a few grumbling coughs but nothing too bad. When I told him about Claire's note though, he hit the roof.

"That doesn't prove anything," he answered with an effort.

"But Gramps, she said someone wanted to kill her."

More coughing, then he replied, "You have no idea how old that note is. It might have been in that book for twenty years for all you know. Even if it is her handwriting it could be from when she was a teenager. Girls are dramatic about everything then."

Didn't I know it. At age eleven I was sure I was an adopted princess spirited away from my real family by bandits. A baby picture of me in the delivery room with my parents couldn't convince me of the truth. I preferred my secret fantasy.

Frustrated by the direction of the conversation I tried to convince him. "What if I show it to the police?"

"Go ahead. They'll probably confiscate the book and the note just to shut you up. That's what I'd have done."

"Maybe I'll keep this to myself for now." My attention went back to the picture hanging on the wall. He chuckled. "You're not going to stop, are you?" There was a pause. His heavy breathing filled the empty seconds. "We'll talk more tomorrow."

"Okay." At least a discussion wasn't completely off the table.

Then he said, "Look for a motive. Love or money. It's usually one or the other, or both."

Money? To my knowledge Claire didn't have any.

Love?

That was another story.

Chapter Eighteen

Early Sunday morning I drove the truck down to Brooklyn, and the assisted living facility where Gramps lived. I'd argued with him about moving from his old brownstone I thought of as home, but he'd insisted. Tethered to his oxygen and prone to episodes of labored breathing, he preferred the activities available at the Colonnades, rather than the loneliness of his house. With three flights of stairs to climb at home he literally had become a prisoner limited to the first floor.

Since the old man was as stubborn as I was, I finally had to stop telling him what I thought he should do and instead start listening to him. Acknowledging the changes in him was hard. Gramps was my hero.

My cousin Kathleen handled the sale of his Bay Ridge brownstone, and helped make the move a smooth one. He still was in the same neighborhood, won money in his regular Friday night poker game, and flirted shamelessly with all the widows. But now there were elevators, plenty of meals and snacks, and transportation whenever he needed it.

When I parked the truck in the lot I called his cell phone, but got no answer. That usually meant he'd left it on the kitchen table or next to the bed.

At the entrance, six Corinthian columns lined the way and had been meant to impress. Wooden benches thoughtfully separated each pair of columns. The automatic doors opened into a lobby that resembled a hotel. A greeter in a navy blue uniform signed me in. She looked at her watch.

"Try the card room," she said, and gave me a wink.

I took the elevator one flight down, then followed the sign on the wall. Groups of seniors sat in large upholstered chairs, clustered around a gas fireplace. Some had walkers, others canes, but most of them were women, their hair similarly coiffed by the in-house beauty parlor. Someone familiar waved me over as I passed. Daisy, the wife of one of Gramps' card-playing buddies, gave me a kiss on my cheek.

"If you're looking for your grandfather, Kate, check the card room. And if you see my Lionel tell him I'm waiting for him," she said. Dressed in a pink suit with matching rouged cheeks, she pointed to her watch. "The bus is picking us up in the lobby in ten minutes." Then she tapped the dial three more times for emphasis.

"I'll tell him."

She tapped on the watch face again and gave me the look—the look that all former teachers give to students they don't completely trust.

I hightailed it out of there. Daisy, according to Gramps, was always scheduling plays and visits to museums and all kinds of little day trips for herself and her husband of fifty years, Lionel. More often than not her hubby would try to dodge them by disappearing right before departure time. Wise to his ways, Daisy would go ahead without him, but he'd hear about it when she got back.

The card room was at the far end of the building. A huge room, it could be divided into smaller spaces if necessary, which is exactly how I saw it today. I peeked through the windows as I walked to the main door. Ladies played bridge or canasta on one side while the men played poker on the other. Gramps had his back to me, but from the cards I saw in his hand, he was about to win big. I stood back and waited for the game to end.

As always, I felt a jolt of sadness when I saw the portable oxygen tank next to him.

The betting, using spare change, continued until Gramps' hand was called. With a flourish he slapped down his full house to groans all around, then slid the pile of coins toward him.

"Watch out, Mick," Lionel advised him. "Those winnings are so heavy they'll pull your pants down over your scrawny ass."

"Just another treat for the ladies," Gramps answered with a smile.

"Look who's here." Lionel popped up out of his chair. "Hello, Kate. Your grampa is on a winning streak here."

A big grin broke out on my grandfather's face when he saw me. "Hey, sweetheart, can you help me with my fortune?" Then he handed me his winnings to put in my backpack, avoiding any future embarrassing experience.

Lionel leaned back in his chair like he had all the time in the world.

"Daisy's looking for you." I delivered the message in a louder than normal tone so the neighboring ladies would hear it. No way I wanted Daisy upset with me.

"You are busted, buddy," Gramps told his friend. "So busted."

"Hummph," Lionel grumbled as he got to his feet.

"Let's blow this place," my grandfather said. He took the handle of his oxygen cart and started to wheel it toward the door. "Don't leave Daisy in the lurch," he reminded Lionel.

His friend waved a hand, sat down again, and beckoned the dealer to count him in.

Gramps shook his head and continued slowly toward the elevator. Even with the oxygen going I could hear his heavy breathing. Helping some firefighters save a family in a horrible blaze gave him permanent lung damage from the smoke and chemicals he inhaled. My gramps was a real hero, but he paid a terrible price.

"So, where are we headed to, little girl?" he asked me as we crossed the lobby. I noticed everyone we passed had a nod or a smile for him.

The automatic door swung open. My truck was parked in the visitor space, adjacent to the front entrance. "I thought we could go out to lunch, then go to Soho and visit some art galleries." I tried to speed up the last part of the sentence but he caught on right away.

"You're taking me to some art galleries?" He made it sound like a punishment. "What's up?"

I stowed his gear in the backseat and helped him into the passenger seat. "We're on a reconnaissance mission that's right up your alley."

"Right. For that you owe me a beer."

On the drive from Oak Falls down to Brooklyn I'd worried about what Gramps would say. None of the scenarios I ran in my head were close to his reaction. After I updated him on what I'd learned about Claire, there was a silence, then a clicking sound. He always clicked his tongue when in deep thought.

"I think you're right to be suspicious," he finally said. He breathed deeply, sucking in the cold oxygen through plastic tubes. "Loving and caring for an animal for some people is like taking care of a child. Your grandma had a friend, Tish, a widow, who wouldn't go on vacation because she didn't want to leave her dog. Finally, after the dog passed, her daughter booked a trip for the two of them to the Bahamas. They never made it, Katie. Tish died in her sleep the day before they were supposed to leave. Her family slipped the dog's urn into the casket at the gravesite, so they'd be together again."

"That's a beautiful story, Gramps."

"It is that, indeed. A love story of a sort." He stared out the windshield at the road in front of us.

"I agree." We were approaching the bridge and the traffic slowed down. For a while we drove at a stop-and-go pace until we turned onto the West Side highway.

Gramps rolled down the truck window and let in the smell of exhaust fumes, fried food, and a few million people. When we stopped at a light he said, "That scene you described in her apartment sounds like a setup."

"I can't tell you what a relief it is to hear you say that."

"Most criminals can't leave well enough alone. The smart guys do too much, and the dumb guys practically leave a calling card at the crime scene." He rolled the window back up and kicked up the air-conditioning. "Can't you get that cop friend of yours involved?"

"Luke?" I bristled a bit at his suggestion. "Doing what?"

"If this was my case, kiddo, I'd check that car out very carefully. Doors and interior for trace and fingerprints, not to mention the keys, pedals, and steering wheel."

"Why the steering wheel? She wasn't going anywhere."

"It's one of those automatic reflexes you do when you get into a car. She'd also move her seat back to be more comfortable. Most women do. They should print the seat adjuster control."

Now I remembered why Gramps had been such a great investigator. The police still had the car, I believed. I'd tell Luke first chance I got. Real life was proving much more confusing than the shows on television. The actors wrapped up every investigation in sixty minutes, including commercials.

"Don't forget to follow the motive. It's either love or money or both."

That was Gramps' favorite line. I'd heard it a million times.

"Of course, when I say love, I mean both sides of the coin—love and hate."

I slowed down to look for the gallery and thought about what he'd said. That was true, those strong emotions were two sides of the same coin and love could turn into hate so easily.

Gramps had one more story to tell.

"I heard about a woman whose marriage was very unhappy. The husband cheated, gambled away their money and threw things at her and their cat—but she was Roman Catholic and she stayed." Gramps cleared his throat, then continued. "After he died she followed his wishes and had him cremated. He wanted his remains scattered in the ocean, but she had a different plan for them.

"What kind of plan?"

"She poured the bastard's ashes into the cat litter box, and mixed him in."

◇◇◇

I dropped Gramps off near the Webster-Simmons Gallery and found a parking spot around the corner near a real estate office. As I turned onto the main street I saw Gramps up ahead talking to a young girl. By the time I got there she'd walked away and disappeared around the corner,

"Who's your friend?" I asked.

"Nice young thing. Wanted to know if I needed any help. Who says they aren't friendly in New York?"

I took his arm and headed him in the right direction. "Check your wallet," I said jokingly.

"Already did, smarty pants," he answered back.

Cabs whizzed by us as we strolled the short distance on the sidewalk. The display windows of the gallery were very high-tech, with most pictures suspended from clear fishing wire for a floating-in-outer-space look. Chinese red lacquer coated the front door and beckoned you to come in and spend your money.

We opened the vibrant door and stepped into a loft-like space, very industrial, with exposed ductwork and commercial light fixtures. The wall to the right of the entry looked like the building's original brick. Stark white walls contrasted with the wide plank wooden floors, darkened and worn by age. A young couple stood in front of a canvas quietly talking. Her soft leather boots reached up to her thighs.

"Swanky," commented my grandfather.

Unlike at the gallery in Oak Falls, no one immediately scurried over to help us. In fact, it seemed as though we were receiving the opposite treatment. We were being ignored.

"We're getting the bum's rush, girlie." His voice wheezed into my ear. "They think we can't afford this stuff."

I had to agree with him there. Polyester pants for him with a matching oxygen tank, and jeans (not the cool kind) paired with a wrinkled button-down shirt for me, did not scream money. On the other hand Bill Gates looked like he hadn't bought a single piece of clothing since freshman year in college.

With nothing else to do we began making the rounds of the exhibit. One area was devoted to black and white photography with older photographs of New York City and the Verrazano Bridge.

"Hey, I was up there." Gramps stood in front of the image of a steelworker, eating a sandwich on a beam far over the water. The grainy picture was appealing in its black and white authenticity.

"What do you mean, Gramps?"

"I took a second job for a while, honey, while your grandma was pregnant with your mother."

Looking at him now I found it hard to think of him working so high in the air. "Were you still with the fire department?"

"Sure." He shifted his nasal tubing a bit. "Not a lot of money back in those days. Your grandma had to stay in bed so I took another job. My cousin got it for me off the books."

A voice from behind startled me. "Sorry to interrupt, but did I hear you say you were a steelworker, like the one in this picture?" An older gentleman with slicked back silver hair and a thin turquoise chain waited for an answer to his question.

'Well, not when this picture was taken. They opened the upper level in nineteen sixty-four." Gramps coughed a bit. "Only did it, on and off, for a few years. Noreen, that's my wife, hated the idea of me being so high in the air."

"I can't blame her," he agreed in an aristocratic voice. "I think I'd piss in my pants." With that he chuckled and beckoned one of the staff. "By the way, I'm Antoine Simmons, the owner of this gallery. It is a pleasure to have you here Monsieur..."

"Monsieur McCormack," answered Gramps without skipping a beat. His French accent sounded pretty good for a guy from Brooklyn.

Another employee dressed all in black suddenly appeared next to us with drinks and a plate of assorted appetizers.

"Look around. Let me know if you find anything else familiar. Bon appétite." With that he glided away toward another couple lingering in front of a sculpture.

Gramps stocked up on mini quiches, wedges of swiss, and candied walnuts, piling his small plate high as if this was an early bird special. The waiter only smiled then offered us more. "Go ahead. We've got plenty."

We stuffed ourselves while we slowly made our way around the gallery, concentrating on the black and white photos. Gramps narrated many of the scenes for me, visions of long ago suddenly as fresh as yesterday through his eyes. A note of enthusiasm permeated his voice, strong and happy, like I remembered from my teens.

The waiter strolled by again and urged us to take more food.

"Do you work here full time?" Maybe I could find out something about Claire from a member of the staff.

"Nope. I'm an actor," he explained. "I'm up for a part in an off-Broadway revival of *Trouble in Tahiti.* Waiting on tables and this kind of gig pays the rent."

Maybe he knew something helpful about the gallery or its owner. "How is Antoine to work for?"

"Not bad, as long as he keeps his hands to himself." In a lowered voice he added, "Sorry, time to play the part of a waiter."

I watched him work the room while more and more people wandered in. Gramps, meanwhile, had stopped in front of one of the black and white photographs. It showed a dance, with young men in suits standing on one side of the room and slim girls in dresses and nylon stockings on the other side.

His index finger, gnarled with arthritis, hovered over the image of a young woman with a flower in her dark hair. "She reminds me of your grandmother. A gardenia, that's what she always wore in her hair. Even her skin smelled like that flower."

Antoine came up behind us, his face reflected in the glass. "Beautiful, isn't it?"

"Yes." Gramps still stood there, a smile on his lips. "Such a treat to see these images from the past."

"Check our website in the next few weeks. I believe we will be carrying reproductions of most of these photos. A limited-edition book will be offered for the Christmas season which can be ordered on line or by phone, if you are interested."

Gently putting my hand on his elbow I walked him a few steps away. "Antoine, thank you so much for your hospitality today. My grandfather really enjoyed himself." We both turned to see Gramps still staring at the dance, frozen in time, lost in memories.

"He's a grand old fellow." Antoine's clipped tones seemed to slip a little. "Reminds me of my favorite uncle, my uncle Al, who passed away this year."

We stood together in silence for a moment. "It's been a sad year for me too. I believe you knew Claire Birnham?"

Antoine's face tightened. "My lovely Claire. Such a tragedy."

I pressed on. "She was starting her job here very soon, I believe."

"Yes, as assistant manager. Quite an opportunity for someone so young." He shook his head in puzzlement. "Who would imagine things could be so bad that she would…?"

Although I felt uncomfortable questioning him I continued. "Did she seem upset to you?"

Again he shook his head. "No, just the opposite. I spoke to her the day before. She planned on driving down on Monday to start moving boxes into her new apartment. A friend from Julliard sublet his place to her for six months while he was on tour, but she wanted to look for a place of her own."

Gramps turned his head slightly toward us. I realized he'd been listening to our conversation.

"She told you she was looking for a place of her own?"

He seemed surprised I didn't know. "Of course, with her boyfriend, I believe."

"Did she tell you his name?"

"Don't you know? I thought you were a friend of hers." Doubt filled his voice.

I scrambled for an explanation. "Claire was a little fickle in the romance department."

"Ah. That explains her sudden change of plans."

"Right. You mean the..." I waited to see if Antoine would fill in the blanks. He didn't disappoint me.

"Her decision at the last moment to move here early. You know, get into the swing of city life before she started at the gallery in six weeks."

This was new information. Why had Claire decided to leave Oak Falls before her new job started? More importantly, where was the money for an apartment coming from? "Gilda must not have been very happy about that," I ventured.

"Probably not. I'm very familiar with Gilda and how she handles her staff—or mishandles them I should say. Very unprofessional, in my opinion." He turned again in my grandfather's direction then gave his gallery a once over. "A tragedy all around." With a sigh Antoine delicately extended his hand to me. "Thanks again for joining us today. Remember to check our website for those limited print editions. They make wonderful gifts."

"Thank you. We will." I'd learned more than I'd hoped for from the talkative gallery owner.

He started to leave then stopped, as though a thought had occurred to him. "Are they investigating Claire's death up there in the boonies? Because, if I didn't know better I'd swear the dear child was murdered."

Before I could reply he strode toward the back of the room where several young couples had started congregating.

Gramps came up next to me. "So, what did you learn?"

"Something odd. It seems Claire had a mysterious boyfriend."

We walked out into the busy street, then paused for a moment as my grandfather craned his neck to look up at the glittering buildings towering above us. Across the street garbage bags were stacked one on another in the narrow alley. A bum crawled into his cardboard box, angled in the shadows to hide from the cops.

An odor of rotting food mixed with the car and truck exhaust. We stood on the sidewalk for a moment while a group of kids pushed past us, chatting excitedly. My gaze followed them as they stopped at the light. "You know, Claire had a new job to look forward to and told her friend how excited she was. I just don't get her committing suicide."

"You could be right, Katie. No pun intended, but something smells, that's for sure." Gramps wheezed for a moment while horns blared and buses rumbled by.

"I think it smells like a murder."

Chapter Nineteen

Things were almost back to normal at the office. No one had forgotten Claire. In fact, we had a daily reminder in the form of Toto. But day to day life now took top priority.

During the morning I noticed Eugene had been more quiet than usual, which meant he barely said anything, even to me. Maybe he felt strange being back on the job.

"Is everything okay, Eugene?" We had examined a young cat and after putting it back in its cage he pressed his forehead against the bars.

Not sure if he heard me I came up alongside him. His eyes were closed, his breath coming in huge gasps. "Did you hurt yourself?" Maybe the cat had scratched him when he returned it to the cage. Not sure what to do, I waited for a response.

The boy shook his head—no—then slowly moved past me, heading toward the restrooms.

"Dr. Kate, can you look at this for me?" Mari sat on one of the lab stools and gestured toward the microscope. "I think this is a roundworm egg, but it's the wrong color."

With Eugene's back rapidly receding I made a mental note to discuss his behavior with Cindy, then turned to help Mari. The new microscope was a pleasure to use, but already the cover was missing. Focusing in on the sample I saw what Mari meant. "Yes, it's similar in shape to an *ascarid* egg, but it's something much more benign. This is pine pollen."

"You know, I wondered about that. But it's really big."

I scooted off the stool so she could take another look. "Pine pollen is so large you can see it easily with the naked eye. Under some trees it looks like drifts of yellow dust."

"Thanks. I'll remember for next time."

My phone began vibrating in my pocket. I always carried it because of Gramps, and the staff had started to text me in the clinic instead of using the intercom. It was from Cindy, our receptionist.

Can you come out to reception ASAP? Eugene is acting strange.

"Mari, I'll be right back. Cindy needs me." I barely heard her response since all kinds of thoughts were racing through my head, none of them good. But nothing prepared me for what I saw.

Eugene sat on one of the plastic chairs in the animal hospital waiting room almost bent in half, rocking back and forth. The back of the chair hit the pale blue wall over and over in a disturbing rhythm.

"Hurt Claire, hurt Claire," he muttered under his breath.

Cindy and I looked at each other in disbelief. A client waiting with her cat glanced up from her cell phone, then relocated to the opposite side of the room.

"How long has this been going on?" I whispered.

"Maybe three or four minutes. I was on the phone," Cindy put her hand to her mouth. "I heard banging but didn't know what it was."

I quietly walked over to him and stared down. All I could see was the top of his head and the semi-circular scar that ran from his right ear to the middle of his skull. The hard white scar tissue looked like a train track cutting its way through a field of short cropped hair. I knelt down, careful not to touch him. Eugene didn't like to be touched.

"How did you hurt Claire?" I deliberately kept my voice calm and unemotional.

"Hurt Claire. Broke the glass. Didn't mean to hurt her." An anguished sigh rattled in his throat. He began to rock back and forth faster and faster. The drumbeat of the chair became louder. I noticed reddish-brown spots on his white sneakers.

I debated whether to continue to question him, especially with an audience watching and listening. At the very least his parents needed to be informed of this strange behavior. Before I could decide what to do, Cindy spoke up.

"Eugene. Did you hurt Claire?" She peered over the reception desk, a look of horror on her face. "Oh, my God, are you the one who killed Claire?"

"Killed Claire. Killed Claire." He continued to speak in an emotionless tone, but now a noise somewhere between a cry and a grunt punctuated each rocking motion, getting louder and louder. I stepped back, not sure if this behavior would escalate into something violent. Eugene took a daily anti-seizure medication. Perhaps we were witnessing the beginning of an event. Behind me I heard Cindy whisper into the phone. I caught the word "hurry" before she hung up. She must have called 911. I stood up and consulted the list of emergency numbers pinned to the corkboard above the fax machine. As soon as I found Eugene's contact info I called his mother. It went to voice mail.

"This is Dr. Kate Turner. We need you to phone the animal hospital immediately," I said as I left a message for her. "Eugene is experiencing some kind of emotional distress. It has to do with Claire's death." What Wendy would think when she heard the message, I had no idea. I only hoped she could get here before the police.

She didn't. When the police arrived with sirens blaring and lights flashing Eugene became more agitated. He drew further into himself, muttering and rocking back and forth, his eyes screwed shut. The thick muscles in his arms and shoulders tensed, and he clenched both hands into two tight fists. When the officers asked him his name he didn't reply. Then they tried to stand him up, each man holding an arm, but he ignored them and kept up the rocking, locked in his sitting position. Finally an ambulance arrived and an EMT crew transferred Eugene, almost catatonic at this point, onto a stretcher.

When Police Captain Garcia arrived to take our statements I racked my brain, determined to tell him only what I heard directly, with no embellishment. Before I could say anything the client with the cat who'd been waiting all this time whipped out her phone. She had videotaped the entire episode.

"Killed Claire" echoed over and over again in the still room.

Chapter Twenty

We didn't know it at the time, but our client had posted her video of Eugene on YouTube before she turned it over to the police. It went viral, and then the local and national news took the story and ran with it. Television and radio news shows speculated on what turned mild-mannered Eugene into a murdering menace. Every neurologist and pop psychologist the media could get their hands on seemed to have a theory, even if they didn't know him from Adam. Psycho-babble flooded the airways and people wondered why his doctors hadn't locked him up before now.

In the next few days poor Eugene and his family had their privacy taken away from them. Our hospital had to dodge calls from the media all day. After the fifth call from a well-known tabloid, I told Cindy not to bother me with them and their calls and only to take messages. How many times could I say "No comment?" We even had a camera crew camp outside the clinic steps for most of the day, ambushing unsuspecting clients on their way home.

I continued working on automatic pilot, a heavy feeling in my gut. Every few hours I checked my phone, hoping Luke would call me from the police department. Maybe after I spoke to him I would understand what happened. Pundits already predicted there would be no trial. Since he'd been arrested, Eugene had withdrawn into a world of his own making. Part of me wondered if the anti-seizure drug and mood stabilizers he took had contributed to his odd behavior.

By the time the day was over I didn't want to talk to another living soul. Instead of going out I hunkered in and cooked up an omelet full of whatever wasn't moldy in the refrigerator. A marathon of *The Big Bang Theory* reruns made me laugh just enough. After washing up and taking Buddy out I got ready to turn in. Putting aside my latest Lee Child thriller, I paged through one of the veterinary journals lying next to the bed. I'd just turned off the light when the phone rang.

"Did I wake you up?" Luke asked.

"No. I'm not asleep yet." I sat up and turned on the bedside lamp. Buddy opened one eye then grunted and rolled over.

"It sounds like you've had some pretty hectic days."

"You could say that."

"Sorry." His apology hung in the air.

Now wide awake I swung my legs off the side of the bed and moved over to the sofa. "So, tell me what you know so far."

Luke cleared his throat. I remembered then that Eugene was no stranger to him. He must have met him at the stables, and certainly knew him from our hospital. When he spoke, his voice sounded uncharacteristically subdued.

"It's mostly bad. First of all, his prints are everywhere at the crime scene. On the broken vase were traces of Eugene's blood and Claire's blood, and we matched his prints to ones we found on her car keys.

"Oh, no." My chest tightened. I felt frozen in place.

"That's not all. His mother picked him up outside her townhouse right around time of death. He had a bandage on his hand. When she asked what happened he wouldn't talk about it."

I thought for a moment. "What kind of bandage?"

"Only a Band-Aid."

"Who put it on his hand?"

His exasperation with me came over loud and clear in his voice. "We're checking that out, but your kennel help killed Claire. We've got him confessing to it."

"No you don't. I mean, yes, you do. But you don't."

"What the hell does that mean?" He was way past being polite to me.

I took a breath to calm down, then started again. "Eugene repeats words a lot, repeats the last few words you say as the start of his answer to you. It focuses him."

"So?"

"That's what I think he did. Cindy said "Oh, my God, were you the one who killed Claire?" I think he repeated the last two words and said "Killed Claire."

"What are you implying?"

"He just repeated what Cindy said." The words rushed out. "That wasn't a confession."

Luke didn't sound convinced. "How do you explain the blood? The fingerprints?"

My sense of injustice threatened to overpower me. Another deep breath and I felt ready to talk. "I don't know. I'm sure there is a good explanation."

"Face it, Kate. Something snapped. Probably something having to do with his head injury and the way he processes information. Listen, I like the kid too, but he confessed." There was a pause. I could hear him breathing. "I didn't tell you, but I saw him lose his temper once at the stable. It's better like this. At least now there's closure for everyone, including Eugene."

Better this way. If I thought Eugene was capable of murder, I would have agreed. But my heart told me differently.

"So what's next?"

"His mental state is being evaluated. I really can't comment on anything else."

Still upset, I got up and walked over to the sink to get a glass of water. "Thanks for telling me all this, Luke. I appreciate it."

"It's all going to be in the paper in the morning. Captain Garcia issued a statement to the press."

"So, no confidences betrayed to outsiders."

He didn't comment on my remark. He didn't have to. Although I'd had more experience with murder and death than most people I was still an amateur as far as the police were concerned.

"You were right, Kate. It was a murder."

"Please don't say congratulations." My mouth dry, I looked around for my glass of water.

"I knew him before, you know." Luke cleared his throat. "Before the accident I mean."

All the noise momentarily woke up Buddy. I took the phone with me and moved to the kitchen table. "What was he like?"

"He was really, really smart, especially with numbers. A math whiz. But not stuck up at all. A bit of a class clown. One of the popular kids."

An image of Eugene flashed in front of me. Not the Eugene that shuffled a little as he walked from cage to cage, his face set in an emotionless mask. Instead I saw a good looking kid with a grin on his face and an easy confidence. As quickly as it came it faded.

"Sorry. I should have realized…"

"Most of us know him. Oak Falls is a small town."

Just how small a town, I was about to find out.

Chapter Twenty-one

Monday morning it seemed as though every person I met asked me about Eugene. What happened? How he got arrested. Did we suspect he was a killer? Plus, they all had their own rationale on why he killed Claire. She caught him stealing or he tried to rape her, or that his head injury made him go nuts.

Our staff did what they always do when things were rough. They did their jobs. Despite how they felt, there were litter boxes to clean and dogs to be walked and X-rays to take and a million other things to do. It wasn't until closing time that Nick, our other technician and kennel helper, took me aside.

"Uh, Dr. Turner. Can I talk to you for a minute?"

"Sure, Nick. Let's go into the office." Thankfully he had held his questions until our day was over. Because he'd been studying for his finals he hadn't been in the hospital when Eugene had been arrested.

After I sat down he ignored the other desk chair and instead leaned against the wall. Normally a personable guy, his body language read nervous.

"Is it true what they're saying, that Eugene raped that lady?" His gaze made a beeline for the floor.

"No. That's not true. I can't believe all the crazy stuff I've heard today."

"Well, I didn't think that could be true."

"Why?"

Nick fidgeted with his fingers for a moment. "He didn't feel like that anymore."

For a moment I didn't understand what he was talking about. But then I got it.

"You mean, Eugene's sex drive changed after his injury?"

"Right," nodded Nick, obviously relieved I had figured it out without making him elaborate on the subject.

"How do you know?"

"I asked him."

It never ceased to amaze me what people talked about at work. My staff knows who is fighting with their boyfriend, what color Cindy painted her kitchen, and tons of little things I have no idea about. I guess I shouldn't have been surprised these guys were talking about sex while cleaning the kennels.

"How exactly did that come up?" The color in his face started to rise until it was bright red. I decided to let him off the hook. "Never mind, Nick. Did he tell you anything else about his life, or how he felt?"

This time he looked directly at me. "Well, he loved working with the animals, and he liked working with you because you taught him things."

A picture of Eugene flashed into my mind. I'd taught him how to keep a wound clean and how to lavage damaged tissue by a steady stream of saline. As always I cautioned him that a senior technician needed to oversee his work. He learned quickly and best by doing things himself. His speech may have been slow and face a little lopsided, but I suspected his mind was sharper than people gave him credit for. With all his limitations he still held down two jobs, which is more than you could say about a lot of folks.

But all these good thoughts didn't help the predicament he was in. I took another look at Nick, self-assured now, arms crossed. Black curly hair, olive complexion, a thin gold chain around his neck. He juggled college and work, and lots of young ladies with his bucketload of charm. Even our receptionist, Cindy, was wrapped around his little finger. His future looked bright.

Eugene's bright future had been torn from him by a horse's hoof in a split second.

"Nick, do you think Eugene is capable of murder?"

I watched his pupils dilate, his brow furrow, and his posture change from relaxed to tense. When he spoke anguish layered his voice.

"Dr. Kate, I honestly don't know."

◇◇◇

"Eugene's mom is coming by in a few minutes to pick up what's in his locker." Cindy sprang this the next day as I was pouring my first cup of coffee. It was seven-thirty and we didn't start seeing appointments until nine o'clock. "She wants to talk to you for a minute."

"Okay. Let me know when she gets here."

I spent the next twenty minutes checking on my patients and going through the lab test results that were sent to us by email. Most veterinary hospitals now had one or two pickups each day and got their routine results back in less than twenty-four hours. A pathology report caught my eye. Immersed in the oncologist's chemotherapy recommendations, I didn't hear the first knock on the office door.

"Dr. Turner, Mrs. Spragg, Eugene's mother, is here."

"Just a moment." I shrunk my screen and slipped on a white lab coat.

When I opened the door three people stood waiting for me. The older woman with gray-streaked brown hair I recognized as Eugene's mother, Wendy. Next to her, undoubtedly, stood Eugene's father, the passing resemblance unmistakable. Clasping her hand was a woman in her late twenties or early thirties with Down syndrome.

"Dr. Turner, thank you for seeing us so early. I think you know my husband, Karl. And this is our daughter Angelica."

"Nice to meet you. Won't you come in?" I didn't know Eugene had a sibling.

They filed into my office, Wendy still holding Angelica's hand. Before I could stop him, the hospital cat, Mr. Katt, snuck in at warp speed. When he wasn't dive bombing us from above he was extremely fond of both sleeping on my desk chair and decorating it with coughed up hair balls. Angelica squealed with delight, pointed and said, "Kitty."

"His name is Mr. Katt." I explained as he zipped past them. "He lives here at the hospital and loves to be petted." To prove my point the brown tabby came out from under the desk and proceeded to greet everyone.

"Gently, Angelica," her mother cautioned her.

As I watched, the cat rubbed up against the girl's outstretched hand, then head butted it, his signature move.

Angelica giggled.

A smile flitted across her mother's face, then it returned to a somber demeanor. The same expression was mirrored in her husband's eyes.

"We want to thank you for everything you've done for Eugene," she told me.

I didn't know what to say.

"He loved working here and he particularly liked helping you and Nick."

"Eugene is a pleasure to work with," I said truthfully, "and he is especially gentle and patient with the animals."

"He learned patience at an early age," the father commented, his eyes resting on his daughter.

"Do you think you could…?" Wendy Spragg glanced at her daughter, Angelica, then caught his eye.

"Sure. Angelica, let's go see Cindy." He stretched out his hand to her.

"You can take Mr. Katt with you," I told her. "Tell Cindy to show you where his favorite cat hiding place is." I scooped the cat up and draped him over my shoulder. "He likes to ride around like this. Is that okay?" My head gestured in Angelica's direction.

"That's how she holds her cat at home," Karl said. Sure enough, when he landed on her shoulder Mr. Katt started purring big time.

As soon as they left, Wendy shut the door. "Angelica's not quite sure what's going on. We've told her Eugene is in the hospital, which she understands. That's why we came so early, so we don't have to talk to anyone in front of her. She loves her brother."

"I'm so sorry," I began. "Is there anything I can do?"

She shook her head. "We've hired a lawyer, but for now Eugene's at a medical facility being evaluated. He won't even talk to us."

I gestured for her to sit down. "The day he became distraught, I thought he was frightened about something."

"Did anything happen at work? Anything traumatic that could have precipitated this?" Wendy took the chair opposite the desk and put her purse down by her feet.

Other than confessing to murder? I kept that thought to myself. "The staff and I went over everything that happened that day, but we couldn't come up with anything."

"Well, he didn't do it. Somehow we've got to prove it."

"How can you be so sure?" An image came to mind, that day I walked behind him and noticed how muscular his shoulders and arms were.

"I'm sure because he loved Claire. Eugene would never harm anything that he loved."

◇◇◇

Her words stayed with me long after their family left. "Eugene would never harm anything that he loved." My instincts told me that was true. The Eugene I worked with never showed any anger toward any animal or person he worked with. I never felt any subtext or hidden emotions running under the surface. What you saw was what you got. A kind, very focused individual, eager to do the right thing and only frustrated when he came up against something he couldn't handle. I remembered how long he practiced replacing a bandage until his were almost better than mine. He sat on the floor with my dog Buddy and must have bandaged his front and back legs at least twenty times. Always one to follow the rules he made sure one of the technicians checked each time to make sure it wasn't too tight.

Despite the evidence I couldn't see Eugene killing Claire. But how to explain his behavior in the waiting room? Especially after Cindy asked him if he killed her? Maybe the broken vase and the bandage on his hand had something to do with it.

"What's going to happen to Eugene now? Are you going to have to replace him?" My ever-practical technician Mari questioned me while eating an oatmeal raisin cookie. We were in the truck on our way to a house call.

"I'll have to talk to Cindy about it," I told her, trying to miss a pothole in the road.

"Meanwhile Nick said he could fill in and work around his classes this semester. I see you've started your training diet," I joked. Mari could eat some kind of crazy amount of calories because of her running schedule. My biggest form of exercise was getting in and out of the truck and jumping to conclusions.

"Very funny." She reached into the bag again, then took a swig of water. "Just so we split the shifts up. I don't want to end up having to do kennels all the time."

Everyone hated to do kennels, which consisted of cleaning up after the animals, mopping the floors, walking the dog patients and boarders, checking their bandages and helping the medical staff, then doing it all over again. That's why Eugene excelled at the job. He never became bored. Never complained.

Mari interrupted my thoughts with a question. "I'm feeling guilty that I didn't put that client who taped him into one of the exam rooms. Like I'm a little bit responsible for that video getting on the Internet."

Mari usually didn't admit feeling guilty about anything, so I was curious. "Why do you say that?"

"It doesn't seem like him. He's the last person I would suspect of murder. I remember the day he got nipped by that Akita with the broken toe. He just shrugged it off, said it wasn't the dog's fault." She popped another cookie in her mouth. "I know some techs who would have been pissed off."

"Me too. I have to tell you, I don't think he did it either."

"Then why don't you investigate it, like you did the last time?"

"You mean when I almost got killed?"

"Well, this time don't be alone with any suspects. It will be cool."

Cool wasn't how I would describe interfering in a police investigation of murder, but I knew I had to do something to help. After all, I'd worked with Eugene for the last six months. If anyone knew how he'd react to stress it would be me and the other members of the hospital staff."

"Besides," continued Mari with a smile, "you'll be forced to work with you know who again. "What's his name…Larry?" I ignored her as she pretended she'd forgotten Luke's name.

"That never occurred to me," I told her with a straight face.

"Think of it as a perk."

◇◇◇

I started not by phoning Luke but by calling someone tapped into everything that went on in town.

"Hi, Daffy, it's Dr. Kate." My client with the grumpy Chihuahua might not go out much, but that didn't mean she was out of the loop. Her network of informants knew no bounds. The clerk who generated the police reports had her on speed dial.

"Why hello, dear. I hear you've gotten yourself into the middle of a mess again."

Say what you might about Daffy, she was nothing if not direct.

"You're right. But I'm not convinced the police have the right person. Eugene isn't violent at all, in my opinion."

I heard a snuffing sound that I took to be a comment of some sort on my statement. "There are several other people who feel the same way, people who've known him his whole life. In their opinion the police are making a big mistake."

Encouraged by that unexpected statement, I continued. "What can you tell me about the crime scene, Daffy? I couldn't find out anything on my own."

"Well, this is all I know. The body was in her car, parked in the garage. Claire sat in the driver's seat and had a bandage on her hand, the kind made of gauze and tape. There was a broken vase in the trash. That's where they found Eugene's blood mixed with Claire's blood. His fingerprints were all over the apartment. They don't know when Claire cut herself, but they think some time just before she died. The new theory is she had a fight with Eugene, who ended up killing her and staging it to look like suicide."

"So, let me get this straight. The police think they had a fight and broke a vase. Then stopped to put a bandage on the cut, then had another huge fight that ended in murder. And Eugene, although mentally impaired, came up with a suicide strategy on the spur-of-the-moment?"

"That's what the chief's sister-in-law told my neighbor."

Straight from the horse's mouth—not. I hoped we weren't playing that childhood game telephone, where you whisper something to the person sitting next to you and it gets passed down the line and changed until it bears no resemblance to how it started.

"Was there, ah, anything else? Any sexual aspect?" I tried to put it as delicately as possible. I shouldn't have bothered.

"Rape? No, there was no sign of sexual assault. Also no weird stuff in the bedroom." Daffy told me all this as matter-of-factly as discussing the contents of her kitchen cabinets.

Obviously there was no such thing as privacy, even when you're dead. Come to think of it, in a murder everything has to be catalogued and searched. Then it goes into a report and it's anyone's guess how many people discuss it around the water cooler. I made a note to check my own apartment and get rid of anything I wouldn't like people to talk about. I remembered the old saying that two people can only keep a secret if one of them is dead.

One of them was dead now, but to help Eugene we'd have to uncover all of Claire's secrets.

Chapter Twenty-two

I took another bite of my chicken salad sandwich and stared out the window. It was Sunday afternoon and I'd stopped in to the Oak Falls diner after taking a hike to Table Falls with Buddy. The smell of coffee and pancakes hung in the air along with the buzz of people talking and laughing. I'd walked about five miles on the national forest trails and felt that peaceful tiredness you get from good old-fashioned physical exercise. My lungs finally felt clean after breathing all that fetid air at The Rocket bar. After lunch I planned on going home to watch a movie. No sleuthing today.

"Finished Kate?" Ruthie, another of Mama G's granddaughters who worked at the diner, asked. She held a big coffee pot in her right hand. They must go through buckets of that stuff.

"Yes, thanks," I told her.

"Do you want something to go? Like a pot pie for dinner?" She gestured to the to-go boxes as she cleared the table. "That's what I do. It makes the weekends much simpler."

"Good idea. Will it take long?"

She added it to my check and smiled. "No. It's already baked. Just heat it up when you're ready." Like most of her relatives she had Mama G's dark eyes and brown curly hair. I knew Ruthie went to the NY State University at New Paltz and majored in architecture. Her tips went to help pay for books and tuition.

A motion caught my eye as I waited for Ruthie to return. Two birds were fighting over something, a crust of bread maybe. The bigger one settled in like he owned it but the smaller brown finch didn't give up, dancing in and out to steal crumbs.

Ruthie interrupted my thoughts. "Here you go." I slid out of the booth then picked up the paper bag she had brought with my food inside.

"Thanks, Ruthie. Hey, look. The littlest finch won after all." We both watched as the little guy flew off with his prize.

Ruthie headed toward the kitchen while I made my way to the cashier, after leaving a good sized tip on the tabletop. More people streamed past me as I left. I'd parked the truck at the back of the parking lot so I had to listen to my shoes crunch gravel all the way to the end of the lot.

"You mother-jumping piece of crap."

Someone I couldn't see had cursed out someone or something. Noting it was a woman's voice I decided to check and make sure she wasn't in any sort of trouble. By reflex my index finger touched the pepper spray bottle attached to my keys that Gramps insisted I carry.

A short distance away a car engine whirred then went dead. "Worthless. Just worthless," continued the voice. "Buzz, you need to come get me now."

I put the takeout in the truck and moved toward the racket. In the next row I saw orange-red hair sticking up over the hood of a Chevy truck, cell phone glued to her ear. As she turned I recognized the face of Claire Birnham's mother, Beverly.

"Something wrong?" I asked. The stench of gas fumes surrounded the car. She'd probably flooded it while trying to start the older model truck.

"The damn thing won't start." With that she pounded the hood with her fist, putting a little dent in the rusted metal. The dirty blue surface was covered with dings and scratches. I notice the right front tire had no hub cap and almost no tread.

"Do you need a jump start?" I offered.

She walked around the front of the truck toward me. Even though the day was cool she wore cutoffs and a tight stretchy top that showed off plenty of skin. A cigarette dangled from her right hand. Backless black heels and silver toenail polish completed the outfit.

"Naw. It's the carbonator."

When she spoke I smelled the stale stink of beer. "Can I give you a lift somewhere?" I asked, trying to be polite.

Claire's mother didn't answer right away, but instead slowly texted someone, then groaned. "Phone's dead too."

"Maybe you should wait in Mama G's," I suggested, using the locals nickname for the Oak Falls Diner. "You could use their phone."

"Hey, I'm only about ten minutes away. Mind giving me a lift?" Not waiting for an answer she climbed back in the truck cab and quickly got out, toting two six-packs. I noticed one bottle was missing.

"No problem. I'm Kate, by the way." I didn't mention I'd met her briefly at her daughter's funeral. It didn't seem to be the time or the place.

"Beverly, but everyone calls me Bev." She followed me to my truck and climbed into the passenger seat.

"Do you mind?" she asked as she popped a beer on the dashboard. "What the heck, I'm not driving."

While I backed out of the parking lot she raised the bottle to her lips and drank half of it down.

"Celebrating," she commented.

Fate gave me this opportunity to talk to her and I wasn't going to waste it.

"Go ahead." I tried to sound as if my passengers always drank while I drove. "When I get home I'm going to kick back too."

She gave me her address and looked around the interior of the cab. "This thing is almost as bad as my piece of crap."

"Well, I'm borrowing it for now." I honestly think she had no idea who I was.

The bottle tilted up to her lips again and this time it came back empty. She popped it back into the cardboard holder and pulled out another. "I'm getting a brand new truck and a Corvette in about four weeks," she gloated. "Ordered them from the dealer. No more of this used stuff."

"Wow. Did you win the lottery?"

"In a way." I watched her expertly pop the top off the next beer. "I've got a big settlement coming in once the insurance company finishes the paperwork. A life insurance policy. Best thing that stupid husband ever did for me."

"Oh. He left you a lot?" My foot eased off the gas. I didn't want to get to her house before finding out more about this money.

"No. See," she turned to speak to me, "my ex worked for an insurance company. Got nuts about life insurance. Bought policies for him and our kid. Not for me, though, he said I was too much of a bitch to die." This made her laugh. "When he kicked the bucket all the money went to Claire. Trouble was she couldn't touch it until her eighteenth birthday. Nothing came to me, though I had to work like a dog to put food on the table."

"So, your daughter is giving you some of the money?" I asked, confused.

"In a way," Bev repeated. "My daughter passed recently and left me everything."

I took my eyes off the road for a moment. Because Bev abruptly began rummaging through her purse she missed the expression of horror on my face.

Triumphantly she pulled out a lighter and a pack of cigarettes.

"At least some blessing comes from such a tragedy." I desperately searched for something else to say to get her talking again. "When my mother and brother died in a car accident I got Social Security survivor benefits. My father said that's how the system worked."

"Yeah, it's the system. It's not my fault I'm getting the money. I'd rather have my baby back." Her voice didn't sound particularly sincere.

"Of course," I agreed, as she finished her last beer in record time. "Besides, your loved ones would want you to be happy."

"Damn right," Bev belched, then continued. "My fiancé Buzz says we deserve the money after raising her and paying for her clothes and shoes and all that art stuff." She paused and lit a cigarette without asking me. "You can buy a lot of happy for half a million bucks."

Chapter Twenty-three

As soon as I dropped Bev off I scurried back home and began a Google search. Something she said bothered me. I thought that committing suicide would cancel a life insurance payoff. Sun streamed through the side windows as I researched the gruesome details of benefiting from someone's death.

What I read surprised me. There was no one-size-fits-all rules about this. Most policies had a two-year clause. They would pay benefits if the insured committed suicide after the policy had been in place for at least two years. Of course, it also depended on the state you lived in, or died in, as the case may be. New York State happened to be one of the ones that did pay.

Could Claire's death have been about money, not love?

How much did the police dig into Claire's estate, or did they just assume it didn't add up to much? Considering that all her stuff ended up in a yard sale, who could blame them for not looking deeper into a money motive? My foot began to tap under the desk as I thought about what I'd discovered. That money would be a windfall to Bev, still working long shifts at the factory.

The idea of a mother killing her child made me sick, but there was plenty of precedence for it.

The next thing to do would be to find out more about this insurance policy and everyone's financials in general. Without hesitating I called Luke Gianetti. Not because I wanted to hear his voice. This was not a social call.

"Hello." He answered on the third ring. From the background noise he was either sitting in front of the television or in the middle of a party.

"Hi, Luke. Am I interrupting anything?"

The volume behind his voice lowered. "Just studying with the television on. What's up?"

"Did you ever look into who benefited from Claire's estate?"

"What's going on?" His voice sounded more confused than mad.

"Just curious." I paused.

"Well, I'm not active on her case anymore. The chief knows how close our family was and made an executive decision. I can't tell you any more from my side." He waited a moment before he continued. "I'm not sure how you could get this information without talking to the family or the family's attorney directly. Is that what you're planning on trying to do?"

Was Luke trying to steer me in that direction?

"Maybe." I decided to keep Bev's confession about life insurance to myself.

"Please don't tell me about it," he said. "The less I know, the more I can deny if you get into trouble."

I couldn't tell if he was joking or not.

Chapter Twenty-four

"One heart."

"Pass."

"One spade."

"Two diamonds."

"Three hearts."

"Pass."

"Four hearts."

The table I sat at might be covered in a lace tablecloth but I was a roomful of ruthless gamblers. My cards were arranged in front of me since I was the "dummy." Yes, it was Wednesday at six p.m. and I was playing bridge with the Oak Falls Ladies Bridge Club. I'd been partnered with Faith Urskin, who was currently marching toward victory on our four heart bid. Her normal partner, my client Daffy and her Chihuahua, couldn't make it due to cataract surgery. I'd volunteered because, as Daffy put it, there isn't anything that takes place in this town that those old bitches don't know and maybe you can discover something about Claire.

"More iced tea, dear?" Our hostess, Candace Appleton, asked. Unlike most of the other ladies she wore high heels and tight jeans. A leopard print blouse slid halfway down her shoulders revealing black bra straps. Various chains and beads hung around her neck.

"I'm fine," I answered. "These cookies are delicious, by the way."

"Costco," Candace bragged. The other ladies nodded and began singing the praises of Costco, all the while finishing the hand.

"My daughter and I split up the meat packages," Faith explained. Her steely gray eyes, enlarged by the lenses of her glasses, looked like those of a bobble-head doll.

Sylvia, who sat to my right, began to calculate the score. "You have a twenty-point leg on," she told Faith and me, then continued on the Costco theme. "I usually freeze it in individual servings."

The game kept on bouncing back and forth between bids and helpful Costco hints.

Candace refilled the plate of cookies and placed them next to me. I noticed several enamel and silver rings on her fingers as well as bangle bracelets on her wrists, but no wedding ring. Without much else to do I started nibbling on a huge double chocolate chip hoping the sugar would wake me up. I'd been playing for an hour with no opportunity to learn anything about Claire or her family, except they probably went to Costco.

After our hostess moved away, Faith lowered her voice. "Ladies. Lock up your husbands. I do believe Candace is on the prowl again."

"Oh, you are so naughty, dear," retorted Sylvia. Her partner Peggy's face scrunched up.

"What happened to that nice Mr. Buchanan she was seeing?"

"Snatched up by Lisa Franklin. She must be twenty years younger than him, but you know men."

Everyone at the table made a sniffing noise.

"Traded Candace in for a newer model, I guess." Faith entered the points into the scorecard and shuffled the deck. "Typical."

As she began to deal I jumped into the conversation. "Do you think that's why Claire Birnham committed suicide?" Everyone at the table looked at each other, in confusion. "I mean because of her love life going downhill."

All eyes swung my way. Each lady had on reading glasses, which made me feel like I was being scrutinized by giant ants.

No one said anything. Should I prompt them, or stay still? I was trying to come up with something else but Faith began to speak.

"That poor girl."

Murmurs of agreement all around the table as the ladies picked up their hands.

"That mother," she continued. "Always drunk as a skunk. And the boyfriends. One heart."

Sylvia picked up the thread. "Remember the two red-haired cousins? First one, then the other. Pass."

"Pass."

"Hopefully not at the same time," commented Peggy. "One spade."

"Two clubs," Faith said. "Such a dirty little mind you have."

All of them smiled at that one.

"The worst is that gorilla she's with now."

I was lost. "What gorilla? Who are you talking about?"

"Buzz, Bev's current boyfriend. Claire Birnham's mother." Faith said this with a completely straight face, irony being lost on her.

"She calls him her fiancé," Peggy added.

"Whatever," Sylvia countered. "Two spades."

"Pass," I said.

Peggy put down her hand and explained. "Claire was only fourteen when her father died and it hit her hard. Her mom lost it and started picking up guys at the factory or in bars and bringing them home. One of those women who couldn't be alone. Buzz was the latest, which is why Claire moved out. Three spades."

"Her dad left her some money," Faith said.

"Quite a bit, I was told," Peggy continued, "from his life insurance. She set herself up in that nice townhouse and bought one of those Japanese cars. Her mother wasn't too happy, since she didn't have Claire to help with the rent."

"So, why did she kill herself? Pass."

Sylvia lowered her voice and looked around the room before continuing. "There is a rumor that Buzz forced himself upon her. Abused her when she was young." She arched an eyebrow and looked at her partner. "Four spades."

"Okay," Peggy clarified. "It's four spades." We were playing a game.

"Did the police know?" I asked. That could certainly be a motive for suicide I hadn't thought of.

"I don't believe so. Bev says people should mind their own business."

"Like that's going to happen in a small town." Faith said. "Hell, I wouldn't put it past those two to have murdered Claire for the money."

Sylvia laid her cards out. Her partner, Peggy, didn't seem very impressed. My partner toasted me with her cup of Earl Gray tea. "Welcome to Oak Falls." Stories run deep in small towns, but this story was an all too familiar one. Shattered family, neglected child, and a predator who took advantage of them. As the evening progressed my bridge game got better but Claire's story got worse. Fights, running away, alcohol and drugs. Things changed for the better once she made friends with Luke and his sister, plus Mama G took her under the family's wing. An art scholarship at Rhode Island University, working at the diner during the summer, and having as little to do as possible with her mom and Buzz and their chaotic relationship definitely helped.

The game broke up at eight-thirty. Candace fussed around and then handed me a package of cookies wrapped in stiff cellophane and tied with a bow.

"Here, I'm re-gifting. I need cookies like a hole in the head," she smiled. "You made Sylvia happy."

"Really?" The other ladies streamed past me like lemmings.

"Sure, honey. They won. I love Sylvia but she goes for the throat."

We stood near the doorway as Candace bid farewell to the last of her animated guests. I decided to stay behind for a moment and ask her some questions.

"You look like you have something to say," Candace observed, beating me to the punch. "Come over here, sweetie, and let's make ourselves more comfortable." She led me to the living room, furnished in beige, with mahogany wood and glass accents. Not the frou-frou room I expected. It was understated, something you couldn't say about Candace herself.

"Would you like a glass of white wine?" she asked me. Out of a small butler's pantry fitted with a stainless and wood wine cooler, she took out a bottle and two glasses.

"No thanks," I said truthfully, sinking into a comfortable chair. "I have to drive home and the roads are pretty dark at this hour. Not to mention the deer jumping in front of you."

"Ah, country living," she answered. I watched her pour a large glass for herself and dig around for a water bottle for me. "So how do you like our little town?"

Not knowing what she expected me to reveal I played it safe. "It's nice. Very nice."

Candace laughed. "You don't have to be politically correct with me, honey. Some people here stick their noses into other people's business way too much. Like me." Her statement was accompanied by peals of laughter followed by a long sip of wine.

It was refreshing to talk to someone who didn't take themselves too seriously. "Well, then Daffy must have told you I have some questions about Claire Birnham's death."

"Yes."

"To tell you the truth, I'm having a hard time dealing with it, and now Eugene, who works at the animal hospital, is mixed up somehow." The words rushed out of me before I could stop. Curious how she would handle my confession I sat back, sipped some water, and waited.

"What is bothering you?" Her voice sounded intrigued.

"Nothing seems to add up. Claire would never have committed suicide without making sure Toto was taken care of. She loved that dog like he was her baby."

"Did you speak to the police about this?"

"Of course, but they aren't interested in hunches, or feelings, or dogs, and honestly, I can't blame them. Fact. Claire tried to commit suicide before, by slitting her wrists. Fact. They've got a suicide note plus a confession and a lot of circumstantial evidence pointing to Eugene—one of the sweetest guys you'd ever meet."

Candace nodded her head and slipped off her high heels. "Sorry, but my feet are killing me. I wore these tonight just to give the ladies something to gossip about. Now, it seems you have a problem here."

"You could say that again." I drank more water and put the bottle back on the glass-topped coffee table. "I'm working full time plus trying to help get Eugene's name cleared."

Tucking her feet up into the upholstered chair Candace slipped the bangle bracelet off her wrist. "You're working in the dark, not knowing many people here in town."

"That's true."

"Let me do a little snooping around for you. It will be fun. Like those two woman on television. Please, please, please. I'm so bored at the moment."

She smiled across the room at me, all curled up in her arm chair, looking as neat as a cat.

Sure, I thought, what could it hurt? "Maybe you could talk to some of the people who knew her best. I've been trying to find out if she really had a new boyfriend."

"Let me write down some notes."

"Okay, but promise me, if you find out anything important we take it to the police."

"Of course."

Forcing myself to impose some order on my thoughts I sank back into the chair. "Better yet, maybe you could confirm if her ex-boyfriend, A.J. has an alibi for that Friday."

"That's the self-proclaimed rock star."

"Right." Obviously Candace knew more than she let on.

"Then there is Buzz. He's a little too fond of Bev's money."

Candace grimaced. "Buzz the loathsome. That shouldn't be very hard, just hit the bars."

My head was beginning to pound as I tried to concentrate. "Oh, you may as well check the ladies out, too. Specifically an

A.J. groupie, Bella, who lives in Rhinebeck. Someone thought she might be engaged to the guy."

"You said ladies. Is there someone else?" Candace clicked her pen.

"Well, this is a long shot but…maybe you could discretely find out more about Gilda, the owner of the Qualog Gallery? Everywhere I turn she pops up, riding under the radar." My head still aching, I took a couple of Advil. "Oh, she might be having a thing with that Russian artist who has been in all the papers recently."

Candace popped up out of her seat. "Enough already. She padded away on her bare feet then whirled around like a girl. "This is so exciting."

Her enthusiasm was catching. Why I agreed to have her help me I don't know; put it down to being tired, I guess. It ended up being one of the worst decisions of my life.

Chapter Twenty-five

"This should be fun," Mari said, as she plunked down a lunch bag onto the backseat. We were in the truck heading for our first morning appointment—health certificates for a litter of puppies. The sun shone with the intensity you see after a storm. Unfortunately, I couldn't lower the window to smell the fresh air because the truck was jammed with loose bags of potato chips, energy drinks, peanut butter sandwiches, and fruit. My assistant was training for a 20K run and burning calories like crazy. The smells transported me back to my high school cafeteria days. I didn't mind that much, since I lived vicariously through her intense workout schedule. Maybe one day it would rub off on me. Hopefully we wouldn't lose track of any food. One time her banana slipped behind the seat and we didn't discover it until the smell drove us nuts.

"Fill me in again on who we're seeing," I asked while maneuvering the truck around a clump of cyclists. Mari checked the computer, finished a handful of trail mix, then fished out the last peanut before crumpling up the bag and putting it in the overflowing recycle trash bag.

"Looks like we have a litter of four Cairn Terriers for first shots and health certificates."

"How old?"

"Eight weeks yesterday." Mari squinted at the screen for a moment then stuck a hand into her lunch bag. She retrieved an apple and took a healthy bite. The loud crunch preceded the crisp smell of fresh apple.

"Perfect."

"Isn't Toto a Cairn Terrier?" asked Mari, "or should I say Cairn terrorist."

Everyone knew Toto at the hospital. His reputation as a very feisty guy was well deserved since he tried to bite everyone who opened his cage. Everyone but our kennel guy, Eugene, currently under suspicion of murder. For him the dog wagged his little stump of a tail and acted the perfect gentleman. Toto definitely had a new home with Eugene and his mom, if everything worked out. One bright spot in a sad story.

The GPS dinged at the stop sign so I made a turn onto Silver Spring Road. A peaceful street, it ran along the side of Silver Spring, a tributary of the Eusopus River that eventually flowed into the Hudson River, then past the Statue of Liberty and New York City and out into the Atlantic. Expensive homes lined the right side of the street, the left side sloped down across a green space to the water below. Thick walls of trees grew near the bank, periodically thinning to reveal the rippling water below. Three blocks in we found our destination, a two-story brick home with white woodwork and black shutters. A welcome wreath hung on the enameled black door above a polished brass knocker. I saw Mari take in the row of hedges leading up to the granite steps and large porch.

"This is the kind of place I want," she whispered to me as we waited for someone to answer the door.

That surprised me, since Mari never seemed to care about material things, only her animals and her sports. Maybe she secretly yearned to be Martha Stewart.

It took a few loud knocks on the door before a small woman in her late thirties greeted us. She carried a screaming toddler in one arm while tucked under the other wiggled a barking Cairn Terrier that looked just like Toto.

"Hi, I'm Samantha. Call me Sam. Welcome to the mad-house," she said with a grin.

She was right. It took more than an hour to work our way through the litter of four squirming, wiggly, almost identical-looking puppies. During that hour we'd been interrupted countless times by phone calls, children racing through the kitchen and pretending to puke when I gave the puppy vaccinations, a slightly confused grandmother in a bathrobe looking for her pills, and the constant barking of the mother dog who was locked outside, convinced we were hurting her babies.

"Is it always like this?" I asked Sam, as she scooped up her toddler who was intent on transferring everything on the floor into his mouth.

"Pretty much," she told me in a matter-of-fact tone. Despite the chaos around her she remained calm and focused.

Mari entered all the puppy information into our online form and emailed it to the client with my signature. Not for the first time I marveled at how much easier technology had made my paperwork. "Okay, Sam," my assistant said. "I think that's the last one. Go ahead and check your email when you have a moment, and make sure everything is entered correctly. If you have any questions call the office and we will take care of it right away. You should be able to print up the health certificates for each of the new owners."

"Mari, can you bring those puppy starter kits in for Sam?" I'd stocked the puppy and kitten kits in the truck last week. Each kit had food samples and some pamphlets on puppy care and training, plus a canned food lid and information about our hospital and emergency care.

"Okay, be right back," she called over her shoulder quickly sidestepping to avoid a puppy and the determined toddler.

"Do you have homes for these guys?" Sam opened the door to the yard and let the frantic mommy dog back inside. I took my stethoscope off and started putting our equipment away. Below me the puppies, now reunited with their mom, raced around the kitchen, no worse for wear. Mari and I always stayed at least fifteen minutes after we gave any shots to make sure none of the puppies vomited, or showed any other symptom that might mean an allergic reaction.

Being careful where she placed her foot, Sam reached down and picked up the smallest puppy of the litter, a pretty female with a thick brindle coat. "Everybody is spoken for, all but this one. We had a great home picked out for her, but," she paused and gave the puppy a kiss, "it didn't work out. I'm tempted to keep her. If I do I'll call her Claire."

I felt a little shock on the back of my neck. "Was the owner going to be Claire Birnham?"

"Yes." Her voice betrayed her emotion. "This puppy was going to be hers. She and Toto visited several times, to see how accepting he was of a puppy. They got along really well. He's her great uncle." Sam put the puppy down and watched her rejoin her siblings, busy dragging around a colorful toy made of red and blue twisted rope.

Oak Falls astonished me sometimes. Everyone knew everyone.

"We have Toto at the animal hospital. Claire was my client."

"I know. Cindy told me all about it. Eugene is going to be a perfect new owner for him. He can be a little...difficult. Toto is one of those one-person Cairn Terriers."

"So true." I looked around to make sure I'd packed up everything. A puppy slid past my shoe,

Sam scooped down and picked it up. "Do you mind me asking what you think about all this?

I picked my words carefully. "If Claire committed suicide, that was her choice. I personally don't believe Eugene had anything to do with it."

Her eyes dilated. "If it wasn't suicide then it was an accident or murder."

"I guess so."

"That wouldn't surprise me at all. Claire was a little like you, Dr. Kate, in a good way. She couldn't let things go. I can't tell you how many times she butted into someone else's business around here. If she saw a wrong she wanted to set it right."

"Do you know something about this?"

"I didn't know who to talk to," she began. I followed her over to the kitchen table where she moved another puppy from the base of the chair and sat down. "Maybe I should have gone to the police right away, but I was so shocked I didn't think of it until the day of her funeral. They had a suicide note. Everything was so confused. By then I figured it was too late."

"Too late for what?" I asked her.

She continued in an anguished voice. "Too late to tell the police what I knew."

"What was that?"

The sorrow in her face turned into anger. "I talked to her on Friday, that afternoon. She sounded fine and excited about dropping off Toto in the morning. He was going to stay with me for the day and play with the puppies when she went down to check out the sublet apartment in New York."

Again, more proof that the day of her supposed suicide Claire had been in good spirits.

"But this is the worst part," Sam added. "She had to hang up because there was someone at the door."

"Did she say who it was?" Finally some new information.

"No. She said she'd call me back. But I never heard from her." Sam started to cry, clutching a paper napkin in her hand and holding it up to her eyes. "I should have called her back. Maybe if I called her back I could have saved her life." More sobs escaped from behind her hand. "When Eugene confessed I figured it was him at the door, so I didn't say anything."

But it couldn't have been Eugene, I wanted to say. He helped carry some things into her place from the stable that afternoon. They arrived together in her car, which she parked in the garage. After they finished his mother picked him up outside her place.

I waited, knowing sometimes it did more good to cry it out.

"Nice. Well, I think I needed that. I've been feeling guilty even though that's stupid." Sam's red eyes had no peace in them.

"You have nothing to feel guilty about," I told her. "But you should notify the police."

She murmured in agreement, tears in her eyes.

I had more questions I wanted to ask but decided to wait. To take her mind off everything we played with the puppies and talked about their personality traits. Even at this young age it was obvious where they all fit in their pack, from the alpha male to the sweet submissive female, the smallest of the litter.

The puppies scooted by me, then turned the corner of the island, their pudgy tummies almost scraping the floor. Meanwhile the mother dog stood next to Sam's chair, her eyes fixed on her master.

"Good girl," Sam said, reaching down to rub her dog's chin. "She always knows when something's wrong."

"Mine too. He lays next to me and puts his paw on my leg."

Mari came in from the truck and put the puppy kits on the kitchen counter.

Enough time had passed so I was satisfied no one would have a vaccination reaction. Sam called the dogs and they all followed her out to the enclosed patio. After adding more food and water she closed the door and we went back into the kitchen. I asked Mari to call the office and told her I'd be out in a few minutes.

"So," I began after Mari left, "what do you think happened to Claire?"

"I think someone killed her."

I leaned forward. "I've been wondering the same thing. Who do you think did it?"

"Jesus."

That was an answer I never expected. Staring at her face in astonishment I saw nothing odd or strange in her demeanor or body language. Surely she wasn't suggesting some kind of divine intervention? Was Sam one of those people who saw the devil in your eyes and suddenly decided to kill you? Had I found Claire's murderer and been chatting with her all along?

She must have sensed my confusion because she said, "I think they pronounce it Hay-soos, though."

"Who are you talking about?" My voice tensed up.

"Jesus Jicinto Margoles. Claire called him Double J for short."

Who? I'd explored almost every aspect of Claire's life and never came across that name. "Sorry, but who the heck is Double J? "

"The kid that kept hanging around her. She was sketching outside of town by the strawberry farm and saw him eating lunch at the side of the road. When she asked him if she could draw his portrait he pulled out a pad and said he was an artist too." Sam walked over to the desk in the kitchen by the refrigerator. After rummaging through a folder she took out a sheet of paper and carried it back to the table. "Look."

I studied it. A lined piece of paper pulled out of a notebook. Claire stared back at me, a slight smile on her face. The sketch caught the essence of her, vibrant, full of life.

"This is very good," I noted.

"That's what she thought. Claire bought him some real art supplies and showed him some basic techniques. Then he started hanging around her place, usually on the weekend. I asked her if he ever scared her and she laughed at me. They worked in the studio in the garage."

"The garage? That's where they found her body."

Sam shivered. "Which is why I feel so guilty I never talked to the police."

"Where is Double J now?"

"I have no idea. His family helps pick strawberries and other crops around here. They might have moved on by now."

"And he's how old?"

"Sixteen."

The thought of having this possible suspect disappear into thin air upset me. "Did anyone else meet him? Maybe another one of her artist friends?" I asked Sam.

"No idea. Listen, I don't want to get this kid into any trouble. That is if he had nothing to do with her death."

"And if he did?"

Sam's face hardened into a hateful mask. "Then he can fry."

Chapter Twenty-six

At a quarter to six I had my hands full. Two emergencies had walked in the door just before closing time. The owner's two male dogs had fought over a piece of steak that fell on the floor. No one won. The Chow sported a large gash above his eye while his buddy, a Beagle mix, had multiple bites around his neck that were swelling as we spoke.

Following the strange rules of the dog world both guys were wagging their tails and acting like best buddies.

While I was explaining that both dogs needed to be admitted my phone buzzed.

"Hi Kate. Guess what I've been doing all day?" Candace's excited voice bubbled from my receiver. "I think I know who..."

"I'm sorry, Candace, but I can't talk. I've got two emergencies on my hands. Can you call me back later?" Mari loosened the Beagle's collar, soaked with blood, then gestured to me. "Got to go. Bye."

Both Mari and I stayed until almost nine-thirty when both dogs were up and recovered from their anesthesia. We'd worked straight through dinner, raiding the fridge for some leftover chicken soup and slices of pizza.

I closed up after Mari left, turning off all the overhead lights before going into the apartment. After walking Buddy, I collapsed on the sofa to chill with reruns of *The Big Bang Theory* and promptly fell asleep.

Candace didn't call me back.

Chapter Twenty-seven

The next morning I was pouring my first cup of coffee when Cindy interrupted me.

"Daffy is on the phone for you, Kate. She says it's an emergency."

I hurried into my office. Daffy and her Chihuahua, Little Man, were among my favorite clients. An emergency is never a good thing.

"Hello, this is Dr. Kate. Is there something wrong with Little Man?" I could picture them in matching outfits, even this early in the morning.

"No, he's fine." Daffy's voice had an urgent quality to it. "It's Candace. She's in the hospital, in intensive care."

"Oh my gosh. What happened?"

"She was hit by a car or truck. It happened last night."

"Where?"

"In her driveway. She was putting the recyclables out by the side of the road."

That night at Bridge Club I'd had to park on the road and walk down Candace's driveway because there were so many cars. There were no sidewalks and no streetlights that I remembered. A potentially dangerous spot, especially after sunset.

It had been three days since I'd played bridge with her and we'd come up with that dumb list. Less than twenty-four hours ago she'd left a message on my voice mail.

Was there any connection?

Daffy kept talking...no witnesses...hit and run...Police were checking auto repair shops in the neighborhood.

A shiver went through me.

I didn't believe in coincidences.

Chapter Twenty-eight

That night rain poured down on the weathered shingled roof of the apartment, mirroring my mood. You could almost hear each individual drop. Nothing outside but a foggy mist, punctuated by flashes of lightning that knifed through the gray. I wanted to jump into bed and escape the thoughts rolling around in my skull. Pull the covers over my head and try to block everything out. So I did.

I lay there wrapped in my sheets, cocoon-like, for about fifteen minutes. It didn't work. The same question sounded over and over like the booms of the thunder clouds above. Did Candace get hurt because of me? Has Claire's killer struck out at another victim? Stop now, Kate. Stop now before you're next.

Then something else crept into my brain, fed by years of Catholic school and the examples of people admired over the years. Call it conscience, I don't know. If there was some connection—am I going to let them get away with it? That's exactly what would happen if I walked away from the investigation. This creep would get away with it. Maybe sometime in the future someone would piss them off and they'd kill again.

Part of me wanted to stay wrapped up with the comforter over my head forever.

When the phone rang I waited until the sixth ring to pick it up, uncertain of my desire to talk to anyone.

"Kate." Luke's voice warmed me up, like sunshine coming through a frosted window.

"Hey, Luke," I said. No chipper remarks from me tonight.

Maybe he could feel it, or maybe he just knew but he kept his chit chat to a minimum. "How are you doing? I'm sorry to hear about your friend, Candace."

Words always sound inadequate when faced with tragedy. "Can you tell me exactly what happened? All I know is what was on the news."

I could hear his breathing, slow and steady, over the phone. "She was hit by a vehicle just after she returned home. We believe she had gone to the curb with her recycle bin. About six o'clock, they think, because of damage to her phone. Possibly a drunk driver, who panicked and sped off after hitting her. It wouldn't be the first time."

The image of Candace with a car bearing down on her was too painful. Full of nervous energy now, I got up, walked over to the kitchen, opened the dishwasher and started to put the clean dishes away. Anything to occupy my mind with something else.

"What's that noise?"

"I'm emptying the dishwasher."

At first I thought we'd been disconnected since I couldn't hear him on the line. Then I realized he was giving me time to finish my self-imposed task. After a few more clangs from stacking the dishes I spoke up.

"Needed to do something."

"I understand completely. For me it's washing the car."

"I'll keep that in mind."

Buddy snuffed, went over to his bed and started digging in the middle of it, like he was trying to get to China. I walked over to the sofa and dropped down on the middle cushion.

"It's late. Try to get some sleep."

"You too. Thanks for calling." Why did I let my imagination go crazy. The police think it was a drunk driver? My neck and shoulders started to relax.

"I knew you'd be upset." He started to say something, then stopped.

"What did you say?" Only the tension had been keeping me awake. Now I felt exhausted.

"Nothing." There was a hesitation in his voice.

"Luke?" I could barely keep my eyes open. With an effort I dragged myself off the sofa and padded toward the bed.

"Nothing." He repeated in a softer voice. "Goodnight, Kate."

Chapter Twenty-nine

Over the next few days I worked non-stop. Daffy gave me a daily update on Candace's condition, which thankfully improved each day. Her main issue was head trauma, which resulted in a mild amnesia. The days leading up to the accident were a blur, memories which her neurologist said may or may not come back to her. Visitation was limited. Rest and no unnecessary stimulation were doctor's orders.

At eight in the morning I found myself driving to a house call on roads slick with ice. Overnight the temperature had dropped like a rock, and that, combined with a brief rain, was enough to make driving seem like an Olympic event.

Armed with a double latte, I cautiously maneuvered a sharp corner and felt the back wheels slip a bit, then grip down. I wasn't looking forward to my first winter here, especially since many of my Oak Falls house call clients lived in fairly rural areas.

This early appointment sounded pretty routine, exams and yearly vaccinations on two cats and a dog. Since Mari's orthopedic recheck appointment had been scheduled for this morning, I'd be on my own for half the day. The wind kicked up and blew the last few leaves across my windshield. Without Mari chattering away the truck cabin felt strangely silent, and the silence made me think of Claire and Eugene.

What did Claire do or know that made someone murder her? I'd been thinking of suspects so much I really lost sight of

Claire herself. My vow to delve into any secrets she might have had felt more urgent but I had very little free time. Candace, so far, remembered nothing about the days leading up to the accident, or the name of Claire's new boyfriend. Meanwhile, Luke hadn't been in touch with me in over a week, even missing our Tuesday night Chinese food thing. Another gust of wind took my attention away as it rattled the antennae, making it wiggle like a baton.

The GPS chimed to remind me my destination was on the right. I turned down an asphalt driveway and parked in front of the three-car garage. Probably this house would be called a rambler, one level with a chain-link fence in the front yard. With my doctor's bag in hand I rang the bell, wrapping my coat around me against the frigid wind.

Two elderly faces peered at me through the narrow glass panels on either side of the front door. I heard several locks clicking, then the door opened and a rush of hot air enveloped me. It smelled like Christmas, even though it was two weeks before Halloween.

We all stared at each other.

I figured I'd go first. "Hi, I'm Dr. Kate Turner, from Oak Falls Animal Hospital."

"You see, Manny. You owe me five bucks." The woman's face lit up with a smile.

"Yeah, yeah." Manny turned around and gestured for me to follow. Bringing up the rear was a sweet-faced yellow lab, with a cyst on her head like a little hat.

It felt like eighty, eighty-five degrees in the house. That wonderful warmth I'd first enjoyed now became oppressive, so I slipped my heavy coat off. As we walked through the house I spied a wood stove going full blast, the coals inside glowing an ominous orange-red.

The lab stuck her nose in my hand. At least that was cool.

"Glad you could come this morning, Doc." Manny said over his shoulder. "Lily and I like to make sure everyone is up to date with their shots, especially that rabies."

"I bet him you were a lady vet, but he thought you were selling something." Lily cackled to herself. Her knobby arms stuck out of the sleeves of her blouse. "That five makes fifteen for this week, sucker. Don't forget."

"How can I forget when you won't stop yakking about it?" Manny's stomach stuck out from under his sweater vest, as plump as his wife was thin. With a quick gesture he opened a sliding door leading to a glassed in porch. "Don't let the cats out." As if on cue a long-haired tortoise shell female attempted to dart out from under an armchair. The small black cat curled up on a pillow on a ratty looking plaid sofa barely stirred. Because of the door the temperature in this room was bearable.

"Let's see," I began. "Our receptionist pulled their medical records for me before I left." I retrieved three pages of computer notes from my bag. "Let's start with Topsie."

"She's a scaredy cat," Lily offered, "but she won't bite."

"Then neither will I."

Both owners looked horrified for a moment, then burst out laughing.

With the ice broken the exams went along with no hitches. I gave them some tips on grooming the long-haired cat, and complimented the very shiny coat on their other kitty, Blackie. Enthusiastically waiting her turn, Guinevere the lab thumped her tail on the indoor-outdoor rug. All the pets were healthy and obviously well cared for, making for happy clients and a happy veterinarian.

I palpated what most likely was a sebaceous cyst on the dog's head, that gave her a jaunty air. "We should take this off," I cautioned them, "and biopsy it just to be sure. Cysts are usually benign but some abnormal cells can be growing in there. If it gets much bigger it's going to cause her discomfort."

"Hey, Manny, when Guinevere gets her plastic surgery, maybe I'll check myself in for a facelift." They both chuckled, and I guessed that was a long-standing joke between them.

Their dog smiled too.

"We do have one problem, Doc." Manny opened the sliding door and all the animals bolted out. I guess they'd been sequestered in there for a while, in anticipation of their veterinary appointment.

Holding my jacket in one hand, bag in the other I followed him into the hot kitchen. Beads of sweat started to form on my forehead. Manny and Lily seemed perfectly comfortable.

"What's the problem?" Other than feeling that I'd been transported to the equator.

"Our cat Blackie is getting out and we don't know how she does it."

He bent down to pet the long-haired kitty, now perched on a chair grooming herself. The short-haired black cat, however, sat next to the door, thoughtfully looking up. "I'm not quite sure I understand. Is she going through a doggy door?"

"No. We took that out after a raccoon used it one night." Lily nodded in agreement.

The kitchen had two single doors to the outside. One led to a wooden deck, the other probably into their garage. It seemed a pretty straightforward problem. "Maybe she slips out when you open the door?"

"Nope. We always watch for that."

"Maybe the dog did it," I joked.

"Yeah." Lily thought a moment then added, "Manny, wanna bet? Five bucks."

"Meow."

We all turned at the sound. Blackie still sat in front of the door leading to the deck, but now was meowing pitifully. The dog pricked up her ears. Blackie stared at the yellow lab and this time came out with a piercing yowl. Again the dog reacted, tilting her head and restlessly looking from Manny to Lily and back again.

A thought occurred to me. "Let's go into the living room for a moment, and leave the animals here. I want to see what Blackie does when we aren't in the room."

We were in for a surprise. As soon as we left, the lab began pacing back and forth in front of the door. The cat walked over to the dog, stared again, and uttered that weird yowl. As if on command the yellow lab jumped up on the door and pushed the handle with her paw. The door sprang open toward her. Without a backward glance Blackie strolled out onto the deck. Once the cat was out, Guinevere rose on her hind legs and pushed the door shut.

Mystery solved.

"You've got to get this on YouTube," I said, wishing I'd videotaped it with the camera app on my phone. "People are going to love it."

"I'll tell my grandson. He knows all about that Internet stuff."

Lily put a wry smile on her face. She stood on her tiptoes and whispered in my ear, "We should have bet him ten bucks."

Chapter Thirty

Finding out Claire's secrets turned out to be harder than I thought. First of all, you can't just show up at a stranger's door and start asking extremely personal questions about their dead relative or friend. Well, you can, but I don't recommend it. With Candace recovering, still with no memory of the accident or the days before, I was back to square one. Lots of suspicions and no evidence. Mari had recommended I talk to one of Claire's cousins. One look at the expression on Claire's relatives' face stopped me cold.

Her substantial body firmly wedged in her doorway, blocking my view, I couldn't mistake the anger in her voice.

"I'm not comfortable talking about Claire's personal life." Ramona Heyborne's tone implied that I should mind my own business. Of course, she was right. I wasn't the police or a private investigator.

I tried another approach. "The only reason I'm asking is because Eugene Scruggs is now a person of interest. He's one of my employees at Oak Falls Animal Hospital and was a friend of Claire's."

She stared into my face. "We all know Eugene."

Despite the grim look I decided to level with her. "Let me be honest with you, Ramona. The police have found Eugene's blood mixed with Claire's blood on a broken vase in her garbage pail. They can place him in her apartment because he also left fingerprints in the living room. If you know anything that will help prove he's innocent, now is the time to tell someone. Please, if you don't want to talk to me then talk to the police."

She shuffled back and forth, raked her wavy black hair with her hand, then seemed to make a decision.

The door opened a little. Ramona took her time before speaking.

"She had some kind of problem at work in the art gallery."

"That's what I've heard from another one of her friends. Any idea what kind of problem?"

More of the all-purpose glare. "Something having to do with paintings."

Gee, that narrowed it down. Trying not to be impatient I asked her another question. "Did she mention any names?"

"No. She did say something strange one time."

I waited, reluctant to keep prodding.

Another hesitation. "I work at the bank on Main Street. Sometimes we met for lunch, since the gallery is right across the street."

Using all my willpower I kept silent, not knowing where this was leading.

"So she said to let her know if any stranger speaking Chinese came into the bank."

◇◇◇

I was completely stumped. What did a mysterious Chinese person have to do with a death in upstate New York? That made no sense. But since it was almost lunchtime I decided to follow the only local Chinese connection in Oak Falls.

The Chinese restaurant right in the village was the Lucky Garden and I was very familiar with it. Their won ton soup and orange chicken had been a staple in my diet for the last few months. I'd gotten to know the owners, Henry and Su-Lin Chang, fairly well both at the restaurant and as clients at the animal hospital. Their enclosed porch cantilevered out over the river, a quiet oasis at the popular restaurant. I claimed one of their coveted riverside tables and watched the water glide around a large boulder. The sound of the stream running always soothed my spirits.

"What can I get you today, Doc?" Su-Lin Chang's smile always lit up the room. Her round face with deep brown eyes and smooth skin glowed with intelligence and warmth. No wonder her husband fell so hard for her when they were both students at NYU.

"I hate to be so predictable, but I'll have the shrimp in lobster sauce special."

She leaned in for a moment. "That's my favorite, too."

While I waited I looked at the artwork and pottery on consignment. Like most of the businesses in Oak Falls these owners helped local artists by displaying and selling their works, keeping a small percentage of the sales price for themselves. A win win situation for everyone. A series of small pots with some kind of Chinese or Japanese lettering caught my eye.

When Su-Lin came back with my soup I asked her about them.

"You've got good taste, Doc."

"What do you mean?"

"Those are mine." A big grin spread across her face. I couldn't help but return it.

"I can't say I know that much about pottery, or art in general." Although my knowledge of science and biology was pretty extensive, most of my college courses bypassed the liberal arts.

"Don't apologize. Art should affect you emotionally not in your head. I'm flattered you like them."

"Is there much of a market for this kind of work?" Maybe I could learn something from her that would point me in the right direction.

She reached into her pocket and pulled out a glossy postcard. On the front were pictures of the vases for sale, as well as several sculptures. Underneath was a website address and an eight-hundred number. "We're all promoting ourselves now, artists, writers, you name it. The Internet has opened up a global market anyone with a computer can tap into."

I traced the graceful characters with my finger. "So could Chinese artists sell their work to Americans over the Internet?"

"Generally it's more difficult because they must deal with digital firewalls, and censors. Most of my friends are in Hong Kong where they have a huge art fair each year. Social media is popular there, too. She checked to see if I needed anything else.

"We're all digitally connected now." Corresponding internationally was as easy as hitting the SEND button.

"You do have to be careful, though." Her brows furrowed, something unusual for this generally happy person.

"Why is that?"

She leaned in. "Because most of the artworks coming out of China are forgeries."

I barely tasted my soup as I Googled, "Chinese art forgeries," on my phone and told Su-Lin I'd decided to take the rest of my order to go. While waiting I kept scrolling. The number of articles was staggering. Even the prestigious auction houses like Sotheby's and Christie's were caught selling disputed pieces. One buyer refused to pay until he received proof from at least two art experts.

An investigative report stated art crime was now a billion-dollar business, catering to the newly wealthy in China and Southeast Asia who wanted original artworks as a sign of status. One of the most profitable schemes at the moment was providing faked copies of ancient Chinese artists, some from as far back as the fifteenth century. Perhaps Claire, with her art history background, stumbled onto something similar while working at the Qualog Gallery.

Was this the Chinese connection I was looking for?

A lucrative trade in fake Chinese art? If that was the case I was in way over my head. Sitting in my truck trying to finish the article about forgeries, I noticed someone familiar stroll into the restaurant. Russians must like Chinese food too. I could see Andrei Roshenkov standing in front of the cashier. She handed him a slip and he took a seat at the bar.

Who had Candace followed? Buzz, A.J., Bella, and Gilda. On an impulse I backed the truck up behind the restaurant dumpster near where the staff parked. From there I had a great view of the parking lot. I didn't have anything pressing to do, so why not do what Candace did? Follow someone and see where it leads.

About fifteen minutes later Andrei came out with two brown paper bags of takeout. He loaded them into his car, a BMW sedan, and took off. The silver car turned right out of the parking lot. Maybe he was headed for a tryst with Gilda? Or someone else.

I followed, leaving several car lengths between us. He continued driving out of town, then abruptly made a turn off the main highway onto a two-lane road canopied by overgrown trees. The move surprised me, so I drove past then pulled over to the side of the road. As soon as I could I made a U-turn then doubled back.

His car had disappeared.

Determined, I turned the Ford truck onto the side road I'd last seen him on. The road was not in the best of repairs, I noted as I bumped along, dodging a large rut. There were few homes, with most of the land on both sides planted with fruit trees. Sure enough, a sign identified the fields as part of Barnard Orchards. A large gate closed off a driveway leading to what looked like a closed farm stand. The other sign said Dead End.

Not ready to give up yet I parked the truck on the side of the road and decided to explore on foot. I discovered what looked like the end of the road up ahead. By walking just inside the tree line I could see everything, but could duck behind the shrubbery if Andrei came by. And that's exactly what happened. Andrei's BMW paused at the top of an unpaved driveway, then turned right, toward the main road. I quickly moved into the trees before he drove by. His brake lights flared for a moment as he passed my truck. My breath caught in my throat, before he continued on out of sight. Did he know what kind of car I drove? I didn't think so.

Curiosity made me continue. I bent my head to miss a branch and slowly walked up the driveway. It made a sharp curve and cut across a small hill before cresting and running down to a shallow valley. A house stood in the clearing, invisible to anyone on the main road.

I tried to get closer and see through one of the large windows, but before I could I heard the sound of a car coming up the driveway. Panicked, I ran back into the woods, but not before I saw a figure with long dark hair tied in a ponytail sitting at the kitchen table. Was it Gilda?

Or someone new to the game?

Chapter Thirty-one

As soon as they would let me I went to the hospital to see Candace. Since it felt strange to bring candy to someone often called Candy, I opted for a potted plant.

Her room was on the third floor of the Kingston Hospital. When I got off the elevator I was pleasantly surprised. The hallways had been painted a soothing blue, and landscape paintings were hung along the wall. So much nicer than my last memories of a hospital.

The door to room 304 stood open, but I knocked anyway. It was a two-person room, but only one bed looked occupied. The drapes were partially drawn and a human-shaped lump lay under the covers.

"Candace?" I whispered, afraid she was asleep.

"Yes?" Someone answered directly behind me.

To my surprise Candace stood there, wrapped in a white fluffy robe with artificial leopard trim on it. Not standard hospital issue. She looked great.

"Oh, I'm so happy to see you." With relief I began to give her a hug.

"Ouch," she cautioned me. "Broken ribs."

"Why don't you hand me the plant and then we'll go out to the sitting area." She reached over a little gingerly and placed my Martha Washington geranium on the nightstand, next to a vase of mixed flowers.

When we walked together she held my arm, moving a little stiffly on her left side. I'd imagined all kinds of horrible things and now it felt great to see her up and about.

"Candace, I'm so happy you're doing well. I was worried that…you know…this had something to do with our snooping around."

"What snooping?" She sat down in a gray upholstered chair and gestured to one directly opposite her.

Now I was concerned. Had she forgotten that day we played bridge at her house? "We talked about Claire?"

"Well, didn't we talk after bridge? The conversation is a little hazy. Sorry, I don't have much memory of the days before the accident. Plus, I don't remember being hit or anything until I woke up in the hospital. It's pretty normal, they tell me, after a head trauma. At least, that's what my neurologist told me. Usually it comes back in pieces." Her blond hair looked fresh from the beauty parlor, and I noticed she wore makeup and a small pair of pearl earrings.

"It's amazing you don't have more injuries," I told her.

"Here's what they figured happened. I was putting out my recyclables at the curb and somehow I managed to pull the pail between me and the vehicle that hit me. So although the pail and I went flying I landed on a whole bunch of empty pizza boxes and plastic bottles." She laughed at the irony of it.

I joined in. "I guess in your case it really pays to recycle."

We spent an enjoyable half hour talking, until I noticed she started to get a little tired. Not wanting to stress her I walked her back to her room. The person in the bed next to her was in the exact same position as before. If she didn't periodically let loose a snore I would have called the nurse.

"Are the doctors satisfied with your neurological status?" During our conversation I had heard nothing to be concerned about except the memory loss.

Candace straightened her robe and leaned back on her pillow. "Yes, for the most part. I suffered a concussion and some superficial bruises. The cracked ribs are the worst of it and they're more of a nuisance than anything else."

"I think you're pretty brave."

Someone walked past the room and she glanced up for a moment, then dropped her voice. "There's a silver lining to all of this, Kate."

"What's that?" I couldn't imagine anything positive associated with a hit and run.

"My neurologist. He thinks my mental status is delightful."

That confused me for a moment. Delightful wasn't really a medical term.

She quickly explained. "He's divorced and a few years older than me. I'm being released tomorrow and we're going out to dinner tomorrow night." A wicked smile lit her face. She raised her hand to offer a high five.

"Way to go."

"Hey, somebody's got to check my reflexes."

Chapter Thirty-two

Relieved that Candace had landed on her feet, I ran some errands and then returned to the apartment. Being with her had reminded me of something I'd meant to do. Gramps was notoriously difficult to buy presents for, but I thought I'd found something he would really like.

The phone at the Webster Simmons Gallery in Soho rang six times before someone picked up.

"This is Antoine. How may I help you?"

I was surprised the owner of the gallery had answered the phone himself. "Mr. Simmons, this is Kate Turner. My grandfather and I were in your gallery a while ago. I'm calling about a photograph we saw there."

"Are you Mick McCormack's granddaughter?"

"Yes." I looked around for my purse. "I can't believe you remember us."

"Of course I do. Did you know your grandfather visited us the other day with some friends of his? Such a lively bunch, I might add. One of them bought a rather intricate wooden puzzle box for their grandchild."

"That must have been Lionel and Daisy."

"Yes, I believe that's them. A very outspoken couple."

"That's a very diplomatic way to describe them." I could think of a whole bunch of adjectives like argumentative, bossy, opinionated...

A polite silence followed. "So, Ms. Turner, how may I help you today?"

Spying my purse under some newspapers I picked it up and brought it to the kitchen table. "My grandfather was particularly taken with a photograph there, a black and white of a dance."

"Mmmm." There was a pause. "I believe I recognize the one you are referring to. There is a woman in the foreground wearing a gardenia in her hair."

"That's the one." After digging around a moment I pulled my checkbook out. "I'd like to buy that as a surprise for my Gramps, but it wasn't on your Internet site."

"We don't have everything posted up there yet, since we're a little short-staffed here. I think we have fifty of that particular photographer's work available."

"Unfortunately one is all I can afford right now."

He excused himself to check on something, so I waited on hold to find out how much it cost.

When he returned I was surprised and happy to find all the black and white photos were on sale. I arranged to have it shipped directly to the animal hospital, excited to have found Gramps a birthday present I knew he would like. So much better than another pair of socks.

"Is there anything else?" Antoine asked.

On an impulse I decided to question him about his experience with art forgeries. He was surprisingly verbose.

"You know, it's the bane of every gallery owner now. Like it or not, probably a certain percentage of the works I sell are fake and I have no way of knowing. Reputable auction houses and dealers are being deceived all the time. Why, there was a Chinese artist turning out fake Modigliani and Renoirs in a garage in Brooklyn." His voice dripped with distain.

"A Chinese artist?" I repeated.

"Yes. The poor fellow was hired to paint both copies of the great masters and pictures in the styles of well-known artists. Then the thieves created a fake persona with an art collection for provenance, and sold it for an insane profit.

"What happened to the artist?"

"Oh, the police arrested him. It turns out he had been an art instructor in China. Extremely well trained, like so many of the Chinese. The poor fellow. They're not quite sure how much he understood." Antoine voiced his distain. "They kept him there almost like a prisoner."

He paused, then added, "The police think he just painted to order."

Chapter Thirty-three

"What are you guys watching?" Cindy came into the treatment area with a fistful of messages, most of them for me and caught us all playing hooky, staring at my phone.

"That's so cute." Mari laughed and clapped her hands, eyes still on the screen. Manny and Lily had sent me a copy of their video of the black cat escaping with the dog's help. With their grandson doing the uploading it had been posted onto YouTube.

Mari handed the phone to her and hit the play icon. Within a minute Cindy was in hysterics. There's nothing like a good animal video to pick up your spirits.

"I think I'll put a link to this on our hospital website." Scribbling down the address she muttered, "Good publicity for us."

"So funny." Mari wiped her eyes with her sleeve. "So they thought it was the cat that did it, but it was the dog helping the cat. Who would have thought?"

I nodded my head in agreement, my mind more focused on the messages Cindy had handed me. Maybe I could squeeze some callbacks in before the next appointment.

"Finished?"

"Yes. A good laugh always makes me happy." Mari flashed me a great big smile.

"Getting through all my callbacks will make me happy."

My technician picked up an empty coffee mug from the desktop. "Okay, I can take a hint. But listen, if you have any time tonight, drop by Judy's Place. It's open mike night."

I waved goodbye, and by the time she closed the door I had already called the first name on my list. With each call I pulled up the medical record on the computer and jotted notes. That way the staff would have access to whatever the client discussed with me on the phone.

My hand stopped halfway through dialing when I saw the next name. Luke Gianetti. The same Luke Gianetti I'd been arguing with since Claire's death. I wondered if this was a personal call or a professional call about my patient, Gatto, his grandmother's cat. Suddenly the desk chair didn't feel comfortable anymore. I stood up and started pacing the room.

I've found out through bitter experience that putting off things you don't want to do doesn't really help. Instead of spending more time worrying, just do it and get it over with. So I sat back on the chair and called him. The number he'd left didn't seem familiar.

His warm voice answered after three rings.

"Luke Gianetti here."

"Hey, Luke. It's Kate." I panicked for a moment. How many women named Kate did he know? "Kate Turner, that is, from the animal hospital."

"Yes. Thank you for getting back to me."

From the tone of his voice I figured this wasn't a personal call. He sounded pretty matter-of-fact. I adjusted my response to match. "What's up?"

"I wanted to tell you and your staff that Eugene is being charged with manslaughter."

My stomach felt like someone had punched me. "Oh, no," was all I could muster.

"Chief Garcia is releasing the news to the media as we speak. It's not my case, you understand, but I thought I'd give you a heads-up, so you don't have to hear it from strangers." Luke sounded almost apologetic.

My mind raced. "Does he have a lawyer?"

"He's been assigned a public defender."

After briefly dealing with one law firm in town I didn't know if that was good or bad. "This is like a nightmare you can't wake up from."

There was a moment of silence. I thought I heard a faint sigh, but then Luke spoke again, all business. "Any updates on this case will be handled through Tina, Chief Garcia's secretary and public relations contact. Is that clear?"

Before I could react he was gone.

I worked the rest of the day and finished up at six o'clock. Exhausted I started toward my apartment to walk Buddy when Mari caught up with me.

"Hey, Doc. Did you hear anything else about Eugene?"

"Only that they brought charges against him." The fluorescent lights at the back of the hospital gave off a slight hum that only added to my worsening headache.

Mari's face scrunched up in distress. "It was on the local TV news."

The headache went up another notch. "That figures."

My technician's brows rose. "Are you okay?"

"Actually, I have one heck of a headache." Inside my head it sounded as though I was shouting. "I think I'm going to go lie down." A weird iridescent sheen glistened across the surface of my coffee, abandoned on the counter. I took a sip. Very bitter. A little coffee sometimes helps a headache by constricting blood vessels, but too much can make it worse.

"Feel better. Don't forget about open mike night." Mari strode off leaving me leaning against the wall.

◇◇◇

I must have dozed off, fully clothed on top of the comforter. Unfortunately I'd had a crazy dream. Claire at her easel, her hands splashed with paint, as always—then something else drips on the canvas—something crimson and thick. Blood. She doesn't notice but starts humming a tune I don't recognize. Abruptly she faces me, her face cherry red from carbon monoxide poisoning, and says, "It wasn't Eugene. Do something, Kate."

My eyes flew open. For a moment I thought someone was in the room talking to me. Then I remembered and put my hands on my head. My headache was gone, but right then I'd rather have a headache than another one of those ghostly dreams.

A glass of orange juice brought me back to reality. My computer screen beckoned but I needed to be around living, breathing people. Taking Mari's suggestion I decided to go into town and check out the late night scene at Judy's Place. I tried to convince myself the dream meant nothing, just random thoughts scrambled up by a restless brain with a migraine.

I almost succeeded.

◇◇◇

Irish folk music, a ballad about a girl slipping out to meet her sweetheart, could be heard as I tried to find a spot to park near Judy's kitchen. Each time the door opened, the tune escaped. Although muffled the clear notes of a flute floated on the night air.

It took a while for me to park in one of the town's designated parking areas tucked behind main street. For the first time today I relaxed, hoping for an enjoyable time. The downtown historic streets were not very well lit, so I looked down to avoid potholes, and took off in the direction of Main Street and Judy's Place. Another few minutes brought me to the restaurant's front door. Music swelled out like an embrace when I walked inside.

It took a moment for my eyes to adjust to the dim light. People were crammed in everywhere, looking toward the brightly lit stage and musicians. The regular tables and chairs had been clustered against the far wall. Playing on stage an Irish band was lit by two rows of overhead track lighting set at several angles. Some were focused up the walls for effect, while the others served as spotlights on the performers.

I was surprised to realize that all the sound came from only four people who played guitar, banjo, some kind of flute, and what looked like a small accordion or concertina. Most of the audience sang along with the group. From the hooting and hollering I gathered it was a pretty relaxed concert venue. By the time I squeezed through the crowd to prop myself against a wooden post they had finished the number, and, it turned out, their set. When the applause broke out I joined in.

The host turned out to be someone I knew, a client of mine named Henry James. His parents both taught English and gave him the name of their favorite author—but it would have made more sense to name him after their favorite wrestler. About six feet tall, heavily muscled and with a realistic snake tattoo encircling his neck, his appearance definitely made a statement. But appearances aren't everything, which I learned the hard way. In reality, Biker Henry was a soft-hearted guy with a nervous stomach and a profound interest in baking.

"Now for a little change of pace." Henry's shaved head glistened under the lights. "Rosie Gianetti will read one of her poems tonight. Rosie, where are you?" He squinted into the audience.

From a few feet in front of me someone began to move. I spied Rosie's auburn hair with threads of silver in it as she made her way up to the front.

"Go Rosie!" A raucous voice yelled from the back.

"Settle down now, Frank," she yelled back. Henry reached for her hand and helped her up the few steps onto the stage before handing her the microphone.

She cleared her throat. "As most of you know I've been scribbling down my thoughts since high school. I hope you like this one."

The hummingbird buzzes by
Iridescent throat gleaming
and honeysuckles sigh

Finished, she looked out at the audience who stood in silence. Then applause broke out and feet stomped, as if she'd sung a country song instead of spoken a haiku.

"One more time," someone yelled.

The hummingbird buzzes by
Iridescent throat gleaming
and honeysuckles sigh

She bounced off the stage to a wave of applause.

A broad smile lit Henry James' face. "We're gonna take a break here, then continue in about fifteen minutes. Don't forget to support your fellow artists, guys. Profits go toward renting this space." He turned off the mike and placed it on a tall stool that stood against the wall. People started to mill around, most making a beeline over to the bar.

I made my way toward the soda machine to buy a bottle of water. Coming back I almost knocked into Rosie, but stopped just in time.

"Hey, Kate. How are you?" she asked me.

"Great. I loved your poem." Rosie's cheeks turned even rosier with the compliment.

"Thanks. It's sort of a haiku without the seventeen syllables."

"You could have fooled me," I answered truthfully, raising my voice to be heard over the crowd. "Do you read your poetry here often?"

A bellow of noise drowned out her answer. She gestured me to follow her. Like a little buzz saw she cut through the room and toward the door onto Main Street. I dropped some money in the donation basket at the entrance and followed her outside. The cool night air felt luxuriously crisp.

"Boy, it gets pretty stuffy in there." Rosie turned toward me. "I'm kind of a regular now. We try to hold it twice a month. It lets all us locals blow off some creative steam."

Moonlight bathed the buildings. Across the street it glistened off marble tombstones in the old cemetery. The silvery glow made the shingles on the church spire resemble snake scales.

"This is fun. I had no idea there was an open stage spot in Oak Falls." Lifting the bottle of water to my lips I drank some to get the stale air taste out of my mouth.

Other patrons pouring out of the club during the break stopped and complimented Rosie on her poem.

"Usually I can't sit still for poems," a young girl with lots of bangles on her wrists happily volunteered, "but yours are just right."

"You and me both," Rosie volunteered. "I like to keep it short and sour."

"I thought that was you, Dr. Kate." A booming voice behind me caught my attention.

Henry James loomed in front of me, the moonlight blanching him out like a ghost.

"Hey, Henry. Good to see you. You never cease to surprise me, first baking now being an emcee." Dressed all in black to match his Harley persona, he dwarfed little Rosie.

"So Doc, what are you doing here?"

"Somebody told me to check it out. It seems like a lot of fun." I noticed that people were starting to filter back in.

"Are you going to perform?"

"What do you mean?"

"Everyone who watches has to join in at some point."

Horror shook me to the core. "Everyone? What if you don't have any particular talent?"

He looked at me and raised his left eyebrow. The silver ring in it glittered. "Of course you have a talent, albeit a strange one. The whole town knows your special skill. You solve murders."

◇◇◇

I thought about what he said on the way home. I'd only helped solve one murder and that happened almost by accident. Basically, I'd uncovered a whole slew of suspects with varying motives, none of whom ended up being the murderer.

But maybe that was part of my talent. If you stirred the pot enough something or someone was bound to rise to the surface.

Chapter Thirty-four

Morning light glowed behind the lace curtains.

My hand felt wet. Lying in bed I fought to wake up. Was this another dream? Confused, I was convinced something was terribly wrong. Then I realized what had happened. Buddy decided it was time to get up, and used his doggy tongue as an alarm clock to wake me up.

"Okay, let's go outside." As soon as he heard "go outside" my dog started his happy dance, hopping his way to the door. My watch confirmed I'd slept almost eight hours, unusual for me.

Instead of being relaxed with the extra sleep, I felt groggy.

After feeding Buddy I went into the hospital to check on my patients. A familiar barking reminded me that Eugene's family still hadn't taken Toto. An image of my kennel worker in a cell made me cringe. Being a creature of habit, unfamiliar things made him anxious, or at least that was my experience. Before we did anything together I always explained what I needed to do, step-by-step and how he would be helping me. I doubted anyone would take the time to explain much in prison.

The message light was blinking on the office phone so I played it back.

This message is for Dr. Kate. It's Wendy Scruggs, Eugene's mom.

I was hoping we could pick up Toto sometime this weekend?

Eugene is home and I thought Toto would be good company for him.
Thanks.

I made a note of the phone number and immediately called her back.

About an hour later the hospital doorbell rang, even though I knew that Eugene had a key. After a quick peek out the front window I opened the door.

"Hi, everyone." Wendy came in first, holding her daughter's hand. Eugene followed, his head down. He looked like he had shrunk into himself.

The mom was putting up a brave front for her children, but the shadows and puffiness around her eyes told a different story.

"I'm sure Toto is going to be very happy to see you, Eugene." Not even the sound of the Cairn's name got a reaction.

"Thanks for letting us come on a Sunday. I know it's your day off." Wendy took hold of Eugene's arm and guided him into the reception area. Head hanging, he still hadn't said anything.

"Kitty." Eugene's younger sister had spotted Mr. Katt lounging on the reception desk.

"Why don't you go ahead and play with Mr. Katt while Eugene and I get Toto?" My thoughts were that the hospital routine might make him come out of his shell. "Eugene, can you help me with Toto, please?"

Without waiting I turned and started toward the treatment room. "I think your lab coat is hanging up in the break room."

I felt, rather than saw, a slight hesitation on his part, then the familiar walk-shuffle of his steps. "After you get your coat on, go ahead and wash your hands, and then take Toto out of his cage."

From behind a chart I watched him go through the familiar steps.

Toto ecstatically greeted him, licking his face and making happy whimpering noises. Finally I saw a smile on Eugene's face.

"I'm so happy you are adopting Toto. Let me take a quick look at him before he goes home with you."

Eugene immediately lifted the dog up, and brought the little Cairn Terrier over to the exam table. Despite the dog wiggling from excitement I began my exam. As was my habit I talked as I checked him out.

"Heart and lungs good. Eyes nice and clear. Those bite wounds have all healed up." The dog was so happy, he forgot to growl at me. "Let me check those ears." I took the otoscope and slid it down each ear canal. "Perfect." I sensed Eugene relaxing as we proceeded with the check-up.

"I'm going to recommend you feed him a senior diet." I brought out the scale and Eugene placed him in it. "Twelve pounds, so he's lost a little weight. You can increase his treats for now, since everything in his life has changed so suddenly." Putting the scale back on the shelf I tried to make my next statement casual. "I think he misses Claire. Do you miss her, Eugene?"

"Yes. My mother says she's in heaven now."

In my head I could hear Luke and Gramps advising me to stop right there, but I ignored them.

"I'm sure she is. What happened to Claire, Eugene?"

In a whispered voice he answered my question. "I killed Claire."

Keeping focused on Toto I pressed on, something driving me forward.

"How did you kill her?" Again I didn't look at him, but continued to examine the dog, checking his feet and toes.

Would he answer the question? I wasn't sure. Toto looked up into the boy's face and whined, eager for his physical to be over.

"I put the bandage on her but nobody checked it. It killed her."

Confused I stopped what I was doing. "Why would that kill Claire, Eugene?"

"Nick said I always had to have someone check the bandage. If it was too tight it could kill them." He stopped and made a choking sound. "It must have been too tight because everyone said that she's dead. So I killed her."

That simple answer produced an unexpected wave of relief. Nick, the weekend technician, had tried to impress on him the dangers of a too-tight bandage, which could lead to tissue death and gangrene. Eugene didn't differentiate. To him death meant death, plain and simple. Claire had a bandage on her hand, Luke had told me. Eugene probably applied it in her townhouse that Friday afternoon.

"Why did Claire need a bandage?"

His soft eyes stared into mine. "I knocked over her vase." He demonstrated with his elbow. "She picked up the pieces and cut herself, so I bandaged it for her."

"That was the right thing to do."

"My finger got scratched but it stopped bleeding pretty fast." As if to demonstrate he held up his hand to show a thin pink scar on his index finger.

Toto put his front paws on Eugene's chest and did what he could do to help. He gently licked the finger of his human friend to make it all better.

Chapter Thirty-five

After Eugene's revelation my first instinct was to call the police, but his mother Wendy called their attorney instead, and I respected her wishes. After all, I was the only one so far he had spoken to about his actions on the day of the murder. The stakes were sky high. Wendy confided that their family home was the collateral for Eugene's bond of two hundred thousand dollars. Given his health issues, medication needs, close community ties, and clean record, even the prosecutor had not opposed bail for the manslaughter charge, but lawyer's fees and court fees already added up to an alarming amount. In the justice system even the innocent had to pay the piper.

But before I spoke to the lawyer I sat Eugene down.

"You didn't kill Claire, Eugene, by putting a bandage on her cut." I said. "What Nick told you was only for animals. Not people."

Eugene didn't say anything.

"If you put a bandage on a person, that person will check to see if it's too tight. Do you understand?"

He stared down at the floor.

"Does your mother have to be there when you put a bandage on your knee, or finger?"

"No."

"Or when your sister has a cut?"

"No. She puts her own Band-Aids on." This time he raised his chin.

"See. That's one of the differences between animals and people. Right?"

"Right."

"Also, they're covered with fur."

That brought a smile to his lips.

The lawyer hoped Eugene might be able to testify on his own behalf, but wanted to put his explanation on videotape, just to be sure. After taking my statement over the phone, then warning me not to talk to the police, the attorney hung up.

◇◇◇

With Eugene, Toto, and his family gone, the office resonated with silence. It was only me and Mr. Katt. The hospital was so quiet I could hear the fluorescent lights hum.

How could I solve this murder? On television it only takes sixty minutes, including all the breaks for commercials. Real life isn't that convenient. I'd solved a murder before, but had come upon the truth by being in the right place at the wrong time. I didn't want to rely on that same dumb luck again. An innocent young man's life hung in the balance.

I decided to do two things: try to track down the young Hispanic boy nicknamed Double J, and learn the identity of Claire's most recent boyfriend.

After pacing back and forth I decided to go into town and start there. Buddy thought any reason was a great excuse to go for a ride in the truck. Tail wagging, he took his customary place in the passenger seat, wet nose pressed against the glass.

"So, what do you think I should do, Buddy?" Like most animal owners I frequently had conversations with my pet. Taking the role of therapist, Buddy cheerfully refused to give me his opinion.

Fall had rolled in with a vengeance over the last few days. Crisp air, cloudy skies, and sharp shadows gave the landscape a clearer focus, like an optometrist changing out one lens for another. Bright crimson and golden leaves punctuated the usual green, bringing different parts of the forested areas to life. As I drove I thought about Claire. What was unique about her murder disguised as a suicide?

"The killer didn't want Claire to suffer, Buddy." I slapped my hands on the wheel. My dog swung his head around and gave me a puzzled look. "There was no violent fight or sudden attack. So, she knew her murderer, maybe was friends with him or her? No forced entry shows she wasn't afraid of them." My attention went back to the road in front of me. I thought about Claire's mother, Bev, buying a Corvette for Buzz with the insurance money. Would a mother kill her own child?

Sadly, I knew the answer to that question was…yes.

It was then I realized I was right down the road from Bev's house. The day I dropped her off I didn't pay much attention to her place but now…now I'd like to see where Claire grew up. I also had a perfect excuse to drop in. Toto had a new home and I wanted to tell her.

The driveway to the older ranch house was deserted. Someone long ago had converted the garage into living space, so they used a modified carport to park the cars. A shed butted up against the space creating one of the structure's walls, while a heavy tarp closed up the front. In the side yard a big old truck was pulled up onto the lawn. It looked like someone had tried to change a tire and quit mid-job. The large front grill dripped with caked-on mud.

After I closed the Ford's door I made a big show of stretching and looking around in case anyone was studying me through the blinds. I don't know what I expected to see. Picking my way around more mud, I made my way to the front door and rang the bell. A buzzer chimed in the distance.

Where on earth would Bev and her boyfriend park a Corvette and an SUV? After ringing the bell a few more times I decided to walk around to the backyard. Maybe there was a barn or outbuilding.

"Hey, you." A man's voice boomed directly behind me.

When I spun around I recognized the big guy from Claire's funeral who accompanied Bev. The shotgun in his hands was something new.

"What are you doing here?" His voice sounded menacing. The shotgun pointed directly at me.

"I'm looking for Bev and you can put that thing down." I didn't appreciate having a gun pulled on me. "You must be Buzz. I'm Dr. Turner. I met you at Claire's funeral."

He lowered the weapon, showing no remorse. True to his nickname he wore his hair buzzed short. "It's not loaded, so you don't have to worry. We've got to be careful out here."

I didn't believe him but we weren't playing a game of show and tell. "Is Bev home? I wanted to tell her Toto has a new home."

Now he relaxed, his gun butt balanced on his military-style boot. "Okay, I'll tell her."

"I'm curious. How long did Claire live here with you?"

His body language immediately changed from relaxed to suspicious. "Why do you want to know?"

"No reason. Just curious I guess." I forced myself to look directly into his eyes. Tension radiated off him. His back rose, arms and shoulders bunched with muscles.

"Curiosity killed the cat. That's what I told Candy too."

Was that a threat? Did Candace find out something Buzz didn't want anyone to know? It was then I noticed the ham-sized hands holding the shotgun were splattered with paint.

I got out of there as fast as I could. Buzz didn't stop me, he just laughed. Next time I talked to Luke I'd ask if the police ever got an alibi for Bev's fiancé. Maybe he'd traded a human life for a Corvette.

Feeling like I needed to keep going I went on a search for Double J. The farm where Claire's cousin said they met was about one-half hour past town. By the time I got there all of the agricultural workers had left, the fields were silent. Early morning would have been the time to catch them at their work. Then I noticed some summer bungalows all in a row at the back of the farmland. Several small children played outside.

I turned into a worn, rutted road and slowed to a crawl. Dust billowed up behind me as I made my way down along the fields.

I could see tractor treads in the hardened earth. As the truck got closer, the kids stopped playing and stared.

"Hello, there." I jumped out of the truck, then took off my sunglasses so they could see my face. "I'm looking for Double J. Is he around?" One of the little girls pointed at me, then said something to her friend. I realized I had my stethoscope on, had plucked it from the rearview mirror out of habit and draped it around my neck.

"Are you a doctor? Is Double J sick?" The little girl with big dark eyes spoke flawless English.

I squatted down to get on her level. "No, he isn't sick, and yes, I'm a doctor—but only for animals. There is something I need to ask him, about a friend of his. He's not in any trouble." My instincts told me that too often these children associated local adults with problems.

Someone stuck their head out of the closest house and saw me. It was a woman about thirty or forty. I couldn't tell, because her brown skin was dry and shiny from being out in the sun.

"Lupe. *Ven aqui.*" A gesture with her arm reinforced the command. The little girl reluctantly kicked at the dust as she walked to her door.

"Could you tell her I need to talk to Double J for just a minute?"

The child nodded then started speaking rapid fire Spanish to the woman.

A short argument took place, with the older woman glancing at me several times. Finally, decision made, the two of them disappeared into the bungalow.

Then my secret weapon poked his head out the driver's side window.

Buddy was a much-needed icebreaker. Once he began wagging his tail and fetching for all the kids, most of the adults came out of their homes, including Double J. What no one had told me was how slight the boy was, barely five-two and not weighing more than one-twenty, tops. His slim hands and curly dark hair made him look far younger than sixteen.

We talked for a while, but he didn't have much to add to what I already knew. The few times he'd hung out with Claire was on the weekends, and they painted or sketched together. She gave him some books on drawing. Every single time his mother came along as a chaperone and knitted.

"Ask your mother if she ever saw Claire with a man, a boyfriend possibly?" He went into his bungalow, and after a few minutes an elderly woman came out, even smaller than he. Her face was very wrinkled, wizened up like a walnut.

He bent down and said something to her, then gestured to me.

The woman pinched her son's cheeks, then spoke. He in turn translated her words to me.

"She saw somebody, once. He drove up to the townhouse and parked across the street. Claire was in the garage with me." His mother added something, then gestured as though holding something up to her ear. "Okay," Double J continued, "Claire's phone rang. She answered, then smiled and waved to him. He blew her a kiss and drove away. My mother was sitting under a tree in the shade."

"Can she describe him?"

More chatting back and forth. "He was a gringo, blue eyes and yellow hair. Blond."

"What did he drive?"

This time the his mother gestured, more animated. "He drove a big truck, grid on the front, plenty of muscle to haul a load of sweet potatoes." Her smile revealed small stained teeth.

I thanked them both and offered Double J my phone number, in case he remembered anything else. To rule him out I casually asked where he was on the Friday Claire died.

"That's easy. We had a field trip that day, to the Museum of Natural History in New York City. How could I ever forget? We didn't get back until eight o'clock at night."

As the scenery rolled past I felt a weight lifted off my shoulders. Double J wasn't a suspect, and most importantly, we had proof that Claire and her ex were still in contact with each other. I wondered if the beautiful but jealous Bella had suspected her rocker boyfriend still carried a torch for his high-school sweetheart—and decided to douse the flame. On an impulse I decided to swing by Claire's townhouse and take another look around the area. The day of the yard sale the place had been full of people and cars, I hadn't gotten a sense of the surroundings at all. My cover for being there? I could walk Buddy while I checked everything out and no one would think anything of it. Claire's unit bordered the lower parking lot, and after a few wrong turns I found her cul-du-sac.

Squirming with happiness, Buddy waited for me to put his leash on before jumping down from the floor of the truck. Once on the ground he lifted his chin at me as if to say, "What now?"

I noticed some cardboard boxes stacked on the sidewalk next to her mailbox. More stuff to get rid of, I supposed. For a moment I thought about scooping up the boxes and transferring them to the truck, but then the front door opened and someone holding yet another box started walking toward me. Red hair stood up like an electric shock victim. I couldn't see the face but recognized the hair. It was Bev, Claire's mom, and if Buddy and I didn't move she'd slam right into us.

Bev peered around the box. "You can't take anything here. This stuff is for St. Vincent de Paul pickup." Clutched in her hand was a small cardboard sign that said the same thing. With the new box balanced on top of another, she whipped out some scotch tape and secured the sign.

Satisfied, she began to pat down her pockets until she pulled out a pack of cigarettes, then started the pocket pat-down again.

I watched the whole thing, hoping somehow to talk to her.

"Got a match?" Her face didn't look very hopeful.

"Yes, I think I do." I walked over to the truck, parked right next to us, and fished a pack of matches from the glove box.

Bev briefly looked at the cover before lighting up. I realized it was a souvenir from that rock 'n' roll club in Rhinebeck, where Claire's ex-boyfriend was playing.

"My real estate agent won't let me smoke inside."

So the For Sale sign on the other side of the driveway must be for Claire's townhouse.

"I think they do that to appeal to the widest group of buyers." The streams of smoke Bev produced floated away from me.

"Too many damn rules and regulations." A cough punctuated the statement. "If I want to smoke somewhere, the government shouldn't stop me." The wind shifted and smoke blew in my face. That's when I noticed the underlying hint of alcohol, which meant she'd been drinking. Bev definitely had relapsed.

"Do you need any help with those boxes?"

She squinted and took a good look at me. "Don't I know you?"

"Yes, we met at your daughter's funeral. I'm the vet, Kate Turner." Her face stayed blank. "I gave you a ride from the diner when your car wouldn't start."

Her eyes squinted up at me. "Right."

My mind started racing through reasons I would be standing on the sidewalk outside her daughter's home but I needn't have bothered.

"I've got some stuff on the second floor to bring down." Without any more explanation she threw the cigarette butt on the ground and headed back inside.

I smashed the still smoldering cigarette under my boot, let Buddy back in the truck, and rolled down all the windows. At sixty degrees outside and cloudy I didn't have to worry about him overheating. Making sure his water bowl was full I ordered him to stay. He immediately poked his head out the driver's window, tongue hanging out. Sometimes I wondered if he pretended he was driving when I left.

Bev had disappeared in the direction of the kitchen, but I heard her drop something and curse.

"I'll go upstairs and get a box." I fought to make my voice sound matter-of-fact.

She answered with a grunt.

I walked up the stairs remembering how Claire's place had looked during the yard sale. Her colorful paintings and bold furniture choices gave the space life and spirit. Now nothing remained but dingy white walls and memories.

Each room had been packed up, the cartons stacked neatly in the middle. Someone had run a vacuum cleaner over the rugs, leaving long streaks behind. No wonder Bev asked me to help. There must have been six or seven more boxes up here. I didn't think I could safely manage more than one at a time so I lifted up the first one and carefully walked down the stairway, my vision impeded by the corner of the box.

"Where do you want them?" I called out in the general direction of the kitchen.

Bev answered back something unintelligible. I picked a spot by the front door, started a new pile, and went back up the stairs. After the fifth box, and the fifth time I'd maneuvered the steps, I needed a break. Short of breath I rested on the bottom step and hung my head between my knees.

"What's the matter with you?" Bev appeared out of nowhere. I could hear her cracking a big wad of gum.

"Nothing. Just taking a break." She wasn't fooled. Instead, Bev started laughing at me.

"Not in great shape are you, college girl?" She came as close to chortling as I imagined anyone could come.

Winded, I simply nodded in agreement.

"Claire is the reason I didn't go to college. Got pregnant in my junior year of high school."

Okay, where was this going?

Bev was on a roll now. "You're judging me like everybody else. Look at the drunk."

"No, I…"

Pain shone behind her eyes. "Go ahead. I'm used to it. Maybe that's the only way I can keep going. How else am I going to get up every crappy day and go to a crappy job and see nothing ahead of me but more crap?"

"Bev, I'm sure that…"

She interrupted me. "Well, now I've got my chance and I'm not gonna blow it. As soon as this place is sold I'm out of here."

"That's great." I wondered if Luke knew anything about this.

"Want a beer?" Her anger had disappeared.

"Isn't it a little early?"

"Nice and cold." Bev sang the last word.

"Sure. What the heck." Last time alcohol loosened her lips. Maybe it would work again. Bev scooted into the kitchen, and after a moment came back with two tall ones in her hands. Then she parked herself down on the stairs next to me and took a very long swig. I wondered how many beers she had on an average day and if she didn't like to drink alone.

"Asses backwards." Bev belched, not bothering to cover her mouth.

I moved further over on the step. "What do you mean?"

"Chief Garcia and his boys in blue got their asses on backwards. That's what I mean."

"If you say so." I toasted her bottle with my bottle, then kept quiet.

"Running around in circles with their damn asses on backwards." This produced a belly laugh, followed by a burp, followed by another fit of laughing. "A mother knows what a mother knows."

Completely confused now, I ventured a question. "Are you talking about the investigation…?"

She interrupted me, fury in her voice. "Yes, the *investigation* if you can call it that. My baby is dead and they got NOTHING." Her anger reverberated in the empty room.

In two minutes she'd gone from laughing to crying. I didn't know which was worse.

"I'm sure Eugene had nothing to do with it." There, I'd told her my opinion whether she liked it or not. To my confusion she agreed with me.

"Of course Eugene didn't do it, the poor dummy. He loved Claire." Bev finished her beer and looked suspiciously at mine. "Want another? Helps you keep hydrated."

Yeah. That's a great excuse to drink beer all day. Except alcohol dehydrates you. Now who was the one running around ass backwards?

Except now was no time for a lecture. "Okay. I just need to use the bathroom."

She pointed her chin toward the hallway. "Down there."

After she meandered toward the kitchen I sprinted to the bathroom, beer bottle in hand. Making sure to turn on the fan and shut the door I poured the beer out, saving a little on the bottom, then added some water. With the dark glass camouflaging the color, hopefully it would fool someone not looking too closely. Next came flushing the toilet and washing my hands in the sink with soap to camouflage the beer smell. I hurried and beat her back to the stairs.

"Goes right through you, doesn't it? Cleans you out." She smiled with approval as I tossed back the rest of the doctored bottle. "Here you go."

The cold bottle was beaded with sweat and so was I. Stumped on how to handle the situation, I went for broke.

"Do you have any idea who killed your daughter?" My hands rose toward my face in case I had to ward off a boozy blow. Instead she acted like it was no big deal.

"People ask me that all the time." I noticed she'd broken one of her long fingernails. Bev caught me looking and stared back at me with a suspicious look.

"So, what do you tell them?" I lifted the bottle to my lips and pretended to drink. At this point I had no idea what she would say. If she said she thought it was the Dalai Lama I wouldn't have been surprised. Luckily the holy man didn't seem to be involved.

Her eyes glittered and Bev licked her lips. "Not A.J. He would have punched her lights out like he did before, the nasty sonofabitch."

Okay. Still at a loss.

"It was one of those snooty-snoot types she started hanging out with."

I wondered who Bev considered to be a snooty type. Someone who drank their beer from a glass? She continued without any comment from me.

"Those people from the art gallery, acting like they're better than everyone. Looking down their noses at us locals." She punctuated the statement with a another belch. "They aren't as special as they think they are. Especially that bitch, Gilda."

Lifting my bottle in the air I kept the ball rolling. "You can say that again. Not special at all."

"Claire told me one time," she lowered her voice conspiratorially, "one of them was a phony. A phony baloney." Bev cracked herself up with her rhyming.

Who was a phony? And what exactly did Claire mean by that?

"Phony baloney." Laughing again at herself, Bev got up and stumbled into the kitchen. I suspected she'd had a little something else besides the relatively sedate beers.

"A real baloney sandwich sounds pretty good right now, don't you think?" Her voice carried in the small space. "I ordered two from the deli and brought them with me, with extra mayo. "

While she did something in the kitchen I sprinted into the bathroom one more time to dispose of the second beer. Then I yelled, "What do you think Claire meant by phony?"

"What did she mean?" Bev repeated what I asked, never a good sign.

The doorbell chimed, breaking any moment of camaraderie I'd tried to build.

"Bev, are you here?" The woman's raspy voice sounded familiar.

Sure enough, when the newcomer came in I recognized her from the yard sale. This was Evie, the best friends forever, fanny pack and all.

"It's about time you got here." Bev sounded annoyed. "I just about gave away your sandwich to what's her name here." She gestured with the brown paper bag from the deli.

"Kate." No one appeared to listen.

Evie looked around the kitchen and into the hallway. "How much more is left to do?" Both women watched me.

"There are only two boxes left upstairs."

"Can you get them, honey?" All of a sudden Bev's voice

became syrupy with concern. "My knees can't take those stairs and Evie's knees are older than mine."

"You wish."

After some half-hearted name calling the two then started arguing about the sandwiches. I decided to finish moving the last boxes. Maybe then I could get a little more information about that "phony baloney" Bev mentioned.

Refreshed from my fake beer break I bounded up the stairs only to find the last two boxes were the heaviest. What did she have in here? Claire's rock collection?

It took a couple of stops on the landing, but finally both boxes stood in the hallway. I noticed someone had written "books" on the side of the cartons. That explained it, but it gave me an idea.

Going into the kitchen I noticed the two women had gone through another beer in the short time I'd been gone. Not to mention devoured the sandwiches.

"Bev, what are you doing with the two boxes of books?"

"Everything's going to St. Vincent de Paul. Why?" She fixed a bleary eye on me, then smiled. I guess she'd reached that mellow point. Doubtful she'd stay in that zone for long I asked, "Do you mind if I take them home and pick a few books out? I'm out of books to read."

She smiled at me again. I felt like I'd won the sociability lottery. "Go ahead. Take some then drop the rest off in their donation bin next to the church. Okay?"

"Good idea. What are you doing here anyway?" Evie commented, then wiped a sandwich crumb off her faint mustache.

"I, uh…" How was I going to explain this?

"Knock it off, Evie." Bev rose to my defense for some unknown reason. "She was walking her dog and offered to help me with the boxes. At least she's not after my money like some people."

Her friend started to sputter and protest but Bev cut her off.

"You think I don't know? Being so nice now I've got some cash." She poked a hot pink nail in Evie's face. "Just kidding. Not."

"Don't listen to this old bag." She pushed Bev's hand away and picked up her purse. "You wouldn't have found out nothing about him if it hadn't been for me." She started to say something else, glanced in my direction, then thought twice about it.

"Who needs you?" Bev yelled, shoving her face uncomfortably close to the other woman's face.

"Drop dead. It's Buzz you got to worry about, not me." Evie flounced out the door, slamming it shut for good measure.

Bev's eyes were mere slits when she turned on me. "Don't you start."

I held my palms up. "I wouldn't think of it."

"That's right." Bev reached into her pocket and pulled out a thin metal flask. The distinctive tang of whiskey perfumed the air as soon as she twisted off the cap. The woman poured it into her quarter full bottle of beer, then drained the whole thing, elbow bent toward the ceiling.

My reaction caught her by surprise. "Nice way to make yourself a boilermaker. My gramps' favorite drink."

"You want a hit, college girl?" This time "college girl" sounded like a nickname instead of a put-down.

I raised my hand in protest. "Sorry, I've still got some work to do."

"Your loss."

Watching Bev made me wonder if she was as nasty and selfish as she appeared to be. Some people live their lives with grace while others want to grab the universe by the throat and strangle it.

"Your daughter Claire was a wonderful person. I'm sure you miss her terribly."

Tears sprang into her eyes but she quickly put her head down, concentrating on the bottle in her hand. "Yeah. Shit happens."

The quiver in her voice betrayed her. Underneath the prickly exterior Bev was a grieving mother. Or she was acting up a storm?

"Just one more question. When Claire talked to you about fakes, did she say anything else? Did she mention China, or Southeast Asia at all?" I knew I was grasping at straws here, probably another dead end. Every clue I'd stumbled on recently revealed a blind alley.

There was no immediate reply.

With her head still down Bev rubbed her eyes. Her shoulders slumped and gave the impression she'd collapsed like a balloon from the inside out. Pretty sure she'd reached her limit I stood up to go, my muscles already aching from the unaccustomed work. "Do you need a ride home?"

"Nope. Evie will be back. She always comes back."

"Alright, but if she doesn't I can swing by and drop you at your house."

"Wait."

I turned around. Bev still sat in the same position, staring at the floor.

"It was a different word, not fakes, but something like it I think."

After waiting a moment I saw her shake her head in frustration. Maybe this mystery wouldn't have a happy ending for anyone. I gathered up my things, not looking forward to lugging those books to the truck.

"I remember now. The word wasn't fakes."

I held my breath. Please let her remember.

"She said forgery."

◇◇◇

Once home, with the evidence piling up I prepared myself for a stern lecture on keeping out of police business and called Officer Gianetti. Thankful to get his voice mail, I mumbled a message and hung up.

Then I hunkered down on the sofa and waited for Luke to call me back.

Chapter Thirty-six

Luke and I met up in an unlikely spot, the old cemetery next to the historic Episcopal church in downtown Oak Falls. Shaded by immense trees, the grass felt slippery under my feet. The parish had stopped active burials on the church grounds over one hundred years ago. Today most tourists visited to wander through the grounds or try their hand doing rubbings of the early tombstones. Most of the carvings were weathered, difficult to read. Except for a few more recent white marble slabs, the bluestone grave markers presented a strangely uniform and peaceful sight. A solitary oak, leaves bright scarlet, colored the landscape.

Luke stood in front of a small gravestone. As I drew nearer I saw it read "Gianetti, Antonio d.1836, wife Prudence d. 1851."

"A relative of yours?" He started when he heard my voice.

"We're not sure. My cousin is supposed to be checking into it." After one last look we strolled toward a small hill that led to the back of the cemetery. "Most of our family came to America around the 1900s. I'm not sure what an Italian immigrant would be doing in a Protestant graveyard."

"Maybe he fell madly in love with Prudence."

We lingered in front of a newer marble slab decorated with carved angels. "Maybe he did."

A crow began to caw in the trees above.

"What about your family history, Kate?"

"My mother's side are mostly Irish and Welsh, but my dad's family is a mix of Swiss, Dutch, German, and who knows what. We think his family originally settled in Pennsylvania way back in the 1700s."

"A daughter of the American Revolution?" He laughed, then steadied my elbow after I slipped on a moss-covered stone.

"Not that I'm aware."

The hill leveled off, giving us a view of the mountains. Luke let go of my arm. The air smelled of wood smoke and damp earth. The dead were resting in peace. Not a bad place to discuss murder.

"So, Kate. What is this meeting about?"

I couldn't tell if he was annoyed or not. "Before she died Claire told her mother she'd discovered a forgery."

"What?" His brows rose and doubt creased his forehead.

"I'm not sure, but it's possible the gallery she worked for is selling fakes." I remembered how eager the Qualog Gallery owner, Gilda, welcomed my friend Tim's credit card. "By the way, I think Gilda is having an affair with that Russian artist."

He pulled out a small notepad and jotted down something. "Did Beverly say anything else?"

"Just that it had something to do with a fake or forgery."

"Was she sober at the time?" His voice reflected uncertainty.

The wind kicked up for a moment, twirling the leaves under my feet. "Sort of. It's hard to tell."

He walked away from me for a moment, then paced back. "This is a strong accusation, Kate. You could ruin someone's reputation and business with this kind of talk. Any evidence behind it?"

"No. That's where you come in." I smiled at him, trying to be as charming as I could be. He wasn't buying it. "There's more. Bev's boyfriend, Buzz, thinks he's going to share in all the insurance money, but I think she's getting ready to dump him."

"Bev's been dumping him and getting back together with him for the last fifteen years. No surprises there."

"Alright. Maybe this is some kind of love triangle murder. A.J.'s new girlfriend, Bella, is smart enough and rich enough to get away with murder."

"And maybe you've been reading too many books. Thanks for all the help, Kate, but let the police do their job." His brown eyes caught mine.

"All right, all right. I get the picture." As attractive as Luke was he sure could make me mad. "Can you at least try checking some of this out. Quietly?"

He took my hand. "Please believe me. I'd do anything to help Eugene and his family. But I've still got to follow the rules. You may think the police are slow but eventually we get to the bottom of things."

His hand felt warm and comforting, but his words chilled my heart. Eventually didn't cut it. Unless the killer was caught and Eugene cleared of any wrongdoing, the specter of murder would hang over his head for the rest of his life.

Chapter Thirty-seven

That night I felt frustrated for several reasons. Walking in the cemetery reminded me I hadn't visited my mom's and brother's graves in a while. That kernel of guilt I always carried around with me weighed on my conscience like a lead sinker. Plus, being with Luke was unsettling, because despite what I told myself, feelings for him kept rising up. Obviously, we were only destined to be friends.

Meanwhile Jeremy's last posting to me had been extremely brief. That's after I'd missed two Skype sessions and forgot to respond to an email.

With so many people annoyed at me, remembering lives cut short made me even more melancholy. I didn't want to add Eugene to the list.

Buddy nuzzled my hand and jumped up on the sofa next to me. My untouched glass of white wine sat on the coffee table. I'd stacked the boxes of books from Claire's condo in the living room, planning to go through them on the weekend. When the phone rang I welcomed the distraction.

"Hello, Katie. What are you up to this lovely evening?" My grandfather's voice rang out clear as a bell. Usually I could hear his breathing between sentences.

"Hey, Gramps. You sound great."

His laughter almost carried into my living room. "I'm feeling much better. The doctor put me on a different medication, plus I've lost some of my beer belly."

"Good for you. Are you still taking that yoga class?" The idea of my Gramps in a classroom practicing yoga brought a smile to my lips.

"I never thought I'd say it, but it's helped me a lot. I even drag Frank to it."

How his buddy Frank, a retired NYPD detective, could get his six-foot-four three-hundred pound frame into the lotus position was beyond me. The senior center they both belonged to really did a great job for their members.

Pausing for a sip of wine I gave Buddy a kiss on his nose. "Hey Gramps. What do you know about art forgery?"

"That came out of the blue. What's up?"

Knowing he'd be mad at me for investigating the murder, I camouflaged the truth a bit. "Someone might have sold fake artwork here in town."

"Well, it's a big deal. All the auction houses like Sotheby's and Christie's here in the city have had to deal with it. I read in the papers about a painting that was sold but the owner won't pay for it until it is verified by art experts."

"Did you ever hear about fakes coming out of China?"

I heard him grumble as he maneuvered around in his favorite chair. "Sure. The *New York Times* ran a big article on forgeries of early Chinese masters by Chinese artists. They make everything else we buy. Why not art?"

"I guess I never thought about it, since that kind of expense isn't in the budget." My eye caught Claire's painting hanging on the wall nearest the kitchen. That impulsive purchase was the most expensive piece of art I'd ever bought.

Gramps laughed. "You and me both, kid. Except for my original Kate Turner abstract on the living room wall."

"That's right. I almost forgot about that."

"Well, I haven't. Not my granddaughter's first finger painting. You had almost as much paint on your clothes as on the paper."

Now it was my turn to laugh. "Do you still have that picture of me while I was painting it?"

"Sure. You've got a mile-wide smile as you show off your hands to us. Your poor mother had to wash you twice to get all the paint off, once in the shower and once in the bathtub."

He stopped talking, remembering those happy times I hoped.

"If you want to learn more about crimes in the art world there's a special unit here in the city…fakes, forgeries, antiquities, selling stolen works…you name it, they do it. Most of it is coordinated with Interpol, since these guys are global now. Like Fed Ex."

He chuckled at his own joke. It was great hearing him sound better, less wheezing and coughing.

"Goodnight, Gramps."

"*Vaya con Dios*, Katie."

Just before I went to sleep I thought of Claire. If she stumbled on some kind of art forgery scam worth lots of money, would she threaten to turn the scammers in to the police? Or try and cut a deal?

Chapter Thirty-eight

When I walked into the clinic the next day it looked like all hell had broken loose. In a way, it had. Our trusty septic system for the old part of the building was backed up. Mari scurried by me with a bottle of bleach in each hand. The staff members were in damage control mode. The renovated hospital area was fine, but the old kennels and runs had to be closed down while the plumber did his magic.

"Our leach field is saturated, especially from last spring's thaw and the rain." Cindy took a moment out to explain. "I told Doc he should invest in a new system when he gets back.

"Anyone in those old runs?"

"No. We only use them for overflow boarding now." At major holidays Doc usually ran a boarding special for his clients so they could travel and not worry about their pets. The runs were an older design but they were large and had elevated beds and access to the outside, depending on the weather.

The smell of bleach was everywhere. "What can I do to help?"

"Well, we rearranged your schedule so Mari can stay here and help. She'll be available to work with you this afternoon, though."

The smell of fresh coffee cut through the bleach and reminded me I needed a cup. A big cup. "What time do I start?" Mari took pity on me and handed me some java.

"Your first house call appointment is at nine, so you have about a half hour before you need to leave."

Suddenly out of nowhere something big and striped hurtled down in front of me, howling like a banshee, before darting for the office. Momentarily startled, I quickly recovered without losing a drop of my java.

"What's up with Mr. Katt?"

"He absolutely hates it when we bring out the bleach."

"Cats have a very sensitive sense of smell," I reminded everyone. "Yet another reason to keep the cat box clean." Finished with my first cup I reached for the carafe and a refill.

The ringing phone drove Cindy back to her reception desk, while I went to check my email and the morning lab reports. Mr. Katt lay at my feet, his bushy tail thrashing against my ankles as he commented on his morning so far.

"I'm with you, guy." I addressed my comment to the furry dude now rubbing his head on my foot. "I hope this isn't how my entire day's going to be."

◇◇◇

It started off easy enough, a recheck appointment on a big goofy dog to remove his stitches. My clients purchased a home with twelve acres from an auction. Unfortunately, they found out the previous owner had a slight hoarding problem. They'd had to haul off all kinds of junked and rusted farm equipment, mowers, car parts, and sharp metal objects from the property.

Fluffernutter, the dog, stumbled over a rusty scythe while chasing a rabbit on the day they moved in. I'd been worried about tetanus and infection, but with treatment he'd done fine.

The rural driveway appeared on the right, an unpaved road that curved toward the farmhouse. At the turn I noticed a silvery pond off to the left, and a large clump of apple trees. To lessen the bumps I shifted into low. Deep ruts from a heavy vehicle guided me along. A woman recognizable as Mrs. Fluffernutter was waving to me from the porch, signaling to drive behind the home.

That's when my adventure started.

After parking the truck I got out and stretched. No one was in sight until a long beak and head poked out from behind a storage shed. A goose. I wondered, idly, what other animals the Fluffernutters had on the property. Maybe a mini farm situation. Still not seeing anyone I walked a few feet in front of the truck.

Several other beaks appeared, then geese started waddling toward me, honking and flapping their wings. I knew geese had been used in Europe as watchdogs, alerting owners of trespassers.

These birds seemed to be on high alert.

Now a small sea of noisy geese flowed toward me. I looked the leader in the eye. He looked back and hissed. I checked my pockets for anything to divert their attention but for once they were empty.

"Nice geese."

I stood still to let them get used to me. My brain was trying to remember the client's name. I didn't want to call out Mrs. Fluffernutter.

A sharp beak pecked at my jacket. "No," I said in my authoritarian voice that always stopped dogs cold. The geese hadn't gotten the memo. Another peck at my jacket, this time on the other side.

Then, in unison, beaks were hammering away at my sneaker laces, my toes, my hands and elbows and up and down my legs. Admitting defeat I tried to run back to the truck, but slid on some goose poop. The flock kept coming, waddling toward me, necks bobbing up and down. Pushing myself up I jumped into the truck and slammed the door. Safely ensconced above them I honked the horn to alert someone. The geese immediately began to imitate the noise.

"Dennis, go get the geese." Help had arrived in the form of Mrs. Fluffernutter, the dog, Fluffernutter, and a small boy.

It was the boy, no higher than my waist, who waded into the gaggle of geese and began to swish them away from us with his arms. Miraculously, the heavy fowl acknowledged their young master and noisily moved away toward the pond.

"Sorry about that. They came with the property."

"No problem." I gingerly looked around before stepping out of the driver's seat door.

"Fluffernutter looks good. No limping." His wound had been to the back of the leg, narrowly missing the Achilles tendon.

"Yes, he's back to himself. The sweet little boy." Hearing an endearment thrown his way their pet proceeded to wiggle toward his owner, then sat on her foot and drooled.

The dog resembled a small bear, some mix of chocolate Labrador and Woolly Mammoth. He weighed at least ninety pounds. I hoped she was wearing sturdy shoes.

"Let's go into the house so I can get those sutures out." The location of the wound meant I had to have the mound of living fur lying still. Too bad Mari wasn't with me. She had the whammy on dogs.

My worry turned out to be a reality, with the dog flailing his legs and trying to lick his owner's face while I zeroed in on the tiny sutures. What should have taken two minutes ended up being a fifteen-minute ordeal. More for me than the dog.

"Can I get you anything, Dr. Kate?"

"Maybe a little water, April." I'd finally remembered my client's name, but Mrs. Fluffernutter kept threatening to come out of my mouth. When she got back I gave her some instructions.

"He can resume his normal activity. Just call us if he starts bothering the wound."

"Thanks so much." Fluffernutter raised his face toward me, tongue hanging down over his fuzzy chin. Then a movement caught his eye and off he dashed. We started walking back to the truck. While she chatted I kept watch for the geese.

"You have a lovely property," I commented. "How long have you been here?"

She leaned against the truck, watching her son playing with the dog. "We moved in two months ago. It's been heaven compared to the townhouse."

"It's beautiful. Plenty of land, and a great setting. What is it? About five acres or so?"

Eager to brag about her property April gave me the rundown. They had a barn, a stream, and a lake all to themselves, as well as two fields for grazing. Stone and wooden fences separated the areas. Because of a dip in the real estate market, they considered it a steal.

"Does your son like living in the country?"

"Absolutely. My daughter has some mixed feelings. It's a little far from town and the stable. But we're going to put a horse setup in next spring, and maybe do some boarding."

The fields around the house would be put to good use with a horse or two. "Has she been riding a long time?"

"About three years. She's a student over at Magic Stables." She lifted her hand over her eyes to block a sudden ray of sunshine.

"A client of mine used to ride there, before she passed away."

"You must mean Claire Bingham, such a sweet girl. Fluffernutter used to play with her Toto all the time." I smiled thinking about the huge dog and the tiny Yorkie playing. "Toto used to boss my sweetie-pie around. So funny."

Toto definitely was an alpha male in a zeta body.

"Such a mystery, what happened. Just as she had gotten that new job and was going to buy that apartment in New York."

My head swiveled so fast I thought I'd dislocate my neck. First the gallery owner, now another friend with the same story. "What do you mean, buy an apartment? Someone said she was only subletting from a Julliard student."

April called her little boy over, who was running at warp speed around the truck. "Hey kiddo, you're only going in one direction. Now you should run the other way."

Dennis opened his eyes wide, contemplated his mom's unusual advice, then took off like a shot.

"Kids." April smiled as he started counterclockwise lap number one.

"Sorry to ask you again, but are you sure Claire said she was buying an apartment?"

There was a pause in the conversation, a long pause. "Why are you asking all these questions about Claire? Are you helping with the investigation?"

"Well..." I hesitated trying to find the right words to explain. "Well, sort of." Not good Kate, not good at all.

That seemed enough of an explanation for April, though. She proceeded to tell me about the plans Claire had shared with her while they were walking their dogs. With only a few interruptions I got the whole story. Claire told April she might have a nice chunk of money available to her soon.

"Nothing about where the money was coming from?"

"Sorry. That's all I remember." Once again her attention was distracted by her son, who had stopped running around my truck and was busy chasing the dog.

"Listen, you're right. I am trying to help Eugene and his family by asking some questions. If you do think of anything else, could you call me at the hospital number?"

"Of course."

"Look at me." The shout had her running toward Dennis perched precariously on the pasture fence.

The menacing noise of the geese nearby made me leap in the truck, also at warp speed.

Rumbling down the road I wondered how this new information fitted into the puzzle of Claire's life.

Could the money she expected have been coming from a payoff?

It sounded like Claire had resorted to blackmail to make her dreams come true.

Chapter Thirty-nine

Back home after the attack of the killer geese, I stripped off my funky-smelling clothes and threw them in the hamper. The multiple beak strikes had resulted in black and blue marks just starting to bloom on my legs and arms. Only my pride was seriously hurt. As a veterinarian I felt embarrassed that I ran away from a bunch of geese in front of a client.

Padding around the apartment in bare feet I banged my toe into one of the boxes of books I'd hauled in from the truck. Maybe now was a good time to stop and go through them. I slid the first box closer to the sofa and cut the tape with my keys. Half hoping to find a valuable clue hidden in one of the books, I began unpacking.

Right away I noted that Claire had an eclectic taste in books. Next to the latest James Rollins thriller was a Gunn Zoo mystery by Betty Webb, and a copy of *Gulliver's Travels.* Mixed in with the fiction I found some nonfiction library books, the most interesting being a biography of Wolfgang Beltracchi, famous art forger.

This was the first bit of evidence tied to Claire that hinted at a motive for her murder. But who would be faking art? I decided to do some research of my own, starting with reading all about Beltracchi.

What I read astonished me. Art forgery has been going on for centuries, but the number of fakes estimated to be hanging in museums was astonishing. Time after time experts are fooled by a clever artist who uses an old canvas to paint a "discovered" painting by a long dead famous painter. Picasso, Monet, Modigliani and Matisse seem to be pretty popular on the forgery list. The biggest problem is authenticating the fake, creating a history for the work so it will pass muster by the experts. A solid provenance can add millions to a price.

But what famous paintings had been sold out of Oak Falls? None that I could recall. I'd read nothing about any big art sale in the newspapers or heard anything on the television news. That meant I needed to dig a little deeper into the Qualog Gallery where Claire worked. For that I'd need some reinforcements.

I knew just who to call.

"Hey Tim. How's it going?" Tim and Tina lived across the river in Rhinebeck enjoying a lifestyle I could only dream about.

"Kate. We were just talking about you." In the background I heard high-pitched barking. "Just a minute, someone's at the door."

I hung on the phone listening to a rising crescendo of yipping that stopped abruptly. Then Tim got back on the line.

"The UPS guy. The way the dogs behave you'd think he was Jack the Ripper."

"Well, your dogs are so cute they could probably charm him to death." I was rewarded with the sound of Tim laughing. He thought my jokes were funny, which was one of the many reasons we got along so great all through school.

When he got control of himself I continued. "So what do you know about art forgery?"

"Talk about changing the subject." Tim sounded surprised. "Where did that come from?"

I glanced at the book on Wolfgang Beltracchi sitting on the coffee table. "Well, I'm sort of investigating another murder case."

"Why am I not surprised? How can we help?"

I took a deep breath and explained. My scheme was pretty simple. Have Tim and Tina return to the Qualog Gallery on the pretense of looking for a painting. I'd tag along then and try to poke around while they kept the gallery owner occupied.

It didn't quite work out that way.

◇◇◇

We met on Sunday morning in town to go over my plan. Tim and Tina looked fantastic in their designer duds, all linen and leather. Me, not so much. I'd forgotten to brush the dog hair off my black pants.

"No worries, Kate honey." Tina started to dig around in her giant Coach bag. "I always carry a lint roller with me." She handed off their two Papillons to Tim and dove back into her search.

Tim smiled while the dogs gave kisses.

Triumphantly Tina pulled out a portable lint roller. "You'd be amazed how often this comes in handy."

Seeing that my friends never seemed to travel without their show dogs, I couldn't have agreed more.

Meanwhile Tim wanted to get into the role. "I've got it all planned out. My cousin Natalie is getting married soon, so I'll say we're looking for a wedding present. That will keep it nice and simple, right Tina?"

His wife enthusiastically agreed. "Natalie has a nice little art collection of her own going. It will be easy to shop for her."

"Right." Tim passed one of the dogs back to her. "Maybe we should look for real."

The glimmer in their eyes disturbed me. "Wait, now. You don't have to buy anything." Finished with the roller I tore off the fur laden strip and handed it back to Tina. I was worried they would get a little too caught up in the scheme.

Tim and Tina blissfully smiled at each other. "We know."

I started getting an anxiety pain in my stomach, but Tina grabbed my hand and before I knew it we were walking into the Qualog Gallery.

Tim took the lead by putting on his glasses and carefully reading the card to the right of a familiar looking painting. He gestured for his wife to take a look.

"Isn't that another Roshenkov?" Tina barely hide the excitement in her voice.

Leaving them to browse Andrei Roshenkov's work I looked around the gallery. There must have been fifteen or twenty people milling around in the large space. Quite a good gathering for a Sunday afternoon. Only a few feet away I noticed the art gallery owner, Gilda, in an animated conversation with two older men, one of whom looked Chinese. Her assistant, Roxie, sporting a new day-glo orange streak in her hair, stood in the far corner talking on the phone.

With the coast clear I decided to quickly walk through the room, concentrating on the artwork for sale. On a divider wall all by themselves hung four Chinese lithographs. With zero knowledge of Chinese I took a picture of the prints with my phone, intending to look them up later. The price I could read. Six thousand dollars each.

"I'm sorry, but we don't allow you to photograph the artwork." A high-pitched, slightly nasal voice admonished over my shoulder. Roxie stood behind me, a stern frown on her face.

Trying to find some excuse for my interest I said, "Oh, I didn't know."

Her eyes widened. "Weren't you just here? You're Claire's friend, aren't you?"

"Yes. I spoke to you before."

"Yeah, I remember. You saved me from the dragon lady." She gestured toward Gilda. "This is my last week here and I can't wait to leave. No one ever warned us in art school about employers like her."

I noticed she still kept her voice down. Obviously, things weren't going that well for her at the gallery.

"You're lucky I saw you and not Gilda. She'd probably tear your head off." The assistant stifled a laugh. "Unless you're loaded with money, of course."

"No such luck, I'm afraid."

"Oops. She's looking at us. Pretend to be interested in the lithograph."

"Sure." I moved closer and peered at the tranquil scene of high snowcapped mountains and a winding river.

Roxie began to explain what we were looking at. "This is a

lithograph of a famous ink painting by Qi Baishi. The authentication comes from a gallery in Beijing."

Something puzzled me. "What is an art gallery in upstate New York doing selling Chinese art?"

She laughed. "We sell a lot of works from China. Gilda has connections with several artists in Hong Kong and also works with an art broker based in Beijing. The Internet has made every art gallery a global one. Our catalogue is posted on our website and we feature local artists as well. All the buyer has to do is Google it."

I heard my name being called so I said a quick thanks and walked over to Tim and Tina. They were in some kind of intense powwow with the gallery owner.

"There you are." Tina gestured to me to join her. She and Tim were standing in front of a massive painting, that even I could tell had been done by Roshenkov.

"What do you think?" Tim's eyes shone with excitement. "Beautiful, isn't it?"

The intricate swirls of color vaguely reminded me of Van Gogh, with the paint laid on quite thickly in some places, yet filled with birds and animals seen only in the artist's imagination. My eye was drawn to a fanciful bird with a head like a swan but wings like a butterfly.

"Beautiful, yes, surprising too." It was so detailed I couldn't imagine how long it took to paint. The longer I looked at it the more interesting it became.

"People are starting to notice him," Gilda bragged. "I wouldn't be surprised if he became the next big thing in the art world, a New York show, lots of publicity. Prices could skyrocket. You'd be buying his work at bargain basement prices."

Tina glanced at Tim, then squeezed my hand. "Why don't we go into your office, Gilda, and discuss this? Kate, would you mind watching the dogs? They might need to be walked."

My friends passed the Papillons over to me and then the three of them headed down the hallway toward the gallery office. With the dragon lady safely out of the way I was able to take some quick photos of the other works displayed. I wanted to compare them with the items in her catalogue for any discrepancies.

When one of the dogs started to whimper I realized Tina might have meant what she said. I hustled over to the exit, then put each dog down on the sidewalk, checking that their leashes were properly attached before I let them go.

Both eagerly headed for a small patch of grass in front of the gallery and squatted in unison. Luckily, no plastic bags were needed.

Much to my surprise, a familiar looking French Bulldog came out of nowhere and joined them.

"Those are beautiful dogs. What breed are they?"

I recognized his voice before I turned around. Andrei Roshenkov stood just behind me, watching the dogs interact. Beautifully groomed, as usual, a Rolex glittered on his wrist and his manicured pinky sported a thin platinum band. Mindful of the big wad of Papillon fur that decorated my lavender knit sweater, I picked up one of the dogs for camouflage.

"Oh. Hi there." By the look he gave me it was obvious he didn't know who I was.

"Hello." He checked his phone for a moment, then closed it.

"Papillons." I lifted the little dog in my arms up to eye level.

"Excuse me?"

"That's the breed. They're Papillons. You know, French." That sounded inarticulate even to me.

"Of course, it means butterfly, because of the fringe on their ears."

"Exactly."

The dogs were taking their time doing their business.

"You're originally from Russia, aren't you?" I might as well take advantage of this meeting.

"Yes."

"How do you like living in America?"

Andrei watched the dogs. "America is very good for my art. Very welcoming."

"Where do you work—I mean—when you paint?" His

French Bulldog finally lifted a leg on a convenient tree. "Do you have your own studio?"

This time he turned to look at me instead of the dogs. Was there a hesitancy in those ice blue eyes? "*Da*. I have a studio not far from town, in the countryside. Every day I try to work on something. Maybe I could give you a small tour one day?" This time I recognized the look in his eyes as flirtation and possibly an invitation.

"That would be nice." I decided to flirt back. "You know, I must say you're the cleanest artist I've ever met, Andrei. My friend Claire always had spots of paint on her."

He frowned, voice flinty. "My teachers in Russia punished us for sloppy technique and dirty hands. Paint is for the canvas—not the artist. Your American schools have no such rules."

"I think your teachers were right." Now I turned up the charm and batted my eyes.

In a flash his countenance mellowed and he returned my smile. "Ah, you joke. I did not understand." The sunlight hit his hair, lighting it up like gold. I couldn't get over how handsome he looked. Had he noticed my truck that day I followed him? There didn't appear to be any indication of that.

A very well dressed middle-aged woman walking by almost did a double take when she saw him. He must be used to that kind of attention. Come to think of it, that's two unusually handsome men I've talked to recently. Not counting Luke.

"You are the veterinarian, I believe." His voice brought me back from my daydream.

"Yes. I work at the Oak Falls Animal Hospital."

I felt his gaze on me.

"A doctor for animals, a noble profession." He reached down to scratch his French Bulldog between the ears.

Not sure how to respond I simply said, "Thank you."

He acknowledged my response with a nod of his head, then tugged on his dog's leash and proceeded down the sidewalk toward the Qualog Gallery.

Claire must have enjoyed being around such a good-looking guy. Had she been tempted to do something about it?

Chapter Forty

After surviving the art gallery intact, except for a purchase of another Roshenkov painting on the part of my friends, we celebrated at the local gelato store. Under blue striped umbrellas we succumbed to our sweet tooths.

"Just a sec." The chocolate hazelnut with a biscotti stuck in it demanded my full attention.

Tina didn't even try to talk. She simply raised her eyebrows above a double scoop of pistachio with extra nuts on top.

After a sigh of contentment I addressed Tim's question. "I've got too many motives."

"How can you have too many?"

"You tell me. Her mother stood to inherit a lot of money, and she's got a nasty boyfriend who thinks he's entitled to some of it. Claire complained to her cousin about the art gallery she worked in. Someone there might be selling forgeries. Her rocker ex-boyfriend held a grudge because she dumped him and has a very jealous new girlfriend who doesn't want to share. Let's see..."

Tina began making a noise, her mouth full. She gestured with her hands at me then finally spoke. "I forgot. I've got some news about Claire's ex, A.J. The police showed up at his new girlfriend's condo on a domestic violence call."

"Bella? Is she all right?" For all her bravado the young groupie appeared vulnerable to me.

"I think so." Tina took another spoonful of her ice cream.

"Anyway, she wouldn't press charges and vice versa. Said they both had accidents."

"Both of them?"

"That's what I heard. She gave him a bloody nose and a black eye."

A.J.'s physique indicated that he obviously lifted weights, while Bella looked like a hard wind could blow her over. Apparently she was stronger than I thought. "And her?"

"Mostly cuts and bruises and a cracked cheekbone."

"Terrible." I winced thinking about two people using violence on each other. Hopefully they'll get some help. Being two such obviously physical people could either one have had the patience to stage a suicide?

Finished way before the others, I pushed my empty cup of ice cream away. "I'm not through with the motives, though. Claire might have discovered a forgery at the art gallery, like I told you. The question is did she plan to turn them in or use it to make a profit?"

"Oh no. How horrible." Tina gave the dogs a little lick from a plastic sample spoon.

"Right. We don't know if she was supplementing her income by a little blackmail."

Tim's brows furrowed up. "Do you think she was capable of that?"

"Honestly, I don't know. She needed more than her inheritance money to buy an apartment in New York. Maybe she felt whoever she blackmailed deserved it." A sudden memory of Claire flashed in my brain. Thick brown hair and a brilliant smile. I felt bad thinking ill of the dead.

Tim brought me back to the present. "What do the police think?"

"Well, they have to stick to facts," I joked, "so they aren't getting very far."

Tina remained quiet. Thoughtful.

"What do you think about all this, honey?" Tim reached over and took his wife's hand. I turned and waited for her answer.

Tina's gorgeous brown eyes opened wide. "I think Kate has stepped in a big pile of doo doo. I only hope she can climb out of it before something terrible happens."

◇◇◇

Tina's prediction unfortunately came true the next day when I found myself literally in a big pile of dung. Llama style. Yes, from a herd of llama living in upstate New York.

Mari and I were on a farm call to a pair of sisters whose cottage industry was knitting. They kept cashmere goats, rare breeds of sheep, plus a few alpaca and llama to supply specialty wool. A wide variety of laying hens also wandered free-range around the property.

I'd slipped on my long green rubber boots before walking into the corral. Mari hadn't been so lucky. It was a toss-up if the muck would cascade over the top of her garden-style boots she had stashed in the truck.

"Yuck." Her foot squished as she hit a wet spot.

"Jane." I took a guess as to which one of the identical twin sisters stood just inside the gate. "Where is the fellow with the bite wound?"

"It's Ralph. The big brown and white guy."

I took a long look at the closely huddled group. They were all brown and white. Since that didn't help at all, I clarified my request. "Can you help us put a lead on him?"

All the llamas had halters on, each with little plumbs of brightly colored yarn hanging down from the sidepiece. I'd seen similar headgear on pictures of llamas in Peru and even read about them in a classic mystery by David Dodge called *The Red Tassel.* They looked very festive except for the pissed-off expression in their luminous dark eyes.

"Lorraine." Jane yelled for her sister. A moment later her twin opened the back door of their house and came striding toward us. I found it a little disconcerting, to say the least.

Each woman had the same long bony face, defined by patches of red sprinkled over high cheekbones. Their curly gray hair stuck out around their heads like puffy dandelions. They wore identical clothes, right down to their boots. It was spooky.

Mari said the first thing that came to mind. "I can't tell you apart." Her voice held a tone of wonderment.

The twins looked at each other, their heads turning almost in synchrony, one to the left and one to the right. "Actually, it's easy, once you know the secret."

I knew the twin on the left must be Lorraine, because I'd seen her come from the house. But once I stopped staring at them, like the old shell game—if they switched positions I'd be lost.

"So, what's the secret?" Mari persisted in asking.

Lorraine took a lead from her pocket and stepped into the corral. She made a funny whistling noise, and immediately the entire pack turned their heads and pricked up their ears. Muttering softly the woman walked from animal to animal, giving each one a treat from her pocket. With a practiced hand she clicked the lead into the metal ring at the base of the halter of a large male, then rewarded him with a treat. Finishing up with the last one we heard another clicking-whistling sound and saw Ralph coming toward us.

I immediately noticed the bite wound on his side, which was one of the several reasons for the house call. Moving my gloved fingers gently but firmly around the wound I was pleased to notice that although it was deep, it was clean, with no infection, and had already started to heal. Unfortunately, because whoever bit him yanked back, he'd have quite a scar.

"You've done a good job here. It's not infected."

"We've been doing what you told us, spraying it down three times a day with the saline, and Jane used one of her drawing poultices. Will he have a scar?" Lorraine sounded pretty matter-of-fact.

"Absolutely, unless you want some plastic surgery done to reduce it." I was busy running my hands down Ralph's legs and checking his big flat hooves. So far everything looked great. We discussed diet for a while then she unhooked him. He stood stock still for a moment, gazing at us with a thoughtful stare.

"Was one of the females in heat when this happened?" The small pack looked like they got along reasonably well with each other. However, raging hormones could put a quick end to peaceful coexistence.

"You got it, Doc." Jane yelled from the far side of the corral.

"You can try separating them when the girls go into heat," I suggested, "especially if you only keep one or two males around for breeding purposes. I've got to tell you, though, that the flock will be healthier if you have more genetic diversity. Talk to some of the other llama breeders around."

Again we heard her sister call out. "That's what I keep telling her."

My eyes met Mari's. I'd examined all the animals on the list the sisters had given me. Unless there was something more, we were finished.

Somehow I got behind Jane and Lorraine and darned if they didn't walk in unison, like a pair of matched dapple gray draft horses.

Mari caught up to them, the muck in some places just a couple of inches below the tops of her boots. "I have to ask. What is the secret to telling you apart?"

Again they looked at each other, with that weird synchronous movement, one turning their head right, the other turning their head left. "That's easy." I didn't know which twin spoke. "We're mirror image identical twins."

Poor Mari gave me a look then asked, "What does that mean?"

"It means we are like looking into a mirror. Jane is right-handed, but I'm left-handed. I have a birthmark on my right shoulder, Jane's birthmark is the same but it's on her left shoulder."

Mari's face lit up. "That's super cool."

Her enthusiasm was contagious. I found myself analyzing their differences too.

Then I got an idea that slammed me like a lightning bolt.

Could they have given me a clue to solving Claire's murder?

Chapter Forty-one

It was the "hands" part of the mirror image twins that caught my attention. One pair of hands being mistaken for another. Claire had said "forgery" to her mother. Maybe Gilda had hired one artist to forge the work of another. Maybe the Chinese connection was just that, someone in China producing paintings at a fraction of the cost of what Gilda could sell them for here in the United States. Perhaps something about one of the paintings made Claire suspicious. But which one?

Then I thought, wouldn't there be some sort of paper trail regarding artwork coming into the country? Or did Gilda simply use her online catalogue and have items shipped directly to their new owner.

The only artist at the Qualog Gallery that I'd met was Andrei Roshenkov. What did I know about him? He'd studied at a well-known art school in Leningrad and this local show was the first step in his career. But Andrei wasn't busy forging Chinese artworks; he was concentrating on his own intricate paintings. According to Gilda, his career was on the rise.

And where did A.J., the musician, fit in here? Was the lovely Bella mixed up in the art world in any way? I made a note to find out more background on her. Claire had worked at an art museum in Rhinebeck. What if they'd met there? Maybe that was another connection between them.

Too many things to think about. Claire and her life were tied to so many people, like a silken spider's web that seems to be random, but isn't once you find the key.

For a moment my mind jumped back to the mirror image twins. There was something…but what was it? Another possibility always lurked in the background. Claire could have been the victim of a random killer, perhaps the unknown stranger who rang her doorbell that fateful Friday. In that case, solving the crime might be hopeless.

As I crawled into bed that last thought came to mind. The unknown stranger. Although police statistics indicate that you are more likely to be killed by someone you know, there are always a certain percentage of murders where the victim was in the wrong place at the wrong time.

The comforter on my bed was littered with articles I'd printed from the Internet. Those cheery items weren't going to help me get to sleep. Instead I picked up an old Agatha Christie I'd read millions of times and started to read.

◇◇◇

A loud slam. The walls shook. My bed vibrated. My windows rattled. What was happening? What woke me up? Buddy added to the noise by barking, which made two more dogs in the hospital join in. I shook off sleep, thinking it was an earthquake or a tree limb falling on the roof. I struggled up and threw the covers off. Then I heard squealing tires. The clock on the nightstand read three-fifteen.

Someone was in the parking lot.

My stomach lurched with fear. I flipped the lights on and cautiously slipped over to the window. The motion detector light above the door had come on. Harsh bright light revealed empty asphalt. Whoever had tripped the sensor was gone. Nothing had fallen in my apartment. Buddy yawned as if this was a routine late night event, then settled down onto his bed.

Should I call the police? What would I say? They'd ask me a million questions and I wouldn't get any sleep. It's not like I could give them a description or anything, I rationalized to myself. Buddy grunted in contentment as he curled up, his eyes covered by the long feathers of fur on his tail. Whatever happened it was over as far as the dogs were concerned. Still upset I took another peek out the window. The parking lot light had turned itself off and everything was silent.

Wrapping my blanket tight around me I propped myself up on the sofa and turned on the television. Reruns of the original *Star Trek*. While the crew of the Enterprise set their phasers on stun I clutched my cell phone, ready to call 911 at a moment's notice. After three episodes I finally fell asleep. As soon as I stirred in the morning my dog twirled around like a brown and white flash, eager to go outside and start his day. His enthusiasm didn't match mine.

"Let's go, Buddy." I'd hit my snooze button the maximum three times before getting out of bed. A gentle pounding in my temple warned of an impending headache. Vague recollections of something happening last night began to penetrate my mental fog. Sliding into my flip-flops I headed for the back door and my dog's favorite grassy spot alongside the building.

Buddy tore out of the doorway, but instead of turning to the left to go to his favorite place, he detoured sharply to the right—toward my truck—which no longer stood in the parking lot, but instead had been propelled almost into the side of the building.

"Holy crap." Was it really an earthquake? What the heck happened here?

Gingerly I walked around the old F-150, noting the dent in the reinforced rear bumper and matching dent in the front. Branches had wedged into the front grill, the juniper on the side of the building now hung off to the side while the aspens were smack against the hood. Out of force of habit I always put on the parking brake, even on level ground. My Gramps had drummed it into my head. "You never know," he'd said a million times. I wondered if that and the hedges had stopped the truck from knocking a hole in the wall.

Another car swung around the corner. I recognized Cindy's VW bug. She practically leaped out of the front seat, eyes wide.

"Were you in an accident? Are you okay?" Her gaze ping-ponged back and forth from me standing in the parking lot in my bathrobe to the damaged truck.

She thought I'd somehow lost control and plowed into the thick greenery.

"I'm fine. The truck was fine too when I parked it here yesterday. Someone was joy-riding around in the parking lot and hit me."

"Didn't you hear anything?"

"I guess. About three in the morning a loud bang woke me up."

"Weren't you scared? Did you call the police?" Cindy whipped out her phone and started taking pictures.

"Buddy, come on." My dog ran to my side, tongue out, enjoying the morning. "You know, it was over so fast…."

She interrupted me. "I'm calling Cousin Bobby right now."

I bowed to the inevitable. Cousin Bobby was Robert Garcia, Oak Falls' chief of police. Needless to say I was not on his Christmas list. While I started to protest another car rolled around the corner. All the staff parked in the back parking lot, leaving the front available for patients. Since I didn't feel like explaining everything again in my pajamas I excused myself, "I've got to get dressed."

With a wave she dismissed me.

This was going to be another rough day. After a long hot shower and quick breakfast I stepped into the animal hospital and straight into a clump of police officers having coffee with Cindy. Sure enough, Cousin Bobby was there, along with Luke and another officer I didn't recognize.

"Here she is." Cindy sounded like a game show hostess.

"Riley, can you make sure we're not disturbed?" The chief of police motioned to the young officer I didn't know on a first-name basis.

"Why don't you use the office?" Ever helpful, Cindy opened the door and we all filed in.

Riley closed it behind us. I got the feeling he was standing guard directly outside.

The room felt unbelievably small and claustrophobic, squeezing me and two police officers into a staring contest.

"Can't you just take a quick statement for the insurance company?" I twisted around in the desk chair, addressing the chief.

He eased down in the office chair opposite the desk. Luke remained standing.

"Well, Dr. Turner. Kate. It isn't that simple." Even at nine o'clock in the morning, the chief had five o'clock shadow.

Luke stood as still as a statue, and refused to meet my glance.

Taking my clue from him I turned away and spoke only to the chief. "Isn't the likeliest scenario some joy-riding kids? I heard them take off."

"No cameras out back, I see."

That I did know something about. "Cindy told me Doc bought some cameras to put in the parking lot, plus some other stuff, but never got around to installing them. Our hospital alarm system does have cameras trained at all the exits and on the windows, so if someone tries to break in, the siren goes off. The alarm company then calls to report it."

"What about motion detection? You must have heard the crash and the truck bumping up to the exterior wall." The tone in his voice held some doubt.

"Of course I heard it. It woke me up."

He wrote something in his notebook. "You didn't report it?"

"No."

The chief scribbled again.

I waited, then continued. "Getting back to the motion detectors, we don't turn them on. Because of all the animals."

This time he looked up, a frown on his face. His bushy eyebrows merged into one fuzzy line.

I explained. "We've got our hospital cat jumping all over the place and that would set off our current system. It's an older one, but it still works."

The police chief scowled again, like I was personally responsible for turning off the motion detectors. Or was I feeling guilty again for no reason? I glanced up at Luke, but he didn't look back at me. Instead he was frowning, too. Only it looked way better on him.

"Should we upgrade our system?"

The chief continued scribbling in his notepad while Luke suddenly took interest in the ceiling.

Something wasn't right. I massaged my temples with my fingertips, trying to ward off the massive headache waiting to break free. Then I went for broke. "Okay, guys. What is going on here?"

Garcia looked at Luke and gave a barely imperceptible nod.

"There's no way to sugar coat this, Kate." Luke's voice sounded very official. "Someone lined up their truck with yours last night, and deliberately tried to push it into the building. The dent marks on the back bumper are straight on. No one was doing wheelies and sideswiped you. They probably stopped because of all the barking."

My mind flashed back to three this morning. I imagined some huge vehicle looming in the darkness, the driver hunched at the wheel, shrouded in black.

"Someone is either angry at the hospital…"

Garcia finally addressed me directly, gray patches under his eyes getting grayer.

"Or very mad at you."

Chapter Forty-two

Pie is very comforting, which is why I was wolfing it down in a booth in the Oak Falls diner at almost nine at night. I'd been sitting in my apartment, antsy in the intense silence, when the thought of a piece of pie became irresistible. Unfortunately, it necessitated me getting out of my pajamas and physically driving there. Thanks to the extra heavy-duty bumpers and frame Doc had installed in the old truck it drove fine, despite the deep new dents. The dents in my peace of mind weighed me down more.

Buddy waited in the car, munching his nighttime treat, while I debated asking for another slice of apple pie to go. I was staring out the window drinking my decaf when someone sat down across from me.

"Why am I not surprised you're here?" Luke eyes smiled at me but the rest of him appeared as tense as he was this morning. "Pie therapy?"

"Absolutely." To prove the point I put another forkful in my mouth.

Rosie, my waitress, interrupted us. "Hey, cousin. What are you doing here bothering this nice lady?" It seemed like half the town was populated with Gianettis or their close relatives.

"Getting takeout from the prettiest waitress in Oak Falls."

The cousins obviously had a good relationship. Rosie backhanded him with the menu.

"Alright, I'd like two of the specials, one with salad, plain, and another with the soup of the day. Oh, and a coffee while I wait."

"You got it. Anything else, Kate? More decaf?"

Luke ordered like someone in the food business, which he was. He and his brothers and sisters had all worked in the diner at one time or another. They probably knew the menu backwards and forwards.

"No, thanks." Not in the mood for a chit chat with Luke, I asked for the bill.

Rosie disappeared for a moment, then returned with a coffee for Luke.

"Anyone upset with you?" Luke lifted his mug to his lips, his eyes now hard above the white china rim.

"Hey, we've been through all of this already. I'm tired. Can we give it a rest?" I started looking around for Rosie with my check.

He put his hand on my wrist, to stop me from leaving. "Why do I have the feeling you aren't concerned about this?"

I felt my face start to redden as I shook his hand off. "Just because I'm not whining or crying doesn't mean I'm not concerned. The main reason I'm here is because I don't feel comfortable at home right now." As soon as I admitted it I regretted it.

"Let's do something about that."

"What do you mean?"

"I'll put you on our night patrol for the rest of the week." His face stopped looking so frozen.

Although part of me didn't like the idea, the rational part of me secretly jumped up and down.

My eyes drifted back out to the diner's brightly lit parking lot. "Well, if it won't be any trouble."

"No trouble. We routinely patrol the town and bars at night. We'll add you to the loop."

"Okay."

"Okay."

"So, Luke. Can you level with me for a moment? What's your take on this? Should I be worried?"

He looked everywhere except at me. Finally he raised his head, those dark eyes—sympathetic, and something more. "I don't know."

"That makes two of us."

He finally smiled, that off-center smile I liked so much. Probably all the girls he knew liked it.

"Who's the other dinner for?" Yet another statement instantly regretted. I put it down to lack of sleep, and being really nosy where Luke was concerned.

Rosie came over at that moment with two bags of takeout. She ripped off one check for me and the other for him. "Thanks, Kate. See you kiddo," she told him, with a peck on the cheek.

We both picked up our checks but didn't move.

"It's for Riley. He gets the salad, I get the soup. We're working tonight."

"Oh."

"Kate, I've got to tell you something." He put his head down slightly, like he didn't want anyone else to hear.

My stomach lurched, even stuffed as it was. What was he going to say?

"That mischief in the parking lot. Chief Garcia thinks you've pissed someone off."

Chapter Forty-three

Anger erupted inside me, molten and irrational, like a bull seeing the matador's red cape. I stood up, self-righteously furious.

"I've pissed someone off? So this is all my fault?"

"Wait."

Barely able to control myself I stormed past him, almost knocking over his takeout bags.

"Kate, wait a minute."

By then I'd made it to the front door, right into the middle of a human log jam. Two elderly couples blocked the exit, putting on their coats, hats, scarves, you name it. Before I could get out I felt a hand on my elbow. Impatiently, I shook it off.

"Hey, just giving you your pie." To my embarrassment it was Rosie, my server, who'd come up behind me, a paper bag in her hand.

"Sorry, I thought you were someone else." I clutched the bag and looked over her shoulder. Sure enough, skillfully easing past strangers, coming up along the inside track like the dark horse in a race was Luke, a bewildered expression on his face.

"No lovers' spats in the diner." Rosie winked at me, then turned to go.

"That will be the day," I replied loudly with as much conviction as I could muster.

As she walked away I heard her say something under her breath but I didn't catch it. It almost sounded like a giggle. With the back-up cleared out, and the couples safely on their way, I forged ahead, stomping across the wide porch on my way to the truck. He caught up to me at the base of the diner stairs.

"What's gotten into you?"

He'd asked me who I'd pissed off. Obviously him. "Let's just drop it, Luke."

"No." He twirled me around to face him. "If you're in any kind of danger I want to know about it. I mean, the police department should know."

With a full head of steam in me I wasn't about to stop. I shouted, "Maybe I wouldn't be in danger if the police could find Claire's killer and stop wasting time on innocent victims."

Luke's head and shoulders snapped back like I'd hit him. "We're doing the best we can. There aren't a lot of leads to follow."

"Don't I know it. Every one I've checked out has been a dead end."

His eyes held mine for a moment. My anger started to evaporate. Why was I yelling at him? Unlike most people in town, he'd been a long-time friend of Claire's, and wanted the crime to be solved—as much as me. I'd let my own frustration at Garcia and newfound anxiety lash out at him. Why could he get under my skin so easily?

"I'm sorry." I clutched the paper bag in my hand to my chest. "I needed to blow off some steam."

Relief flooded his face, relaxing the tension in his jaw. "That's okay. It's understandable."

A knocking noise caught our attention.

Sitting in front of the diner window, face squished to the glass, was a young boy, maybe seven or eight years old. He was banging with his fist but after he got our attention he plastered his lips to the glass, smearing it with a messy kiss. As I stared at him, horrified, he did it again. Behind me in the parking lot, I heard someone laugh.

Luke waved at the kid and he waved back. "He wants us to kiss and make up."

A woman's arm reached over and pulled the boy away from the window. His mother had caught on to his antics.

"Well, don't let me stop you," a familiar voice said directly behind us.

Without looking I knew who had seen the whole thing. It was our animal hospital office manager, Cindy—sister-in-law of Bobby Garcia, the Oak Falls chief of police—lifelong resident of Oak Falls and one of the biggest gossips in the entire Hudson Valley.

Chapter Forty-four

After a particularly restless night of stop-and-go sleep, waking up at every little sound, I dragged myself out of bed at seven and slipped next door to get a cup of coffee from the communal hospital pot. I knew I was in trouble as soon as I ran into Mari in front of the machine.

"You look like you had a busy night." Mari proceeded to take my designated cup off the hook and filled it to the brim.

I grunted something noncommittal, then caught a glimpse of myself in the break room mirror. There were circles under my eyes and my normally docile hair stood on end.

Her knowing look followed me back into my apartment, where I unceremoniously closed the door. I'd already walked Buddy at five-thirty, which was about the fourth time I'd woken up. I wondered if the police patrol had somehow triggered my senses and popped me awake. The dogs hadn't barked, but maybe subliminally I knew Luke was out there. Regardless, it was way too early to think about that. In addition I badly needed a shower. With the last of the coffee in me I grabbed my bathrobe and hurried into the bathroom.

Before I went back in to the office I took a little bit more care with my appearance than usual, and even used a colored lip gloss before facing the staff. If I had any doubts Cindy had told them everything, the kinds of looks I got confirmed it. Even Nick, the kennel help, flashed me a grin and a thumbs-up.

"Nothing happened," I said in his general direction.

"Sure, Doc." His grin turned even bigger, as though I'd confessed to a wild and crazy night.

"I've got a project for us to do, Nick. We're going to put up all that surveillance stuff Doc Anderson bought that's sitting around. Talk to me later."

He gave me another thumbs-up.

I could only give him one back.

Cindy came in from the front desk, took one look at me, then said, "Rough night?"

"Nothing happened."

"Right." She made the "I'm zipping my lip" gesture big enough for the general world to see.

Raising my coffee mug to them I took a fresh slug. "Okay, you've all had your fun. Now let's get to work." I walked to the treatment board to review the two cases currently in the hospital. They both happened to be spays, older purebred dogs who had had multiple litters. Their operations were necessary not only to control the dog population but to cut down on the chance of their developing mammary gland tumors further down the road. Thanks to early spaying, veterinarians no longer saw as much breast cancer in dogs. Happily the ladies, one a Golden, the other a Chesapeake Bay Retriever, felt great, wagging their tails and gobbling up their breakfasts. After examining them and checking their incision lines, and with Mari finally back to normal, I wrote up their release orders and took a quick look at the house call appointment schedule for the morning.

It was going to be a three cups of coffee or more day, I figured. The staff had squeezed in some rechecks along with the medical cases, so I'd be going nonstop until late afternoon.

"Let's do it," I called out to Mari. On my way out I noticed a small puddle of urine on the floor in front of a cage. One of the dogs must not have been able to hold it before being walked. Automatically I reached for a paper towel and the spray bottle of bleach, bent down and cleaned it up. A furry torpedo launched itself past my head, screeching in anger, momentarily startling me. I'd disturbed Mr. Katt's karma.

"We've got to do something about that." Mari said, the laptop we used on our house calls in her hand. "Maybe some form of behavior modification? I think it's getting worse."

"Personally, I think he's having fun pouncing at us." Mr. Katt had retreated to the far corner of the treatment room and now gazed innocently at us from behind the portable dental unit.

"How does he get up there anyway?" Nick joined us, having witnessed the sneak attack. He focused on the tall storage cabinet that stopped only a few feet from the dropped ceiling. Mr. Katt had found an ideal spot from which to dive-bomb us.

Mari searched the area. "I think he jumps up over there by the sink, then climbs onto the shelf, and walks behind all the cat carriers and stuff, then leaps onto the top of the big cabinet. If he lies down up there you can't see him at all.

"Maybe that's where he hides when we want to put him in his cage at night." Besides being an escape artist, Mr. Katt also seemed to possess an invisibility cloak—never in sight when the staff was trying to find him.

"Hey, Mari, remind me to block the top corner of the ledge off with something."

"Will do." She stopped at the biologics refrigerator to refill the supplies on the truck, then opened the food refrigerator and took out her lunch. There were strict guidelines for storage of our veterinary products—no egg salad next to outgoing lab samples allowed.

I checked my pockets to make sure I had pens, my stethoscope, phone, a notepad, phone, assorted animal treats, and a paper clip for rebooting the laptop if necessary. "Okay, I'm ready." As we walked out to the truck I patted down my pants pockets and jacket pockets again. Our truck always carried plenty of extra stuff, from duct tape to catnip, so most likely if I'd forgotten something it was duplicated in our supplies. A vague feeling of uneasiness came over me, like I'd definitely forgotten something. Between last night's crazy dreams and that whole incident with Luke, I felt knocked off my game.

It wasn't until we were almost at the first house call that I remembered.

This morning was my Skype date with Jeremy. I'd missed it again.

Fortunately I didn't have time to worry about my love life, or lack of one, because the first appointment of the morning was a recheck on a very stinky but much loved Cocker Spaniel, Bitsy.

Althea, her owner, opened the door with an enthusiastic greeting. Mari and I cautiously sniffed the air. To our surprise it no longer smelled like stinky feet mixed with old cheese. In fact, only the welcome smell of vanilla blend coffee perfumed the air. Meanwhile, Bitsy, who had been the source of the bad odor, was wiggling and wagging her stumpy tail like crazy.

"My friends tell me it's a lot better, now." She guided us into the cheerful kitchen accompanied by her happy dog. The paintings of fruit I'd admired last time still hung by the table.

I gave my patient a pat on the head, noticing her floppy ears had been shaved. The groomer also removed most of the hair on the inside of the flap as I had suggested. Her general coat looked better, and she'd lost weight.

"Althea, she looks fantastic. Are you having any problems with this new protocol?"

Poor Bitsy had developed a mess of small problems that added up to one gigantic one. First, she had inherited lots of thick fur on both sides of her ears from her Cocker Spaniel parents. The weight of them made her ear canal never see the light of day. Also, her thyroid gland didn't produce enough hormones, so that affected her skin health, making it dry and prone to infections from all kinds of bacteria and yeast. I'd taken a shotgun approach, meaning I was treating all her problems at the same time. A hypoallergenic reducing diet, thyroid hormone, weekly medicated ear cleanings at the office, and grooming away her excess hair had made a significant difference.

"No problems so far. She didn't like the food at first so I added the low sodium chicken broth and warmed it up to tempt her like you told me. The thyroid pill she takes in a little ball of low-fat mozzarella, which she loves."

"Are you still measuring her food?"

"Every day. Her scale is right over there." Althea pointed to the countertop. It helped that Bitsy was an only dog and wasn't in competition for food with other pets.

"Okay. I consider this a success story." My technician gave me a thumbs-up, the second one I'd gotten this morning.

"Do you want to change her treatment orders?" Mari had booted the computer and was typing in notes.

"Yes. I think we can go with maintenance ear medication. Let's schedule another recheck at the office, and we'll go over how to incorporate ear care into your daily schedule."

As Mari took care of the paperwork my eyes drifted to the paintings on the wall. I remembered that Althea had taken classes with Claire.

"Would you like some coffee before you go?"

"Absolutely." I stood up and went over to the sideboard where the coffee was brewing.

"Me too," Mari echoed.

When I poured it steam rose up, a sure sign it was too hot to drink. I let it sit for a moment, warming my hands on the cup. Satisfied I wouldn't spill any I sat down at the kitchen table overlooking the backyard. It felt good to get off my feet. The bad news was it was only ten o'clock in the morning.

"Thanks so much for taking such good care of my baby." Bitsy's owner pushed a plate of oatmeal raisin cookies over toward me. I slid them over to Mari.

"Believe it or not, Bitsy's health issues are pretty common in Cocker Spaniels."

"Well, she's much happier and so am I." Althea joined us at the table.

I noticed she had purple under her nails, and a spot of vermillion on her arm.

"Have you been painting recently?"

Her eyes followed mine and she ruefully scratched at the dried paint on her arm. "Yes, I've been doing some *plein air* work."

"What's that?" Mari sandwiched her question in between bites of cookie.

Our hostess stopped a moment to drink her coffee. "It's a technique of painting in the outdoors, working directly in nature. Claire and I did it together a few times."

With the mention of Claire her face caved in a little.

"I wonder if I have one of those open air paintings. It's a river scene, called *Life's Little Surprises.*

Althea clapped her hands. "We both worked one morning down by the stream in town. I painted the mountains with the river in the foreground, but she painted the crossing rock."

"Crossing rock?"

"That's what everyone calls the big flat stone there at the bend. It's the best one to use to cross the river." She jumped up and went to refill the plate of cookies. I raised my eyebrow at Mari but she pretended not to see it.

Mentally giving myself a cookie limit I remembered someone else mentioning that rock. For the life of me I couldn't remember who.

"I've hung several of Claire's paintings on my studio wall. Would you like to see them?"

Mari rolled her eyes but I immediately jumped at the chance. "I'd love to."

We got up and followed Althea and Bitsy down the hall to what probably was a spare bedroom, now converted into a small artist's studio. The floors were a pale polished hardwood. Two easels stood next to each other, both with unfinished paintings on them. Canvases of all different sizes leaned up against the wall, the painted surfaces facing away from us. Althea gestured toward the far wall.

I recognized the very abstract and colorful painting style, similar to those I'd seen in Claire's apartment. Other pictures were more realistic, mostly outdoor scenes. One captured the spirit of the old graveyard in the center of town, but an unusual portrait caught my eye.

The portrait was of a woman with a beautiful face, made angular by the artist. She stood in three-quarter profile, in front of a gilded mirror, her reflection caught in the glass, dark hair cascading down her back. Claire had captured the image of her boss, Gilda, at the art gallery very well. But why did the reflection look so strange? Why did the face in the mirror that stared back at us look Chinese?

Mari excused herself to get ready for our next appointment. Althea stood biting her lip her eyes resting on first one canvas then another.

"Is that Gilda, from the art gallery, in this painting?"

Althea shook her head, yes. "It's a good likeness. She's quite a lovely woman."

I took a few steps toward the picture and studied the reflection in the mirror. The artist deliberately softened the image, but, I could swear the cast of the face gazing back was Asian. A paintbrush hung from the figure's hand.

"The figure in the mirror…"

Althea spoke up. "I asked Claire about that. The reflection in the mirror isn't Gilda."

"Then who is it? What does it mean?"

"She told me it was a secret, but I'd know soon enough."

Another secret. Everyone involved with Claire had a secret.

Althea turned to go. "I'll treasure this always. She gave it to me the day before she died."

"Are you sure she wasn't seeing anyone, Althea? It's very important." My eyes went back to the painting. Why did Claire give this particular piece to her?

"She spent some time with that Russian artist, but that was while working on the show. Nothing fancy, takeout, pizza, quick stuff while she oversaw the design for the show." Althea became agitated as she tried to remember. "Oh, she ran into A.J. one day in Rhinebeck. I asked her if they hooked up but she only giggled at me. I had the impression there may have been someone else but she didn't share that with me. Did that help any?"

"I guess every piece of information helps."

We were on our way back to the kitchen when Althea stopped suddenly.

"Wait a minute. Claire said something else to me that day. I know—she said that picture of Gilda should be called *My Insurance Policy*. Then she laughed."

Chapter Forty-five

"I don't know what it means, Gramps. I just know it means something." I'd paced around the apartment for almost forty-five minutes before calling my grandfather. As always he brought me down to earth pretty fast.

"Hold on." He took a moment to catch his breath. "This is very intriguing, but again, it's not evidence. Remember, the police want hard evidence."

Buddy sniffed around my feet, then looked up expectantly, hoping for some chips or a snack of some sort. Seeing nothing of interest in my hands he gave up and jumped on the sofa.

"That's why this investigation is taking so long. There's no evidence, just rumors and conjecture and something someone thinks they overheard." Frustrated I went over to the kitchen and took a fistful of corn chips from the bag on top of the refrigerator.

Buddy woke up and wagged his tail. I slipped him a broken chip and sat down next to him. A tuft of dog hair gently rose from the cushion, then settled back down.

"Katie. Listen to me." Gramps voice gentled, like when I was a kid and needed comforting. "Conjecture only leads so far. I learned that the hard way investigating fires. Sometimes things point one way, but mean something different. Finding out the truth takes a lot of time and patience. Don't forget, the bad guys don't want to be caught. If they can lead you astray, they will."

Lead me astray. Something about that phrase resonated in my head.

Who had led me astray?
Obviously, the killer. But maybe someone else had.
Someone who hadn't meant to at all.
Like the victim.

Chapter Forty-six

Sitting on the sofa, pen in hand, I decided to make a list. Lists impose some kind of order that you can see. But instead of nice regimented columns my fingers began to draw doodles all over the page. Claire interacted with Andrei all during the set-up of his show, so why did he pretend he barely knew her?

Without thinking I drew a big eye and a question mark.

Then there was Gilda, with her Chinese connection staring at us from the mirror. All that talk about forgery and fakes. Now a series of dollar signs danced across the page.

Add to the mix a nasty pair—Buzz, currently engaged to Claire's mom—and A.J.'s girlfriend, Bella. Both had opportunity and motive, money for Buzz, and jealousy for the beautiful Bella. Under the eye I drew a Corvette logo and a knife dripping with blood.

The drawing didn't help unlock my subconscious. Instead it made it obvious I could benefit from art classes. Someone killed Claire, and my gut told me I had all the clues. I only needed to put them together in the right order. Buddy lay upside down in his bed, snoring away. Restless and frustrated I instead made a list of items I needed at the grocery store, pulled on my coat and climbed into the truck.

◇◇◇

After wandering around the supermarket for almost half an hour, I loaded everything into the backseat and began driving home. All the people involved in Claire's life, and possibly her murderer crowded into my consciousness. The ladies made it to the top of the pile. Gilda, the art gallery owner, might be a bitch of a boss, but was she also making money selling fake Chinese works of art? Potentially there could be millions involved—and piles of cash makes a dandy motive. Did Claire leave us a clue in that odd portrait of her boss? The other top contender was Bella, the old boyfriend's new squeeze. She knew he still had a thing for Claire, his high school sweetheart. Crazy love is a dangerous state of mind, and jealousy always a powerful emotion.

They had the strongest motives, but something didn't add up. Still wanting to make sure the man in the car who visited Claire was her ex, I decided to call Double J again. No answer. Disappointed, I left a voice mail. As soon as I hung up, my phone rang—the number I'd just called was calling me back.

"Hello." I turned on the speaker phone.

"Dr. Kate. This is Double J." His voice sounded like it was coming out of the bottom of a barrel.

"Hi there. How are you?" I pulled off the road and into the gas station parking lot, glad he returned my call. "Can you speak up?"

"Is that better?" There still was a small echo, but his words were clearer.

"Yes."

"My mother remembered something about the man she saw at Claire's condo that day. He wore an expensive watch that glittered on his wrist. His arm hung out the window and he wore a knit shirt"…his voice trailed off for a moment…"like a shirt for golf."

The wrist to shoulder artwork on A.J.'s arms were vivid in my memory. "Did she see any tattoos?"

He must have turned away to question her. Muffled Spanish could be heard in the background.

"Hello? There were no tattoos. The gringo was *peinado*, very neat and well-groomed. His shirt didn't have many wrinkles like most *Americanos*. My mother approved."

It had been Andrei that day at the townhouse. I'd been stupid—not realizing what my unconscious was trying to tell me about mirror image. Two separate people, two men who were the flip of each other. Someone had even commented on it to me. Claire was attracted to the same kind of guy physically, only one was a tattooed grungy rocker and the other a cosmopolitan artist meticulously groomed. Both had sculptured cheekbones, blond hair, blue eyes, and similar builds.

Were both of them also prone to violence?

Andrei had lied to me about his relationship with Claire, saying he barely remembered her. What else was he lying about?

I'd found our killer.

Now to find out why.

I turned into the animal hospital, headlights shining across the deserted parking lot. All the gossip about Claire moving to New York with a boyfriend and having extra money made total sense. She thought they were in love, but Andrei only loves one person, himself.

Deep in thought I opened the truck door and climbed out.

Someone stepped out of the bushes.

"Stay calm. Hand me your keys." Andrei Roshenkov punctuated the sentence by sticking a gun barrel into my back. "Everything will be fine as long as you do what I say."

The cold metal pressed against my spine. I wondered if he'd said the same thing to Claire before he killed her.

Buddy barked when we walked into my apartment. Andrei pulled a dog bone out of his pocket and asked my dog to sit. Man's best friend happily obliged.

"Into the animal hospital. Now!" He gestured toward the door with the gun. I turned my head. He pushed me forward and I stumbled into the treatment area. My brain kept telling me to grab the weapon, but my arms and legs felt like they were made of lead. Shock had set in.

My foot hit the metal base of an IV stand, one of several around the room. A bag of saline hung from the hook, the plastic tube line looped next to it. Capping it off was a green top eighteen-gauge needle.

The Russian moved closer, murmuring softly, "Why didn't you stop? I used my truck to warn you and your friend, Candy, but, no—you kept on—following me to my studio. Peeking in the window." He suddenly screamed at me in rage. "Talking about my hands being so clean."

I kept eye contact while inching my way closer to the needle.

His right hand lashed out at the heavy IV stand, slamming it into my left side before it careened past me. Off balance I tripped and hit the floor hard.

Andrei towered over me, enjoying his dominance as he explained his plans. "All I needed was one more week. One more week and the gallery show would be over. I'd be free to go anywhere." He started pacing in front of me, barely glancing down, one hand squeezing into a fist, the other aiming the gun directly at me.

Pain radiated along my ribs and hipbone. Desperately I fought to catch my breath. I needed to keep him talking until I could fight back.

"What painters did you copy? Monet? Picasso?" It hurt to breathe. My voice sounded ragged but I forced out the words. "You never told me what your scam was."

A look of amusement replaced his anger. "No, I didn't. Get up." He motioned with the gun.

I crawled toward the IV stand on its side. My hand rested on the plastic tubing, covering the part where the eighteen-gauge needle attacked. "Did someone supply you with those Chinese lithographs at the gallery? Is Gilda in on it?"

This time the look on his face was one of contempt for my investigating. "Not even close. I said get up."

Slowly I moved, wincing in pain, pretending I was badly injured. My mind focused, sharp and alert, as an ancient instinct kicked into action. The instinct to survive.

I hauled myself up, back against the wall, the needle now palmed in my hand. Forgery was the word Bev had used. Forgery.

Andrei's hands, Chinese, straight dark hair. All the pieces clicked together and suddenly I knew.

I measured out my next words, diverting his attention from my cupped hands. "Claire told her mother someone at the gallery was committing forgery. That was you. You didn't paint any of those paintings. What did you do? Hire a poor Chinese artist to paint them for you?" I taunted him. "You took the credit and the money. Is that it?"

"Stand still."

"Claire didn't trust you. Did you know that?" Tiny side steps brought me closer to the countertop.

"You are wrong. Claire loved me, but she wanted the world to know the truth. I had to kill her." He shrugged, matter-of-fact.

It took all my courage to laugh at him, push him to get angry again. "She knew you had no talent."

He bellowed and rushed me, free hand clenched in a fist, gun raised to strike my head.

I twisted left, knocked his arm by sliding inside, and plunged the thick needle deep into his neck, aiming for his jugular vein. Blood flowed immediately, running down his pale skin.

Andrei clutched at his throat.

I stamped down on his foot and punched him in the stomach with my free hand as he bent forward. It felt like hitting a block of wood.

Roaring curses in Russian he flung me backwards, sweeping everything off the countertop onto the floor. My head bashed into the wood cabinets. He snatched the needle from his neck and shoved the gun at my chest.

Rolling aside, I grabbed the bulky steel IV stand and hit his arm. His first shot flew wide, blasting the air, hurting my ears. Angrily he kicked out, aiming at my head.

All those self-defense classes Gramps made me take came back. I caught his leg mid-kick, shoving it backward. Off balance, his second shot hit the ceiling.

A spray bottle of alcohol lay within my reach. Clutching it, I struggled to my feet, breathing in raspy gasps, throat raw. One clear shot into his eyes would blind him. I pointed and sprayed.

A fine mist came out, barely reaching him. He laughed, enjoying himself. Silly girl. Nothing to worry about.

I had nowhere to go. Everything ached. Instinctively I raised my hands in self defense.

Andrei's glacial blue eyes narrowed, then he deliberately planted his feet. Both hands now held the gun in a two-handed stance.

"You coward." With the last of my strength I spit in his face.

He wiped it off on the back of his sleeve, then taunted me. "Time to say good-bye."

An unearthly screech pierced the air. A torpedo of fur catapulted into Andrei's head, clawing his scalp. Instantly he reached up, trying to protect himself, dropping the gun. Seizing the moment, I karate kicked my foot hard into his groin. He doubled over and howled in pain, face beet red.

With one step I grabbed the new microscope. Using the two-thousand dollar hunk of metal like a baseball bat, I smashed it into his forehead.

The guy dropped like a rock.

I clutched the counter, ears ringing, pain stabbing my side. Andrei had to stay down for the count. Ignoring my injuries, I duct taped his hands and feet together and kicked the gun out of sight under the surgical table.

My knight in furry armor sat in the corner, grooming his paws.

"This is Dr. Kate Turner at the Oak Falls Animal Hospital," I told the 911 operator. "There's been an attempted murder. We need an ambulance." The cell phone slipped from my grasp.

I'd never felt so tired. Gratefully I collapsed into the lab chair. Mr. Katt, feline superhero, jumped on my lap and began to purr.

"Thanks." My hands automatically stroked his soft fur. "We need to celebrate. The tuna is on me." Sirens sounded in the distance, coming closer and closer. The cat's warm body and loud purr comforted me as he snuggled closer.

With luck, the new audio enhanced wireless cameras in the parking lot and the hospital that Nick and I had installed would contain all the proof the authorities needed.

Claire could rest in peace.

Chapter Forty-seven

Dark clouds threatening to roll in didn't deter the crowd of guests invited to the opening of a new show at Qualog Gallery. After driving up and down Main Street searching for parking I tucked the truck into the last remaining spot in the public lot.

The past few weeks had been a blur. My confrontation with Andrei was played up in the newspapers, giving me an unwelcome notoriety. The Russian had been arrested and charged with first degree murder, as well as attempted manslaughter, hit and run, and a slew of other offenses. To my surprise several ladies came forward, offering to marry him. Perhaps the idea of playing footsie with a murderer appealed to their sense of danger. One person in particular, gallery owner Gilda Treemont, kept her silence. She hadn't known about his scam. Now her gallery was the talk of the town. Claire had figured out Andrei's game, painting it in her "insurance policy." All the while Andrei had secretly romanced both women, playing one off against the other for his own amusement.

Jeremy got back in touch and set up a new Skype schedule.

It felt good to be back to normal. Eugene had returned to work, often bringing Toto in with him. The little dog and I now shared a peaceful coexistence, monitored by his new and doting owner. Zhang Lei, the real artist of Roshenkov's paintings, decided to stay in Oak Falls. Andrei had helped his art school classmate flee China, but then kept him isolated from the world, a virtual prisoner. Now under Gilda's wing, he had applied for a new visa as a political refugee.

After a quick check of my makeup in the rearview mirror I opened the truck door, being careful not to clonk the Mercedes parked next to me. There wasn't much room as I slipped out, balancing on a pair of heels I'd found in the back of my closet. Unfortunately my purse didn't want to join me. Somehow the shoulder strap had become entangled between the console and the seat. With my bottom half pointing out I lay across the driver's side seat, trying to untangle my bag.

"Need some help?"

Of all people to see me like this, it had to be Luke.

"I'm fine." I hoped he could hear me since my head was practically under the seat.

"What?"

Now I saw the problem. The strap had looped around the seat-belt buckle. One quick maneuver and it came loose. I tried to slide backwards in a ladylike way, given I was wearing a shorter than normal black dress. When I turned around Luke stood uncomfortably close, wedged between the truck and the sedan.

"Uh, the purse strap was, uh, stuck, sort of wrapped around the uh…" My voice tapered off.

"Everything okay now?" Luke looked sharp in a black suit with a pale blue shirt and thin dark tie.

Trying to appear casual I checked around for signs of a girlfriend. There was no one else in sight. I shut the truck door and locked it, then we both squeezed sideways between the vehicles until we reached open space.

"Where are you heading?" He stopped for a moment and brushed some dust from the truck off his sleeve.

"The Qualog Gallery for the two exhibits. Claire's retrospective and the new opening for Zhang Lei's work, the artist who really painted Roshenkov's paintings."

"Me too. I've got the whole day off. Thought I'd see what all the fuss is about for myself."

We started walking toward Main Street. Although the clouds threatened us with rain they only delivered a brisk wind. To ward off the chill I pulled my coat tighter and buttoned the top buttons.

"Cold?" Luke carried a tan raincoat, but made no move to put it on. Maybe he was one of those guys who didn't mind winter temperatures.

"Just a little. It's the first time I've been out of my scrubs in months." As soon as I realized what I said my face turned red. What an admission to make to a good-looking guy, even if it was the truth.

He grinned at me. "Comfort is not to be dismissed lightly. As soon as I get home, this suit and tie are toast."

We turned left onto Main Street and continued walking. Up ahead people milled around in front of the gallery. I wondered who from the town would show up.

To my surprise we were whisked inside by Roxie, her hair now sporting orange stripes, like a crazy raccoon nightmare. "Yes, I decided to stay. Gilda's not so bad once you get to know her. Most of her bad temper was because of Andrei," she explained.

It was super crowded inside, with barely enough room to move around. Someone thrust drinks into our hands and took off, serving tray held high. I watched it disappear behind a black curtain.

"Are you meeting anyone here?" Luke had to bend down and almost shout in my ear over the buzz of the crowd.

"I'm supposed to meet some friends, but I don't see them. How about you?"

He held his drink over his head for a moment as a woman wearing a precariously perched hat squeezed by. "Nope. I'm by myself. I can't see much of anything, though, with this crowd."

"Let's move over there. It's less crowded." Holding my drink close to my body I carefully maneuvered through the crowd until we reached a quiet corner. "That's better."

The crowd thinned out a bit as a large group showered air kisses at Gilda and went out into the street.

"I think you'll like the paintings when you see them. They're beautiful, at least to me. Gilda now represents Zhang Lei and someone in the city is working with the State Department on his behalf. For now the staff at the Lucky Garden has taken him under their wing and are working on his English. I can appreciate them even more now that I've met Zhang Lei."

"All's well that ends well."

"Shakespeare. Spoken by Helen, the widow."

"You know the Bard?"

"My Gramps and I read every one of the plays together, and all of the sonnets. It started off as a bet."

He laughed. "Great way to motivate someone."

"I was fifteen and bratty. Of course I thought I knew everything, but Shakespeare taught me differently." The glass in my hand was bumped by someone coming through. A few drops dripped down my hand.

"You bratty? Who would have thought?"

Luke seemed in no hurry to mingle, which was fine with me. Our friendship had taken a hit with this murder investigation. As a police officer he didn't want an amateur, me, investigating things on my own. Especially when I was nearly killed. But now that the mystery was resolved, we'd drifted back toward whatever it was we'd had.

I looked at him closely: dark intelligent eyes, great hair and a quiet air of confidence. Very attractive. He caught me staring at him, so I pretended to be looking for a waiter.

"Maybe we could get together and talk about something other than crime. Maybe a little less dangerous." His voice was teasing. "Like the weather."

"I'd like that."

"Maybe we wouldn't fight as much, without a murder to solve?" He raised his glass to me in jest.

"Murder brings out the worst in both of us." I raised my glass to meet his. "But I wouldn't count on it."

Before I could continue, my phone chimed. A text message. Roxie rushed past us, a credit card in one hand and a receipt in the other. "We just sold another Zhang Lei and two of Claire's paintings." I noticed her day-glo orange striped hair was set off by orange lipstick.

"That's great, Roxie."

"Got to run or Gilda will kill me." She laughed, then took off, elbowing her way into the crowd.

Luke shook his head. "That's a dangerous thing to say around you."

"Don't start." I pulled out my phone to check my message. "Oh, my gosh."

"What's wrong?"

"Nothing. I've been invited to a wedding."

"Sounds like fun. Who's getting married? Anyone I know?"

I hesitated, then tried to explain. "Well, it's a pot-bellied pig patient of mine, named Angel. He's the groom and his bride is a female piggy called Princess Alice."

"His owner is throwing a wedding?" Luke's voice sounded incredulous.

"I guess so. My friend Daffy is designing some outfits for the couple." Another message popped up.

"That's not all." I looked down at my screen.

"I'm the maid of honor."